DEAD RINGER

V. B. Tenery

White Rose Publishing, a division of Pelican Ventures, LLC
www.pelicanbookgroup.com PO Box 1738 *Aztec, NM * 87410

White Rose Publishing Circle and Rosebud logo is a trademark of Pelican Ventures, LLC

Publishing History
First White Rose Edition, 2014
Paperback Edition ISBN 978-1-61116-351-3
Electronic Edition ISBN 978-1-61116-350-6
Published in the United States of America

Dedication

To my Savior who blessed me with Mattie Tompkins
Tenery as my mother. She taught me if you can dream
it, you can do it.

1

Mercy Lawrence wouldn't have noticed the large man standing by the silver Mercedes except for the way he was dressed. Unlike the tourists on the sidewalk, he wore a light gray business suit and tie. Sunglasses hid the upper portion of his face, and the grim set of his mouth detracted from his otherwise handsome appearance. He stood beside the car's open back door, arms crossed as if waiting for someone.

Not wanting to stare, she tore her gaze away. In jeans, T-shirt, and sandals, she blended easily into the vacationers along the boulevard. She'd spent the last five months in this wonderful country, recuperating from a head injury. Most of her memory remained intact after the accident, but dark recesses still refused to reveal their mystery.

But tomorrow, like a good soldier, she would return to Houston and report to her new job at Sabine Oil, the fulfillment of a goal she'd worked towards for the past six years.

The city's main drag ran four lanes wide with a palm-tree-lined median, the sea on one side, shops and hotels on the other. A soft wind filled the air with the scent of sea kelp and brine, mixed with a light floral fragrance from the purple bougainvilleas hanging on the walls along the walkway. Seagulls swept low over the water, looking out past the rolling surf for lunch.

She shook her hair loose from the confines of its ponytail clip and turned her face to the balmy sunshine—mainlining vitamin D. Her path took her within four feet of the parked car.

The man moved onto the sidewalk and grabbed her arm.

"Having fun, are we?" He spoke with a slight Scottish burr, the strange question more an accusation than a greeting.

She tried to jerk her arm away. "Let go of my arm."

His grip tightened. "I'll just bet you've been living it up." His voice was harsh, his jaw tight.

No one intervened. Casual observers would think she knew him.

One hand locked on her arm, he shoved her into the backseat, slid in beside her, and slammed the door. His movements were so quick, so smooth, she had no time to struggle, no time to scream or put up a fight.

She swallowed the lump in her throat choking off oxygen. Women disappeared all too often on foreign soil, never seen or heard from again. "Who are you? What do you think you're doing? Let me out. Now!"

He ignored her protests and leaned forward in the seat. "Airport, Fergus."

Blood pounded a persistent rhythm in her ears. He couldn't be police. They had to tell one the charges before making an arrest. Besides, she'd done nothing wrong.

Her heart skipped a beat. She wanted to run, but it was too late for that. Pivoting towards him, she drew back her arm and aimed the heel of her hand for an upward thrust under his nose. The move from a seated position lacked the needed momentum.

He blocked the blow, slamming her back against the seat with a forearm of steel across her chest. "You dropped off the map six months ago. To do what, find yourself?"

"I don't know what you're talking about." She squeezed her eyes shut. This couldn't be happening. "This is kidnapping. My name is Mercy Lawrence and people are expecting me back at my bungalow." She struggled against the vise-like grip, slapping at his hand.

"Stop it, and cut the crap, Traci, or I'll slap you back. Taking a wife, a *mother*, home to the son she abandoned is not kidnapping. Besides, you're not a kid."

2

Hamilton, Bermuda
Friday, May 5

His words startled Mercy into momentary shock. She stopped struggling, and sputtered. "My name isn't Traci. Y-you're crazy. Or delusional. I've never seen you before in my life. My passport and ID are in the bungalow." She pointed to the rear window. "Back there."

"I would agree that one of us is delusional." He removed the sunglasses and slipped one temple arm into the top pocket of his jacket. A cold, dark gaze bored into hers. "Ironic choice of name. We just left your cabin. The forgeries were excellent, but then your low-life friend can afford the best."

"You're speaking in riddles. What friend?"

He ignored her question, and his voice softened. "Traci, Daniel is sick. Three months ago, his doctor discovered he had a damaged heart valve. I started looking for you as soon as I heard. The surgeon repaired his heart, but it may be months before he's fully recovered. He's asking for you. I couldn't deny him—have him get upset. It could delay his recovery."

The man's obvious pain touched her, but it wasn't her fault. "Look, I don't want him upset, but I'm..."

He held up his hand. "I have a proposition. Come home and stay until he's well. Perhaps, no more than a month, or two. When that day comes, you can leave. You can go with my blessings and enough money to keep you in Gucci splendor the rest of your life."

Mercy shook her head. "Look, Mister Whoever-You-Are, I am *not* Traci. In two months, the job I've worked for all my life will be gone. This is some horrible case of mistaken identity. You can verify what I'm saying with fingerprints and DNA."

His jaw muscles twitched. "Spare me the denials. You think I don't know the woman I've been married to for seven years? The hair is longer and darker blonde, but if that's supposed to be a disguise, it fails miserably. Airport facial identification software picked you up. There's no mistake."

That sounded familiar, but she had no idea how it worked. "Then the software is wrong. It obviously has a serious malfunction."

"When you disappeared, I thought Daniel and I were free of you." His tone turned harsh. "But Daniel hasn't forgotten. He still cries himself to sleep, calling for you, and now he's seriously ill. You owe him, Traci. You can't be so devoid of maternal instincts that you ignore him when he's sick."

If what he'd told her was true, his wife must have been a piece of work. That, or her husband made life so intolerable she had to escape. His overbearing demeanor made the latter a distinct possibility. "I'm sorry about your son—"

He growled. "Our son. Don't play games with me where Daniel is concerned."

She shook her head and covered her face with her hands. "For the last time, my name is Mercy. I'm not who you think I am."

He turned a hate-filled gaze on her. "You either

come willingly, or I'll tie and gag you. All I'm asking, all your son is asking for, is two months out of a lifetime to do the right thing—do something unselfish for once in your life."

How could she get through to him? He wouldn't listen and wasn't open to verifying her identity. Perhaps he was psycho. And she had no experience dealing with insanity.

She squirmed in the seat, chewing on her inner lip. "I don't have two months to spare. If I'm not in Houston on Monday, I'll lose the job, and I'm not Traci."

He put the sunglasses back on, visually shutting her out.

Sliding to the far corner of the seat, she crossed her arms and tried to calm down enough to think straight. She didn't want him to bind and gag her. That would lessen any chance to escape. Inhaling a deep breath, she asked, "Where's home?"

He glanced at her but said nothing. Oppressive silence filled the automobile until they reached a small private airfield near Wade International Airport. The Mercedes rolled to a stop next to a corporate jet poised on the runway. Wallace, Ltd., was emblazoned on the side. The name seemed familiar. She'd seen or heard the name before, but couldn't remember where.

The sight of the private plane kicked up her panic level another notch. The scent of pure fear enveloped her. Frantic prayers seared her thoughts so fervent the words ran together. Letting this stranger put her on a plane headed for a destination unknown was out of the question. He could be involved in human trafficking.

Everything he'd told her could be a lie. Once the doors closed, she would be at his mercy. He could toss her into the sea for all she knew. No one would ever know. Another missing woman among thousands.

He got out and slammed the car door, came around, and jerked hers open, a disapproving sentry.

She slipped into the warm air, scanning the landscape for passengers, airport personnel, anyone to come to her aid.

He had chosen the spot well. The tarmac stood empty. Only private aircraft neatly tucked into hangers dotted the panoramic view.

If she was to make a move for freedom, time had run out. No one would come rushing to her rescue. She'd lied about someone waiting for her. Since he'd been at the bungalow, he already knew that. There were no close friends here, or for that matter, back in Houston. She'd never had time to make friends. Fending for herself came as natural as breathing, and she did not intend to go peacefully into the dark night.

A terrible thought struck her. In all the commotion, she'd forgotten about Paddy. Her cat. He was waiting for her at the cabin and with her gone, there'd be no one to take care of him. She couldn't leave him alone on the island.

Sucking in a resolute breath, she shoved past her captor, dodging as he lunged for her. She dashed down the runway and soon realized her sandals were never designed for sprinting. Feet pounded the cement behind her, the sound growing closer by the second. A strong arm grabbed her T-shirt, lifting her off the ground.

When he turned her to face him, she slapped him with every ounce of strength she possessed. The blow landed with a sharp *smack*. She raised her hand for another strike, but he grabbed her wrist and pulled her in close, arms pinned to her side.

She tried to knee his groin, but he twisted her sideways. Thwarted, she drew her right leg back and kicked his shin.

He swore, and the next thing she knew she was upside down in a fireman's carry over his shoulder.

She dug her fingernails into the corded muscles on the back of his neck. A warm, wetness covered her fingertips. He swore again and two sharp slaps struck her backside, numbing both cheeks.

With her still struggling and kicking, he stomped back to the plane, up the stairs, and into the aircraft's entrance. Somewhere behind them, lights flashed. She scanned the field and watched as a man with a camera over his shoulder disappeared into the trees outside the runway.

Great. Perhaps he had recorded her abduction.

She pounded the man's back with her fists as he marched down the aisle to the back, opened a door and tossed her onto the bed.

Breathing heavy, his face flushed a smoldering red. "You'd best calm down before you force me to do something we'll both regret." He rubbed his neck, stalked out the door, and a lock snapped into place.

She scrambled off the bed. A weapon was her first priority. She checked the lamps. No good—bolted to the desk. A computer desk in the corner held possibilities. In one of the drawers, she found a letter opener and a metal stapler. She placed the opener in the back waistband of her jeans, the stapler under a pillow.

The aircraft rumbled down the runway and lifted off, tossing her back onto the bed. She brushed the hair from her face and moved to the leather chair in the corner. All she could do now was wait for his next move.

Hours later, the door opened, and his frame filled the entrance. He had changed into jeans and a long-sleeved polo. "If you're over the hysterics, there's food and drink in the galley. You'll have to help yourself. There's no steward aboard."

She shook her head. "No thanks."

"It's up to you." He leaned against the doorjamb. "Where's Rossellini? I didn't find him or his clothes at your bungalow."

"I'm not surprised. I don't know anyone named Rossellini any more than I know you."

He shot her an icy glare and shook his head. "Daniel worships you. Why, I have no idea. You've never had time for him. But by all that's holy, you will see him through this or suffer the consequences." He turned to leave.

"Wait. My cat. Paddy. No one will feed him."

He came farther into the room. "I didn't see a cat at the bungalow."

"You wouldn't see him. He'd hide. He doesn't like strangers."

He gave her a your-giving-me-a-headache look. "I'll call the rental agency and have them to take care of it."

"How do I know you will? I have no way to check."

"You know because I said I would." He bit out each word. Straightening, he took a step towards the door. "It figures you would have more compassion for a cat than you do for your son." Then he was gone, leaving the door open.

She leaned back against the soft leather. What

now? Could she stab him with the letter opener? Yes, if he tried to harm her. So far, he hadn't, except in retaliation from her attack. She'd have bruises on her backside for weeks.

The room began to close in on her. She rose from the chair and walked out into the main cabin.

As she passed him, he held out his arm to stop her and jerked the letter opener from her waistband. "I thought you might find that."

∂∾⚮

Thomas Wallace sat across the aisle from his wife. Buckled into her seat, she stared through the porthole into the darkness. She had the frustrating ability to turn any situation to her advantage. He almost believed her denial, and he had experienced all her tricks.

She knew well who Ricco Rossellini was. Her half-Pakistani, half-Italian lover. Rich, handsome, and dangerous, he attracted women like kittens to cream.

Pushing a weary breath from his lungs, he relaxed against the headrest. Whatever new game she played would do her no good. The airport security systems had picked her up. Bermuda authorities had notified him when their system raised a red flag. There was no mistake.

He'd called in favors from his past to get her programmed into airports with the SDK technology. Payback would be right around the corner. He didn't know when the call would come, but it would come. None of that mattered, now.

Daniel needed his mother. When the boy recovered, they'd be well rid of her.

Misplaced affection had cost him years of denial, loss of self-esteem, and possibly damaged his son beyond repair. Yet here he was, dragging her back home.

How had he become entangled with a woman like Traci? The answer tasted bitter in his mouth. She had been an addiction, a habit he thought he'd kicked until today. But the drug still had the power to draw him back in. Love and hate—two faces of the same coin.

She sat across the aisle, face wearing a sullen sadness, like that of a child denied a treat. The nightlife of New York and Rome had more appeal than caring for her son. How she would hate returning to the island's dull pace.

Perhaps she'd married too young. Maybe she had needed to spread her wings more before settling down to marriage and a family. She was twenty-eight, now. Time for her to grow up and accept responsibility.

Thomas ran his hands through his hair, letting his fingertips massage small circles at his temples to ease the on-rushing tension headache. He reached into the console, extracted two aspirin, tossed them into his mouth, and swallowed them dry.

He stole another glance. In seven years of marriage, she'd never worn anything but her favorite designer-of-the-moment. The longer hair and informal clothing gave her a younger, softer look. He had to keep reminding himself he needed her for Daniel.

"When did your son...when did Daniel have the surgery?" Her voice sounded soft in the quiet cabin.

"Two months ago. I started to look for you before that. I thought you would want to know."

Thomas had cleaned the wounds on his neck with alcohol wipes and applied antibiotic cream, but it began to sting again. He unfastened the seat belt and went back to the restroom to reapply the ointment.

When he returned to the cabin, she rested her head against the seat, her gaze focused on him. He couldn't read her expression. Perhaps fright. She, of all people, should know there was no reason to fear him.

How could someone with such an angelic countenance behave as she had? Embarrassing the family in public without regard for propriety. Abandoning her only child.

He pushed the button on the seat to the recline position. Introspection could take him just so far. It wouldn't solve his problems.

3

Wallace Island, the Aegean Sea
Saturday, May 6

The airplane dropped altitude, and a small dot on the ocean changed into an island with ten or twelve miles of sandy beaches and green foliage. Along with the scene below came the reality of her plight, and she was unsure of what to expect when the plane landed. From the birds-eye view, the only escape route would be by aircraft or boat. And she had no clue where this insane man had taken her.

Wheels touched down with a hard thud. Home. Wherever that might be.

Bright sunlight flashed through the window. She squinted and rubbed her eyes.

A shadow fell across her face. Her captor held out a cup of coffee.

The aroma of fresh-roasted beans wafted to her nose, and she accepted the hot brew. After a tentative too-sweet sip, she shuddered and handed it back. "I drink it black."

He went to the galley and returned with a steaming cup, black as his soul. "Still believe a woman can't be too rich or too thin?"

Why try to explain she always drank it straight? That she appreciated the unenhanced flavor. He probably didn't care.

He took the seat across from her, his expression tight. "Daniel is mobile now, slowly regaining his strength. He won't be up when we arrive. Get your shower and change. Try to be a concerned mother. Anything else will be unacceptable." His jaw muscles flexed. "I'll be watching you, and so help me, if you show Daniel any sign of rejection, I'll give you the thrashing you never got as a child. That's a promise."

What his idea of a thrashing was, she didn't have a clue, and had no interest in finding out. "I'm not afraid of you, and I would never be cruel to a child." She looked down at her wrinkled shirt and jeans. "I have nothing to change into unless you packed my clothes while you were rummaging through my things at the bungalow."

"Your wardrobe is still here. I figured you'd come back sooner or later, so I didn't toss your clothes out, although I should have."

Mercy turned her gaze away. On the long flight, the little boy's needs crept into her thoughts. She didn't know what the next few days held for her, but she wouldn't be the only victim here. The child could get terribly hurt. This mistaken identity fiasco might delay his recovery. Children were smart. He might realize she wasn't his mother at once, even if his father refused to accept the truth.

Why did this man insist she was Traci? Could her resemblance to his wife be strong enough to fool the airport security system? How was that possible?

The aircraft door opened, and he waited for her to unfasten her seatbelt and stand.

She stepped to the entrance, unable to stop her hand from shaking. At the top of the steps, a man she recognized as the chauffer reached out his hand. "Watch yer step, lass."

Legs unsteady, she accepted the offer. "Thank you."

The old Scot's eyebrows rose almost to the plaid cap he wore, but he said nothing. This was her first good look at him. He must have flown up front with the pilot. His clothes were rumpled but clean. A big man, with a weathered face that held the same disapproving glare his boss wore.

A brusque voice came from behind her. "Fergus, will you see to the luggage?"

"Aye."

A long stone path led to steps and then to a plateau. Her host guided her up the stairs and moved up beside her.

At the top, she paused, taking in the Italian villa spread out over what seemed an acre, all white arches sparkling in the morning sun. An enormous white diamond set among a field of sapphires. Unique perfume that smelled of honeysuckle and roses filled the air around the terraces dotting the grounds. The sea, a blue backdrop, could be seen from every point of view.

Eyes narrowed, he glowered at her. "You act like you've never seen it before."

She met his unflinching stare. "I haven't."

Behind them, Fergus uttered an almost inaudible, "harrumph."

As they reached the villa's entrance, the lord-of-the-manor motioned her inside. A wide staircase rose in the center of the marble foyer, tall, potted ferns placed artfully on each side.

He guided her to the second floor and turned

right. "I called ahead and had your things moved next to Daniel." He swung the suite's double doors wide and turned to leave. "You know your way around. If you need anything, just let one of the staff know."

Of course, there would be servants. Would they help?

He left without closing the door. No reason to lock her in. She had no way off the island.

With urgent steps, she crossed the room, locked the door, and searched the area for a telephone. Her breath caught when she spotted one on the nightstand. She lifted the receiver and listened. No dial tone—an intercom house phone.

What did it matter? What could she say if she found a way to reach the outside?

"Hello, my name is Mercy Lawrence, and I've been abducted."

"Where are you?"

"I don't know. An island somewhere."

"By whom?"

"I don't know."

They would write her off as a nutcase.

She stood in the middle of the room and surveyed her cell. Certainly unlike any jail she'd ever seen. The room was huge, with white walls and a white marble floor. A king-sized bed on a raised platform dominated the center of the room. Sheer white and sapphire panels flowed from a silver cornice board centered over the bed. The bedding was white with blue, red, and silver throw pillows.

A thick scrapbook rested in the middle of an antique writing table in the corner, and on the opposite side, a plush, oversize chair sat next to a reading lamp. Elegant French doors led out to a balcony with lounge chairs and tables.

A platinum prison.

Mercy shuddered, kicked off her shoes, and found the bathroom, bigger than the living room in her Houston apartment. Rummaging through one of the vanity drawers, she found a supply of new toothbrushes. That solved one problem. In the shower, she mulled over her meeting with the little boy. Best let him set the tone.

She wrapped a large towel around her body and stepped into the closet. One thing was certain. The lady of the house had great taste and an unlimited budget. Racks of clothes with matching accessories, arranged by casual, dress, and eveningwear, seemed to go on forever.

She selected white slacks and a blue silk top that fit as if made for her. Even the Italian footwear in rows under the matching garments was her size. How was that possible? How could he have known her size? Even the style suited her taste, although designer labels had never fit into her budget.

She shook the doubts away. Despite the head injury, she couldn't have forgotten all this. She was not Traci. Her name was Mercy.

Dressed, she stepped into the hallway and turned around to get her bearings. Not a soul in sight to show her the way. Following instinct, she located the second-story landing.

Descending to the main floor, she found it as empty as the upstairs hallway.

Her gaze drifted into the great room, drawn to the enormous fireplace and the portrait centered above the mantel. She moved in closer. The portrait was a mirrored image of her.

He hadn't lied. In every detail, the woman in the painting resembled her own features—blonde hair, sun-streaked and shorter than her own, the sapphire blue eyes, and the light olive complexion. This was beyond strange.

Knees weak, she backed up to the closest chair and sat on the edge. She placed both hands on each side of her face and shook her head. Could the things she remembered be Traci's memories? She knew nothing of Traci's background. Had she studied geology, been poor before her marriage?

Chin raised, she stood and straightened her spine. She knew herself better than that. She wasn't Traci. If everyone had a double, then she must be Traci's doppelganger. That was the answer. She would never desert her own child as she'd been abandoned.

Muffled voices echoed from across the entryway.

She tore her gaze away from the portrait and followed the sounds down a short passage into the dining room.

An elegant older woman and a small boy, perhaps the most beautiful child she had ever seen, stood at a buffet table filling their plates from silver serving dishes.

Conversation stopped when they spotted her. The two exchanged a look, the boy's expression that of a child who had torn away Christmas wrapping and found a train set.

The china in his hand crashed, sending shards and food bouncing onto the pristine terracotta tile. He froze in place for a second and then bounded across the space between them and grabbed her around the waist. "Mummy, oh, Mummy! You came home."

The woman, tall and slender, silver hair pulled

back into a smooth chignon, had the classic features of a Greek statue. Her skin wore a freshness many younger women would envy. There was something oddly familiar about her. She moved forward with an effortless grace and then pulled up short, blue eyes glistening. Her face formed a welcoming smile. "Traci, it's good to have you home. Thomas said he'd find you."

Perhaps she should have expected this, but somehow, Mercy wasn't prepared.

They labored under the same delusion as the man who snatched her from Bermuda. They believed her to be Traci. After viewing the painting, she could understand why. Despite the identity confusion, a useful piece of information fell into place. She now had a name for her abductor. Thomas Wallace.

She paused for a moment. How should she respond to the child? This wasn't her son. She had no feelings for him. Yet something, perhaps the woman in her, empathized with this little boy who had been so ill without a mother to comfort him. She knelt.

His arms flew around her neck, his head resting on her shoulder.

She pulled him close and whispered against his blond curls. "Hello, Daniel."

A now familiar voice spoke from the doorway. "Don't knock your mother off her feet, son. I know you're happy to see her, but let her get breakfast."

"Daddy!" Daniel released her, shot across the floor, and leaped into his father's arms. "You're home!"

Thomas held the boy close, laughter in his eyes. The harsh man transformed. Lines in his face softened, and he glowed with pride as he inspected the boy. "We arrived a little while ago. You must be careful, son. You're not well, yet." He tousled the boy's hair. "I think you've grown an inch while I was away."

Daniel wiggled out of his father's arms and came back to Mercy.

She smiled and took his hand. "Shall I help you clean up the food and broken glass?"

Thomas dismissed her offer. "The staff will take care of that. Sit down and eat with Daniel." As if awaiting summons, a maid scurried from the kitchen, dustpan and broom in hand, to remove all signs of the mishap.

"In that case, Daniel, may I help you get your breakfast? What will it be? Shall we start with pancakes?"

A smile tipped the corners of his mouth, and he nodded.

She filled his plate and one for herself from the buffet table, and sat beside him.

The absurdity of the situation hadn't escaped her. Yesterday, she had been an orphan. Today she sat at a family breakfast, pretending to be a wife and mother to people she didn't know. It was like a strange dream where one wakes on stage in front of an audience without ever having read the script.

Daniel's adoration-filled eyes never left her face. It unnerved her. She had done nothing to warrant his devotion. Her heart ached for him—the neglect he endured from his mother. Yet his actions carried no reproach. Only a soft expression in his innocent blue eyes, so like her own. "No school today, right?"

Thomas cleared his throat. "We're declaring a week long break from school next week, since you're home, an official holiday in your honor."

The undercurrent of cynicism in his tone eluded the boy, but the woman across the table caught it. Her bright, intelligent gaze darted to Thomas and then back to Mercy.

Daniel couldn't contain his excitement, wiggling in his chair. "You and Mummy, both?"

"We're at your disposal for the next seven days. I'll have to get back to work the following week, but for now your mother and I are yours to command."

Over breakfast, the woman watched Mercy with the same attention Daniel expressed. Mercy shifted in the plush chair, not knowing how to address her. Her kind, well-defined face held a serenity belying the turmoil Mercy sensed in this house. She didn't look like a governess. Much too elegant. Perhaps a grandmother. There was a strong family resemblance to Daniel.

The need to be outside to collect her thoughts swept over Mercy. All the stress of the past twenty-four hours pressed in on her. "After I take a run on the beach, would you like to show me your favorite places on the island, Daniel?"

He ducked his head and nodded. "Yes, ma'am."

As the meal ended, Mercy caught Thomas's eye. "May I speak to you for a moment?"

He placed his napkin on the table and stood. "Of course. Let's go to my office."

After leading her down a wide hallway lined with muted paintings of beaches and harbors, he stopped at an open doorway and ushered her inside.

She waited until the door closed and rounded on him. "I've seen the portrait, and despite the resemblance, I'm not your wife. You can't just throw me in the midst of this household and expect me to meet everyone's expectations. Can't you humor me, and consider the possibility I'm telling the truth? Who is the older woman? What is she to Daniel, to me? What do I call her?"

He sat on the edge of the desk, one dark brow arched. "Don't you think you're carrying this charade too far? Nanna is the grandmother who raised you. As you are well aware."

Mercy dropped onto the sofa near the desk, resting her head in her hands. "I am not well aware. I don't know you. I don't know them, and I'm beginning to doubt my own identity."

He stood and grabbed her shoulders. Pulling her to her feet, he shook her. "I know who *you* are. That's all that counts. Make no mistake, Traci. You will fulfill your obligation to your son until he is well. There is no way off the island unless I take you. Your boyfriend won't pick you up. As far as I know, he lost track of you, too. If you decide to run again, I will have you committed, and you know I have the connections to do so. That is not my first choice, but I will do what I have to do for Daniel. Two months, that's all I'm asking."

Heat burned her cheeks. "I've told you, two months, and I lose the job of a lifetime, because you're too stubborn to admit you made a mistake." She stormed from the room, slammed the door behind her, and moved into the corridor.

This man was playing with her life, her future. She could understand his concern for Daniel. Heartless as it seemed, it wasn't her problem. She wasn't Daniel's mother.

Nanna stood a few paces away. She took a step forward. "Traci, don't be too hard on Thomas. You've caused him and Daniel a great deal of pain. Thomas has been crazy with worry about the boy." She paused, seeming to search for the right words. "I've prayed for you to become the woman your husband and son need. Please try, Traci, for my sake. For all our sakes. I'm getting too old and too tired to clean up behind you."

The haunted look in her eyes struck Mercy like a physical blow. How could her double have caused so much heartache, crushed so many spirits?

"Nanna, I'm not..."

Nanna removed a white lace handkerchief from her pocket and held it to her eyes. She sniffed, and then patted Mercy's arm. The woman disappeared down the corridor, looking like Atlas with the weight of the world on his shoulder.

Warning bells went off in Mercy's head. She'd spent most of her childhood without parents or grandparents, and this ready-made family could fill that void. That would be disastrous. Traci Wallace was alive somewhere, and Thomas Wallace came with the package.

She dashed back and changed into sweats and running shoes. On her way out, she stopped at the scrapbook she'd noticed earlier, and flipped it open. Page after page of Traci's exploits unfolded in tabloid headlines.

A wedding picture and article dated seven years ago captioned, "Wedding of the Year."

Sorry ladies, but party girl and fashion model Traci Montgomery, has captured the heart of Thomas Wallace, heir to the Wallace Oil Machinery fortune. The couple exchanged vows Saturday in a private ceremony with five hundred of their closest friends on Wallace's private island.

A year later, another photo of Traci holding baby Daniel, with Thomas smiling in the background. The caption read, "Wallace Heir Arrives."

More recent stories turned ugly. Pictures of Traci and a Latin-type male leaving her London apartment. A topless Traci sunbathing on the yacht of an American playboy. Traci arrested for disrobing down to her underwear in a Paris fountain. A drunk and uninvited Traci joining the singers onstage at an Italian opera house. A public affair with a man named Ricco Rossellini, the man shown in the London photos.

And on and on.

Surreal, seeing her face below the tawdry headlines. Mercy closed the book, heat searing her face. Who would save such disreputable publicity? Did she take pride in her escapades? Keep them around to punish her husband? The scrapbook left Mercy with no doubts about her identity. She could never have been involved in such behavior.

"Browsing through your press clippings?"

She jumped and swung around to face the man.

Thomas leaned against the doorframe, his expression a mask of stone. "I guess I should thank you. There has been no notoriety for months. I've kept Daniel secluded here on the island to shield him from such unsavory publicity. I never want him to see you as you are. A woman without honor, pride, or morals."

4

Wallace Island, Aegean Sea
Saturday, May 6

After the confrontation with Traci, Thomas stood at the window overlooking the beach. Electric blue surf pounded the sand, leaving behind starfish and an occasional turtle. Seagulls perched on large rocks jutting up from the sea and on driftwood along the shore. Past the beach, palm trees with heavy, verdant leaves swayed in the wind.

The view from the window was serene, unlike the emotions churning in his gut. He'd overheard the meeting between his wife and Nanna in the hallway.

Traci had never shied away from a screaming match with her grandmother. Yet she seemed...what was the word...almost gentle. She'd never shown a compassionate side since he'd known her. Why the change?

He shook his head. People didn't make a one-eighty turn in temperament. Not a woman like Traci. She was a chameleon who adapted to her environment, sticking a finger in the wind to see which way it blew. What was her game this time?

She'd made a hefty income before their marriage as one of the top fashion models in the world. Not enough to support the lifestyle he'd provided, but well into six figures. After she disappeared, her face vanished from the covers of magazines and the other fashion rags. He'd checked with her modeling agency when he learned of Daniel's heart problem. The agency was also looking for her.

Appearances suggested Rossellini hadn't contributed to her support in Bermuda. The bungalow was far below either of their expensive tastes. Whatever her scheme, it had to be about money. With Traci, it was always about money.

He stopped mid-pace, something he hadn't done since she left. The woman was home less than a day, and his blood pressure had risen twenty points.

He snatched up the satellite phone and checked in with his office in Edinburgh. Had to let his assistant know he wouldn't be in until next week. When they finished, he asked to speak to his father. He answered after a short wait. "Dad, I'm going to be away from the office for a week. Traci and I are going to devote some uninterrupted time to Daniel."

"Traci's back?" There was a chill in his voice.

"Yes, just until Daniel is well. He was asking for her, so I brought her home."

At the mention of Daniel, his father's tone softened. "Fine, son. Nothing here we can't handle until you get back."

A couple hours later, Thomas had cleared his desk. He stood and flexed his muscles to ease the stiffness. He punched his hands into his pockets and moved to the window.

Traci and Daniel came into view, stark against the white sand, strolling hand in hand, picking up seashells. Daniel let go of her hand and rushed ahead as if he'd spotted a prize specimen.

Must have finished her jog, something else he'd

never known his wife to do. Exercise had always been limited to lifting a glass of sangria.

For a long moment she stood, staring out at the sea. What was she thinking? Already bored with the island and missing the nightlife?

Daniel dropped an object into his pail and skipped back to slip his hand into hers.

Finding his wife had cost him. From this distance, the look on his son's face was worth everything he'd paid, and more.

Thomas's gaze moved on to Fergus, standing on a bluff watching the pair. He would keep a watchful eye on them. His old friend distrusted Traci more than Thomas did. The old Scot had argued about bringing her back. "Let sleeping dogs lie," he'd said. Fergus doted on the boy, and he knew Traci's ability to hurt the vulnerable child.

With a shake of his head, Thomas proceeded to the kitchen and hailed the housekeeper. "Edda, have someone prepare a picnic basket for me."

The housekeeper greeted his entrance into her domain with a smile. A slim woman in her mid-forties, Edda Hoffman's stiff personality lacked warmth, but she was efficient at her job.

"Certainly, Mr. Thomas. Stella made some nice fried chicken, potato salad, and an apple pie for lunch. I'll have her see to it right away."

Thomas couldn't suppress the smile that creased his face as he hurried upstairs and changed into shorts and sandals.

Whenever Traci came home to the island, fried food and rich pastries appeared on the menu. The household staff detested her, for good reason. They sabotaged her diet in every way possible. It would cost them when she retaliated, but they fought with the only weapons they had.

Ah, home, sweet home.

Lunch in hand, Thomas headed across the terrace and down to the beach.

Traci and his son watched his approach and waited.

"Anybody hungry?"

Daniel ran over and placed one hand on the basket. "Me, Daddy. Want to see my shells? We found some shiny gold ones."

"Great, you can show me your collection while we eat." He spread a blanket on the sand and placed the food on top.

Thomas reached inside the container and handed Daniel a chicken leg. He grabbed a plate and added potato salad and a slice of pie for the boy.

He turned to Traci. "What will you have?"

She looked into the well-laden container. "Whatever's handy. It all looks good. Your cook is quite an accomplished chef."

He tilted his head, glad she couldn't see his eyes through the sunglasses, filled a plate, and handed it to her.

Mockery? If so, she hid it well.

Daniel spread his shells out on the blanket for Thomas's approval.

"Nice specimens, son. They'll be great additions to your collection."

Daniel refilled his pail and wandered nearby to build a sandcastle

"Have you been ill?" There was more than a little sarcasm in the question, but she gave him a startled glance.

"How did you know?" She raised a hand to her hairline. "Ah, you noticed the scar."

He scrutinized her brow. A thin, white line began just at the hairline and disappeared into a thick mass of blonde waves. Invisible unless pointed out. "What happened?"

She lifted her right shoulder, shrugging off the question as if it was unimportant. "An automobile accident. That's why I was in Bermuda. The doctor ordered rest."

"Where did it happen? The accident, I mean?"

"In Houston. The other person's fault, or so the authorities said. Lucky for me. His insurance paid all my medical bills, including the rehab in Bermuda." She stared into his eyes. "What makes you so sure I'm Traci?"

"You mean aside from the airport's SDK system?"

"You mentioned that before. What is it?"

"In layman's terms, it's software that almost all airports have since 9/11. A photo is loaded into the system, usually those of criminals or terrorists. Facial measurements are taken, width between the eyes, length of the nose, hairline, etc. It then snaps pictures when passengers come through customs and makes a comparison. You were a match."

"And it's infallible?"

"Close enough."

"If your wife disappeared—"

"You are my wife."

"Whatever—six months ago, why did it take so long to find me? Why didn't it pick me up months ago when I left Houston, or when I first arrived in Bermuda?"

"You were only programmed into the system two

weeks ago. My last ditch effort to find you."

Perception dawned in her brilliant blue eyes. "That would have been when I returned from Houston after filling out personnel forms for Sabine Oil."

Thomas lay back on the blanket and propped his head on his elbow, keeping an eye on Daniel. "Why Sabine Oil? Why not modeling?"

She scoffed. "Because I'm a trained geologist. I really need that job. What happens after two months? You take me back to Houston, and I join the ranks of the unemployed?"

He shook his head, deciding not to play the game. "How's the outing going?"

"Don't change the subject. I want to know what happens when you discover I'm not who you think I am. And how do I get my cat back?"

He threw his napkin down, feeling the hot flush of blood rushing to his face. "When Daniel is well, if you want a job, I'll see to it. I already told you I'd take care of the blasted cat."

She nodded and looked out across the water that almost matched the deep color of her eyes. "Daniel...he's very intelligent for a six-year-old, with an active imagination. But he's too serious for a child his age. It's like talking to an adult. When's he's better, he needs children to play with. Are there other families on the island?"

She should know the answer, although to be fair, she rarely left the villa when in residence. "Only the staff who works for me and their families live here. They have housing, but I'm not sure how many children there are. There's a small makeshift village, which isn't much. A ramshackle pub for the men and a few fruit and vegetable stands. My pilot and Daniel's tutor live in apartments behind the villa."

"Is there a church?"

"Of sorts. A padre who has a small chapel. Father Paul is older than dirt, but he still holds services every Sunday morning. He came with the island when my grandfather bought it after my dad was born."

"Do you attend?"

This was a discussion he didn't want to have. Especially not with a secularist like Traci. "I did once, but I gave it up. Too much evil and pain in the world for a loving God to let it continue."

Her blue gaze searched his face. "Evil and pain aren't new. They've been around since the beginning of time. Does Daniel go?"

"He and Nanna attend regularly. Why all this sudden interest in religion? As far as I know, you haven't set foot inside a church since you were a child and Nanna made you go."

Before she could answer, Daniel ran back and plopped into her lap. "Know something, Mummy? You seem different since you came back. You smile more." He scooped up a shell from his plastic bucket and examined it carefully. "I didn't use to think you liked me, and I wondered why I made you mad all the time."

She smoothed the hair from his brow and turned his head so he had to look into her eyes. "There would have to be something very wrong with *anyone* who didn't like you, Daniel. You are the smartest, sweetest, most handsome little boy I know."

Thomas's throat constricted at the glow that seemed to settle on Daniel's face. That one compliment from his mother did more for his self-esteem than a thousand from someone else.

God help her if she ever did anything to crush his spirit again.

❧❧

The long day finally over, Mercy retired to her room to follow her usual routine. Shower, brush teeth, and slip into her pajamas.

All the comforts of home. Who was she kidding? Her home had never been anything like this.

She stepped into the tiled enclosure, turned on the rain-shower head full force, and stood there, letting the water run from the top of her head down over her face.

Everything that had happened to her since yesterday seemed bizarre. One minute she was walking down a Bermuda street, the next minute whisked in a private plane to a lush island, told she was the wife of a man she'd never seen before and mother to a six-year-old boy.

Would anyone believe it? Even she didn't believe. What could she expect going forward? So far, he had treated her well. Royally, in fact. Perhaps she should be afraid, but somehow she wasn't. She had the impression Thomas Wallace no longer found his wife desirable. He'd probably moved on. Who could blame him?

Thomas Wallace didn't appear to be insane. Somewhat delusional? Yes. But not crazy. He appeared to have good reason for his delusion. She wondered about his wife. Of course, with his looks and money, he would have no trouble finding women to share his affection. He probably had to beat them off with a stick.

She was here for Daniel's sake. Nothing more.

Water therapy didn't help her confusion. She reached for the shampoo and washed the sand from her hair and then pulled on a thick, white robe. Standing in front of the elaborate dressing table, she towel-dried her hair.

Should she go say good night to Daniel?

Of course. He thought she was his mother.

She slipped into blue silk pajamas and a matching robe and went next door. She knocked. "Daniel, may I come in?"

No sound came from inside the room. As she turned to go, the door opened. "Mummy?"

"I didn't wake you, did I? I just wanted to say good night. May I come in?"

He smiled, nodded, and dashed back into bed.

She followed and pulled a chair close to the bedside. "Are you feeling well?"

He nodded.

"Do you say prayers before you go to sleep?"

"Yes, ma'am."

"Would you like me to listen while you say them?"

In answer, he jumped to the floor and knelt beside the bed.

She joined him on her knees.

He peeked through his fingers and began. "Thank You for the world so sweet, Thank You for the food we eat. Thank You for the birds that sing. Thank You God for everything. And God, thank You for Mummy coming home. Amen."

She swallowed, waiting for the tightness in her throat to loosen. "That was beautiful, Daniel. Thank you." With a kiss on the top of his head, she tucked him in.

Back in her room, she flipped off the lights and slipped between the cool sheets. She tossed for an hour, unable to shut off her thoughts of the little boy. Outside the open French doors, the incoming tide pounding against rocks on the shore called to her. She put on her robe and slippers and walked out to the balcony. She stood at the rail, arms crossed in a body hug.

The moon was huge, hanging low just above the sea, making the tips of the waves silver in its brightness. The island was an oasis in a world gone mad, filling her with the illusion nothing bad could ever happen here. Safety was important. The memory of why wasn't clear, but darkness frightened her.

The sound of breaking glass startled her introspection, and she peered through the shadows around the pool, its waterfall hidden in the darkness of palm trees. Seeing nothing, she turned back into the bedroom and knelt beside her bed.

God was in control. He always had been, always would be.

She didn't believe in happenstance. There must be a purpose for her presence here.

❧❦

Thomas sat in the study in his oversized lounge chair and poured two fingers of brandy into a snifter. He swirled the amber liquid in the glass and then downed it. What was wrong with him? Traci had lost her hold on him years ago. Ever since he'd found out about Rossellini. She'd tried to entice him back into her bed, but he refused, unwilling to share his wife with another man. He splashed another drink into the snifter, empting it in one gulp.

He grabbed his glass and the brandy bottle and headed for the pool. Fresh air would clear his head. He weaved his way to a deck chair, filled the glass again, and placed the bottle on the cool stone deck.

In the east wing, second-floor bedroom, a light flicked on. Traci's room. She came out on the balcony and stood in the moonlight. An old familiar ache washed over him. Why was he finding himself drawn to her again? Still the same Traci, and yet she wasn't. She reflected innocence, a vulnerability that had never been part of her complex personality.

He had to avoid her. Stay out of her way until she left the island. Before he did something stupid.

Seizing the snifter, he hurled it against the rocks at the waterfall's base. The sound echoed in his ears, and glass shards gleamed in the dim lighting.

He dipped his head under the fall, letting the cool liquid run down his face, wetting his shirt. Drunk as a barfly. But not so intoxicated he didn't realize he'd have to have someone clean up the glass in the morning. The waterfall was one of Daniel's favorite places to play.

5

Wallace Island, the Aegean Sea
Saturday, May 13

The next to last day of the proclaimed holiday in her honor, Mercy dressed for breakfast.

There had been unusual activity on the island yesterday. The plane left early and returned late last night. Perhaps a trip for supplies. Somehow, taking a plane to do the grocery shopping seemed a little extraordinary. But this was not a normal household.

She stepped into the downstairs entryway.

Nanna waited for her. Dressed in a pale shade of lavender, she smoothed an imaginary strand of silver, perfectly coiffed hair and pulled Mercy close, whispering. "Do you know what's going on? The men have been acting strangely since yesterday, and Thomas told me not to come to breakfast until I was summoned."

Mercy shook her head. "I haven't a clue. It's not your birthday, is it?"

With a throaty laugh, Nanna shook her head. "Not unless my memory has gotten worse than I thought."

Thomas appeared in the dining room entrance, a boyish grin on his face. "Good morning, ladies. You may come in to breakfast, now."

An elaborately wrapped package sat in front of one of the chairs, which Thomas hurried to hold out.

"Nanna, this is the place of honor."

She gave him a regal nod, raised a brow in Mercy's direction, and stared at Thomas. "OK, what's the occasion? I know it isn't my birthday, and it certainly isn't Christmas."

He motioned for everyone to take a seat. "In America, they set aside one day a year to honor mothers, always on Sunday. However, since I must return to work tomorrow, we're celebrating today."

Nanna removed the bow, tore away the paper, and pulled out a beautiful, silver and gray Hermes scarf. "Thank you, Thomas. As always, you have excellent taste."

Thomas gulped down a swig of coffee and nodded at his son. "Daniel and I had a difficult time deciding what to get for two women who have everything. Didn't we, Danny?"

Daniel nodded, put his hand over his mouth, and giggled.

"Nanna was pretty easy. She can always use another Hermes. But you—" he glanced over at Mercy, "—were difficult. We did find a gift. However, it couldn't be gift-wrapped. Danny, would you like to give your mother her present?"

Mercy sat speechless as Daniel ran from the room and returned with her cat, Paddy.

The cat jumped from Daniel's arms and dashed to rub his head against her leg, rumbling a deep purr.

Mercy's throat tightened, and she mouthed a silent *thank you* to Thomas. Bringing her cat revealed a chink in his hardened image. A man who would go to such trouble to keep a promise couldn't be all bad.

She pulled Paddy into her arms, tears stinging behind her eyes. "Hey, you old reprobate. Have you been making it OK without me?"

Thomas laughed. "When Frank brought in this battle-scarred old tomcat, I thought he'd gotten the wrong animal. I was expecting to see some white, blue-eyed pedigree, and he brings home this old warrior."

She smiled, nuzzling the cat's fur with her nose. Getting a Mother's Day present was a new experience. Diamonds wouldn't have pleased her as much. "He adopted me during a hurricane in Houston." Mercy stroked his fur. "I heard yowling on my patio. When I opened the door, he shot in and took up residence. We became best friends. I named him Patton, after the tough old general, but he became Paddy."

Daniel moved in close. "May I pet him, Mummy?"

"Of course. He's gentle as can be, and he's always hungry."

Thomas chuckled. "Frank said he ate six cans of cat food on the flight, so I guess we need to lay in a big supply."

Mercy shook her head. "Paddy's a survivor. He's use to scrounging for food. He'll probably catch his own fish and rid the island of mice."

Daniel picked up Paddy and headed towards the kitchen. "Come on kitty, I'll get cook to give you some shrimp."

Paddy's hazel-eyes crossed and turned to her as if he understood Daniel's words. The old street fighter had just landed in cat heaven.

৵৽

Naples, Italy
Saturday, May 13

Ricco Rossellini removed three tabloids from his middle desk drawer, glared at the headlines, and then at the man sitting in front of him. "I thought you took care of this problem, Lorenz. It was a simple task. Get rid of a woman half your size. You blew it." Ricco settled back in the chair. "You came highly recommended, and at an exorbitant price, I might add. You should have made her tell you where she stashed the pictures."

Lorenz Lucci towered over Ricco's own six-feet-one-inch stature. He had the manicured hands of a surgeon, dressed in a tailored gray suit, Italian silk shirt, discreet navy tie and simple elegant jewelry. More like an English banker than a paid assassin.

Despite his name, Lucci didn't look Italian. Ricco figured him as mixed, probably Swedish, with his icy blue eyes. That, or he'd been adopted.

Lucci's cold gaze settled on Ricco. "It didn't go as planned. She put up a fight. Before I could question her, she went off the cliff. She couldn't have survived that plunge, Ricco, with the rocks and surf below."

"If she couldn't survive, tell me how she was seen—" he tapped the newspaper, "—at a Bermuda airport boarding her husband's jet? The photos she took can destroy me. Did it occur to you to make sure she was dead?"

Lorenz glared at him. "No way to scale the cliff, and I didn't think it was necessary. Like I said, no one could survive that drop."

"You didn't think at all. Now I still have a problem to deal with." Ricco gave the two goons standing by the ship's portal a curt nod. "Get him out of my sight."

Lorenz stood. "I'll take care of it. I have a reputation. And, I still have a contact on the island."

"I'm not paying you to re-do a job you bungled in the first place."

"I didn't ask you for money. This is personal, a freebie. A satisfaction guarantee."

Ricco shrugged. The man should finish the job he paid him to do. "Don't mess it up this time. You won't get another chance. You understand what I'm telling you?"

Lorenz didn't flinch. His icy gaze swept over Ricco without blinking. Lorenz was one of the most deadly men alive. He didn't scare. Without a backward glance, he wheeled around and left the cabin.

Topside, Ricco strolled the deck, as his men escorted Lucci back to the dock. Violence wasn't something Ricco enjoyed. Unfortunately, it was a byproduct of his business—a lucrative business that paid for his villa, his yacht, and all the other luxuries he enjoyed.

Ricco gazed across the harbor. Pristine luxury cruisers rolled easily in the cerulean sea. A whisper of breezes brought faint sounds of reggae music and laughter across the water. Seagulls swooped across the clear sky and hovered near fishing boats in the harbor. He relaxed against the deck chair. Days like this brought his thoughts to lazy afternoons with Traci Wallace aboard his yacht.

He had loved Traci's free spirit, her thumbing her nose at social constraints, the wild excitement she generated whenever she entered a room. Even though she betrayed him, a part of him welcomed the news she was alive.

How could he have known the little fool, so lacking in moral fiber, would suddenly develop a social conscience?

He'd never tried to hide anything from her. She had been his soul mate, his equal. Rules and laws were for others. But she'd put the pieces of his organization together and turned patriot, snapping pictures with her cell phone of terrorist leaders onboard his boat.

Those photographs could topple the empire he'd built. He wouldn't allow that to happen. Not even for the lovely Traci Wallace.

6

Wallace Island, the Aegean Sea
Sunday, May 14

Thomas had avoided Traci and liquor for the remainder of the seven-day holiday. He found himself relaxing in his home for the first time since his marriage. Daniel's laughter sounded through the villa's corridors and that pleased Thomas. It was the reason he'd brought Traci home. Not that he trusted her, but whatever her reasons, he welcomed the change.

Past visits left everyone exhausted and glad to see her fly off into the horizon. He'd tolerated her tantrums for Daniel's benefit. Nothing she did dampened the boy's affection for her.

He'd held his breath, waiting for the outbursts that would send the villa into an uproar, but it never came. With luck, it would last when he returned to work.

At breakfast Sunday morning, he found the dining room empty. He filled his plate from the buffet and seated himself at the head of the table.

A kitchen maid brought coffee and juice. "Good morning, Mr. Thomas." She turned to leave.

He swallowed the bite of toast. "Good morning, Lily. Has the rest of the family eaten?"

She nodded. "Yes sir, they were down early. They're upstairs dressing for church." She shook her head. "Imagine that, Mrs. Wallace in church."

He hid a smile at her frankness. "Mrs. Wallace is going?"

"Yes, sir. That's what she said."

Thomas finished breakfast and was on his third cup of coffee when voices in the foyer caught his attention. He brought his cup to the doorway and leaned against the arch.

Traci, Nanna, and Daniel stepped into the entryway. Traci wore a white linen sheath and straw hat, Nanna was in light blue and sported her new scarf, and Daniel looked handsome in short pants, blazer, and tie.

Thomas smiled. The tabloids would have fodder for a thousand articles with this image of his flamboyant wife, dressed discreetly, and on her way to church. He joined them outside where Fergus waited. "Headed to chapel?"

They stopped, and Nanna gave him a teasing smile. "You're welcome to come with us, Thomas. Father Paul asks about you."

"Can't this time. I'm leaving for Edinburgh this morning. Have to get back to work." He didn't want to leave. It was always hard being away from his son for five days. He covered the space between them in a few strides and picked Daniel up. "I'll be home late Friday. Be good and have fun. School starts again tomorrow." He gave Nanna a slight nod. "Call me, if you need to."

Her smile brightened. "I'll call if we have an emergency."

He turned to Traci. "Let Nanna or Fergus know if you need anything. They'll contact me."

Traci looked into his eyes and held his gaze. "I can't imagine anything I could possibly need." The unspoken words, "except my freedom," lay between them.

❧

The chapel was crowded with islanders, many of whom Mercy recognized as staff at the villa. Most nodded with stiff smiles, though a few ignored her. She and her small family moved down the aisle and found seats near the front.

Open windows on each side provided a cool morning breeze as the ancient priest took his place behind the rough-hewn pulpit. His skin, dark and wrinkled by the island sun, highlighted his white hair and luminous dark eyes.

Before beginning his message, Father Paul introduced a young cleric sitting on the dais. 'This is Father Joseph. He will be taking my place while I return to Rome to take care of a few health problems."

Father Paul's sermon spoke of handling troubles when they come. It seemed he had prepared it for Mercy's situation. "There are four things you need to ask yourself in times of trouble. One, did I do anything to cause the problem? Two, what can I learn from the experience? Three, what can I find in this experience to be thankful for? And four, how can I find humor in this situation? Laughter is medicine for the soul."

As he expounded on the questions, Mercy considered her own answers. Was she responsible for her situation? No. There might be a lesson in her predicament, but it hadn't yet presented itself. Being thankful was easy. Thomas Wallace was a stubborn, hard man, but so far, he had done her no harm, if one didn't count making her unemployed. Laughter, she was learning from Daniel.

Father Joseph rose from the pew after the message ended. He wasn't a tall man, but he stood tall, his steps strong and purposeful. He could have been Father Paul fifty years ago, with his full head of black hair, dark eyes, and permanent laugh lines at the corners of his mouth. "As the good father mentioned, I'll be filling in for him until he returns. I know you will miss him, and will pray for his speedy recovery."

After the service, the two black-robed men stood at the door as the congregants left.

"Mrs. Wallace, I'm so glad you came." Father Paul's wrinkled hands clasped her own. "I hope you'll be here for Father Joseph's first sermon next week. Alas, I'll be leaving right after the service."

Interesting. How was the priest getting off the island? There were no other planes or boats on the island, other than Thomas's. At least, not to her knowledge. "We'll be here to give him moral support. How are you getting to Rome?"

"A cargo ship comes to the island twice a month. I've booked passage for this afternoon."

She filed the information away and shook hands with the new pastor.

He smiled, still holding her hand, and leaned in close. "If I'm not being too personal, Mrs. Wallace, when was your last confession?"

"Last night."

His eyebrows drew together and he tilted his head.

She smiled. "I'm not Catholic, Father. But if it helps, I think God is nondenominational."

He burst out laughing, dark eyes twinkling in his handsome face. "You may be right, but don't spread it around. I might find myself unemployed."

The temperature had grown warmer as the morning progressed. A cool breeze whispered into the foyer, giving temporary relief. "We'll keep it our secret. You must come to lunch next week, to celebrate your new post."

"Those are precious words to a man who dislikes his own cooking."

"Do you have a phone here?" she asked.

"A radio, but no telephone."

"Then I'll ask Fergus to pick you up."

"I will wait impatiently."

Minutes later, Fergus pulled the golf cart in front of the church and drove them home for lunch. There were no automobiles on the island and, obviously, no gas stations.

To her surprise, Thomas hadn't left when they reached the villa. His luggage sat outside the front entrance. She hurried inside to catch him before he left. They almost collided in the entrance. "May I speak to you for a moment?"

"You'll have to make it quick. I have an appointment in Edinburgh this afternoon." He turned back and led her into his office.

After the door closed, she picked up pen and paper from the desk, made a note and handed it to him. "This has my name, social security number, and my address in Houston. It will prove what I'm telling you is fact. Just check it out. That's all I ask."

"Traci, I don't have time—"

"Have one of your people look into it. Please." She started to leave, and then turned back. "Can you do me a favor?"

"Another favor?"

She nodded. "Father Paul is very ill. Can you give him a lift to Rome? Otherwise he'll have to spend a day or more on an old tramp steamer."

"To Rome, by way of Edinburgh? You flunked geography, right? I told you I have an appointment...I'm not running an air-taxi service, Traci." He folded the piece of paper and placed it in his inside pocket with a dark look that tightened the lines around his mouth.

She gave him her biggest smile.

He expelled a deep breath. "OK, I can have Frank drop me off, and then take the priest to Rome before he returns to the island."

"What do I do with myself while you're gone? Any special instructions before you leave?"

"You can practice being a loving, caring, mother."

She stood still for a moment.

When at a loss for words, he always fell back on rudeness. Pity. No response was needed and she turned and left the room.

After the plane had gone, Mercy changed into jeans and a T-shirt, grabbed Paddy, and ran down to the dock. The steamer was just coming in. She had no money, but she could tell them she was taking Father Paul's place.

Did Thomas know about the steamer? Probably not. Otherwise, he wouldn't have left her alone today. Heart racing, she stepped onto the dock. In Rome, she could contact the American Embassy. She could be home in less than a week.

"Mummy. Mummy. What are you doing?" Daniel ran and took her hand, his over-bright eyes darted from her, to the ship, and back to her. Almost as if he read her mind.

The pleading look in his eyes broke her heart.

She couldn't do it. Easing out a deep breath, she gave his hand a gentle squeeze. "Just watching the big ship unload supplies. Want to watch with me?"

∂∾⌐

Edinburgh, Scotland
Sunday, May 14

Thomas kept the appointment he mentioned to Traci with the buyer. The man stopped in Edinburgh to firm up connections with Wallace personnel at the conference in Saudi Arabia. The meeting was a courtesy visit with an important buyer. It turned into an early dinner before Thomas saw him to his gate and left the airport.

The last ray of evening sunlight reflected off the car's windshield as Thomas exited onto the highway, turned left, and headed for Wallace Manor, his family home. He stayed with his father during the work week. Edward Wallace had retired, but since his wife's death, he went into the office almost daily.

The property wasn't gated. There'd been no need until after Thomas married Traci—when the Wallace family achieved celebrity status. As a result, photographers often lolled outside the entrance trying to get a photo op they could sell to eager tabloids.

Thomas had never lost the sense of pride that filled him each time his family home came into view. The huge, rambling estate represented two-hundred years of Wallace ancestors, descendents of Sir William Wallace, the leader of the wars for Scottish independence. Sir William died in 1305 without children, but was survived by his brothers Malcolm and John Wallace. The manor, the social focal point of the district while his mother was alive, was now only used for family gatherings.

His father's old manservant met him at the door. "Hi, Henry. Is Dad at home?"

"Yes, sir. In the library, reading, I believe."

Thomas left his luggage in the entryway and strolled down the wide corridor to find his father.

The scent of cherry pipe tobacco and a woodsy oak fragrance from the hearth greeted him when he entered the library.

Edward Wallace sat in a large leather chair, before a hearty fire, his Bible open in his lap. Something he had done every evening for as long as Thomas could remember.

Thomas's loss of faith had disappointed the senior Wallace, but he couldn't fix that. He'd tried. Faith was the cornerstone of his dad's life, and Thomas hated that his own disillusionment caused his father pain.

Edward Wallace's hair had turned white, but his spine was still straight as a soldier's. His eyes sparkled with intelligence and good humor.

Thomas smiled. This would be his own image when he was seventy.

"It's good to have you back, Thomas. Did you enjoy the time with your family?"

Thomas eased into the chair next to him and nodded. "Yes, it was great, really. Traci was on her best behavior, for a change."

Edward Wallace ran his index finger over his lower lip, a small wrinkle between his brows. "I've been happy to see there have been no new escapades in the tabloids recently. Perhaps she's growing up."

"We can always hope so."

"It's none of my business, son, but what are you going to do about the situation if she hasn't changed?"

Thomas rested his head against the cushioned wingback chair. "Dad, I wish I knew."

৵৽৻

Wallace Island, the Aegean Sea
Monday, May 15

Mercy watched her chance to escape sail away. If the ship came twice a month, there would be other opportunities. But the expression on Daniel's face would always haunt her. For the present, she'd just have to make the best of her captivity.

She hadn't met Daniel's tutor. Before lunchtime, she made her way upstairs to Daniel's classroom and stood in the doorway, not wanting to interrupt until he'd finished the lesson.

Ainsley McCrary, better know as Mac, was a tiny man, shorter than Mercy. It seemed a strong breeze could lift him off the ground and carry him away. Close-cropped red hair and large tortoise-shell eyeglasses completed his nerdy persona. But there was more to Mac than met the eye.

She'd overheard a few of his English and history lessons as he often took Daniel outside for classes, sitting under a tree, or on the terrace. Mac had held her spellbound. A captivating storyteller, he wove vivid details and historical tidbits into subjects, making it feel more like a fascinating conversation than a school lesson. Strange that someone with so much talent would hide away on an island.

He must have sensed her presence, as he looked at her and smiled. "Mrs. Wallace, how nice of you to join us."

She stepped into the room and held out her hand. "I thought I'd drop by and introduce myself when I picked up Daniel for lunch. You're doing an excellent job with him. I never have to remind him it's time for school. He's always eager to head off to class."

He gave her a fingertip hand shake. "That's nice of you to say, ma'am. He's a very bright boy."

Mercy smiled. "Do you leave soon for summer vacation?"

He shook his head. "Not this year. I usually teach a history class at Edinburgh University, but I opted to stay here over the summer break to write a book on Scottish history."

"How exciting for you. You must come to dinner one evening and tell us all about it."

"Thank you, ma'am. That's kind of you. I'll look forward to it."

Over lunch, Mercy sat quietly listening to the conversation between Nanna and Daniel as she asked about his lesson that morning. Having them close filled a void she'd long ignored. She needed to get back to her life before the attachments became too strong, if it wasn't already too late.

That afternoon, she and Nanna sat on the terrace and watched Daniel get to know his new friends. Three children his age lived on the island, two boys, and a little girl. She'd kept the playtime to non-physical activities; painting, playing with clay, and puzzles, for the present.

Getting the parents' permission ran into a few bumpy spots. Mothers were less than thrilled to leave their children in the care of a woman with Traci's reputation, and with just cause. The presence of Fergus and Nanna, both held in high esteem by the islanders, decided the matter in Mercy's favor. She would never expose Daniel to bad influences, and she couldn't expect other parents to trust her at the start.

It would be a challenge to win the inhabitants over. For Daniel's sake, she had to try. Perhaps when his mother came home, she would respond to a kinder atmosphere from the people. Living with constant disapproval, even if well earned, could dampen anyone's spirit.

The maid brought a frosty decanter of tropical punch with bits of strawberries and pineapple, and placed it on the table by Mercy.

"Thank you, Lily. tI looks refreshing." Mercy poured a glass for Nanna and one for herself, took a long sip, of the cold, sweetly tart drink, a luxury she'd come to enjoy. Despite her angst at being here against her will, she had to admit the sumptuousness of this place could become addictive. Despite the benefits, however, she would have left, except for Daniel. She didn't belong here—another woman's stand-in.

Nanna observed her over the rim of her glass. "You're different since your return, Traci. A pleasant change, to be sure. What happened while you were away?"

Mercy laughed at the old woman's refreshing honesty. She debated whether to confess her real identity. Thomas wouldn't approve. He would be furious if the truth got back to Daniel. The boy accepted her as his mother. Knowing she wasn't would crush him. Worse, he would probably think she was denying him again.

She wiped away frost from the outside of the glass, searching for the right words. "Have I really changed so much?"

"Dramatically, I would say. If you don't wish to discuss it, that's OK. But you should know you can confide in me. I've always kept your confidences."

"I'll remember that, Nanna. Thank you."

The head trauma from her accident had left blank spots in her memory. Missing pieces she had yet to find. It would take time, or so the doctor told her. But one constant remained. She'd lived a solitary life, a determined career woman, never considering marriage or children an option. One word described her life to this point. Lonely. If she could return to Houston tomorrow and report to Sabine Oil, would it be enough?

She'd spent the time in Bermuda trying to gain perspective. To look at her life, try to understand what lay ahead. She didn't like what she saw. Her life was merely a continuation of the solitary existence it seemed she'd always known.

Over the past nine days, she'd grown close to Daniel. They were kindred spirits. He had grown up without his mother, she without either parent. In that short time period, he'd wrapped his small fingers around her heart and brought out every maternal instinct she possessed. He gave unconditional love, holding nothing back. His innocence exposed feelings she'd never experienced. Seeing the world through his eyes gave her a new perspective on what life could be like with a family. How could she go away—leave him still recovering from surgery, still so emotionally vulnerable?

Later that night, she slid under the silky sheets and

reached for a novel at her bedside. A timid knock at the door made her lay the book back down.

"Yes?"

Daniel's head appeared around the door. "Mummy, m-may I come in?"

She smiled and patted the bed. "Only for a moment. You're supposed to be asleep."

He scurried across the room and slid in beside her.

"Were you frightened?"

He shook his head. "No-o, just wanted to talk."

"What shall we talk about? You choose the subject."

His head rested on her shoulder. "Do you like it here, Mummy?"

She paused, sensing the direction this conversation would go. "Very much. And I like being with you most of all."

His blue gaze searched her face. "Do you like it enough you won't go away again?"

Tears pooled in her eyes. She pulled him close. She couldn't make a promise she couldn't keep. She must leave sometime, at least in the next six weeks. The truth would have to come later. "I don't want to leave you, Daniel."

7

Wallace Island, the Aegean Sea
Friday, May 19

Two weeks had passed since Mercy came to the island.

Thomas returned home on Friday and left Sunday, spending his time with Daniel, ignoring her for the most part. He still seemed convinced of her identity as Traci, never saying if he checked out the information she gave him.

At the end of her second week of imprisonment, she went downstairs to the pool deck to watch Daniel's morning therapy with Fergus, amazed at the child's swimming prowess.

"How's he doing?"

The old Scot nodded at her. "He's coming along right well." He called to Daniel. "One more lap, but take it easy, lad. Don't rush. It's no' a race."

Daniel was either a natural athlete or someone had spent hours training him. "He certainly has no fear of the water."

"Never had any," Fergus said. "Gets it from his father. And he's getting his color back. He'll be right as rain in no time."

Much as she hated to give Thomas credit, he'd been right. From all appearances, her presence had improved Daniel's mental health. His laughter constantly bubbled to the surface, and according to Nanna, his appetite had improved since her arrival.

The boy's confidence also seemed to grow daily. He approached her with less trepidation, more sure of his reception. Confidence built on the lie that she was his mother. The thought of what would happen when he discovered the truth frightened her.

Paddy walked into the pool area. He avoided the water but liked to stay close. He leaped into her lap, circled until he found a comfortable spot, and began to purr.

Sunlight flashed on the hillside nearest the villa. She scanned the ridge and saw the flash again. Odd. This was something new.

Binoculars?

Had Thomas posted someone to watch her every move?

Fergus's hovering presence followed whenever she left the villa with Daniel on their frequent trips to explore the island. The old Scot drove in another golf cart behind them.

The servants also lurked in the background, especially Edda.

Mercy had grown used to that. The reflection on the mountain wasn't paranoia. And Fergus stood not ten feet from her. He had no need to spy on her from a distance.

Daniel joined her in the lounge chair, wet and breathing hard, claiming her attention. "Is Daddy coming home tonight?"

Paddy jumped down and returned to the villa, unwilling to share Mercy with the wet boy. She took a beach towel and dried Daniel's hair, and then wrapped it around him. His question caught her off guard. The day of the week had slipped her mind.

"Yes, I believe so."

Hostility from Fergus and the staff drained her energy. She'd never been the most popular person in the room, but open resentment was a new experience. And dealing with Thomas's censure added another negative balance to her stress scale.

∽∾

Wallace, Limited, Edinburgh, Scotland
Friday, May 19

Thomas Wallace packed his briefcase Friday afternoon and headed out the office door, stopping at his secretary's desk. "Have a great weekend, Maggie. I'll see you Monday."

She glanced up from her computer, her brown eyes twinkling. "Behave yourself, Thomas. I won't be there to keep you straight."

He laughed. Maggie McNair was the best secretary he'd ever had. Fifty-five and vivacious, not only was she efficient, he didn't have to worry about her getting a crush on him. She bossed him like his mother had.

As he reached the exit, she called out, "Thomas, I just printed off one of the reports you've been waiting on. Want to take it with you or pick it up Monday?"

"I'll take it." He turned back and stuffed the two pieces of paper into the already packed briefcase, giving her a final wave as he left.

Rain pelted the windshield on the drive to the airport. Sixty-two degrees and continued precipitation, according to the forecast. No matter, he would soon be in the island's more agreeable climate. At the Edinburgh airport, he parked the car in the private hanger next to the company jet.

Frank held the aircraft door open and he dashed up the stairs and into the cabin, glad to see the busy week behind him. He was playing catch-up from the backlog caused by his week of absence. That, coupled with his investigation into Traci's actions the last six months, had doubled the workload.

Her accident story checked out. Indeed, a woman named Mercy Lawrence suffered a near-fatal head injury and spent five months in Bermuda recovering. A manila folder lay on the tray in front of him. Flicking it open with one finger, he surveyed the contents. To circumvent American privacy laws, he'd pulled a few rabbits out of a hat to get access to her medical records.

He grabbed a cup of coffee from the galley, settled into the seat, and scanned the doctor's report. After the accident, Mercy was in a coma for a week, and woke up with amnesia. The doctor's diagnosis also mentioned repressed memory. He ordered her to rest for five months before going to work.

Thomas punched the doctor's office number into the satellite phone. It took a few minutes to make the connection and a few more for the doctor to take the call.

"Doctor Moore, this is Thomas Wallace. The patient you treated under the name of Mercy Lawrence is my wife, Traci Wallace."

"Yes, Mr. Wallace. I'm aware of who you are. I spoke with a Mr. Redford. He said you'd be calling. What can I do for you?"

Thomas flipped through the pages of the report. "I'm having a little difficulty with the medical terminology in your diagnosis. Can you break it down in layman's terms for me?"

"I'll try." He cleared his throat. "The head injury caused her amnesia, which lasted slightly more than a week. I believe she also suffered from repressed memory, as well. She regained some of her past, but not all. That's what made me believe she has unintentionally repressed memories, things she didn't want to deal with emotionally."

Thomas leaned back in the chair. "What kind of memories?"

"It could be any number of things," the doctor said. "Repressed memory is a hypothetical concept used to describe a significant part of memory, usually of a traumatic event or events that has become unavailable to the patient for recall. She blocks out a painful or disturbing period in her life. It's not the same as amnesia, but in your wife's case, I believe she suffered from both."

Thomas made a few notes on the report. "Could a head injury such as the one you described cause a marked change in her personality?"

There was a slight pause before the doctor responded. "It's been known to happen. How severe a change are we talking about?"

"A complete about face. From party girl to domestic diva. Her speech is different. Ah...how do I say this...her language was more colorful in the past. She dresses differently, and her temperament is calmer, almost serene."

He sensed the wheels turning in Dr. Moore's brain. "A change that big would not be the norm, but it's possible."

"Could the injury erase past memories and replace

them with new ones?"

The doctor laughed. "No, Mr. Wallace. That's unlikely. I've learned over the course of my medical career to never say never, but it's highly improbable."

Thomas thanked the doctor for his time and clicked the phone off. He leaned back in the seat, trying to digest what he'd learned.

How should he proceed with Traci from this point? If she legitimately didn't know who she was, he needed to approach her a little less like she was a pariah.

Traci wasn't his only dilemma.

Paul Redford had called in his markers for helping to find her.

❧

Wallace Island, the Aegean Sea
Friday, May 19

The plane touched down on the island, and familiar tension knotted his stomach. He never knew what to expect. Traci's previous residence on the island had family and staff lined up at the front door to greet him with a list of complaints when he returned home.

Suitcase in one hand and briefcase in the other, he keyed the lock and nudged the door open with his shoulder.

No disgruntled mob awaited him. Muscles in his neck unknotted. He dropped his luggage in the entryway, stowed the briefcase in his office, and grabbed a bite in the kitchen. When he'd finished, he went to check on Daniel.

The door to the boy's room stood ajar, his bed

empty, covers turned back and rumpled. "Daniel. Daniel!"

This time of night, the boy should be in bed. Every dreadful possibility ran through his thoughts. Had he taken a turn for the worse? Surely, someone would have called.

He stormed into the hall and beat on Traci's door, his heart pounding like the surf in a tropical storm. Not waiting for an answer, he jerked the door open and stopped.

Daniel sat beside his mother in bed, surprise written on his face.

Traci dropped the book she held and placed a hand over her heart. "You almost scared us to death. What's wrong?"

"I'm...sorry. I panicked when I found Daniel's bed empty."

"Come in, Daddy. I'll scoot over and you can sit with us while Mummy finishes this funny story. Then you can tuck me in."

Thomas crossed to the bed and tousled his hair. He glanced at the book cover. "My mother read it to me when I was your age. I'd forgotten it was still in the library."

Daniel's head nestled next to Traci's shoulder. They made a cozy family picture, mother and son reading together. This was the new Traci, wearing silk pajamas and no makeup.

She placed a marker inside the book, closed it with a snap, and then kissed the top of Daniel's head. "That's enough for tonight. I didn't realize how late it was. We'll finish it, later."

Thomas tore his gaze away from her, picked up his son, and carried him back to bed. Daniel's arms went around his neck. "It's good to have Mummy home, isn't it, Daddy?"

He brushed his son's hair back and smiled. "If you say so. It's very good to have her home." He tucked the boy in, and strode back down the hall, hesitating at Traci's door, unsure whether to approach her. Thomas muttered a familiar line from Shakespeare under his breath. "Cowards die many times before their death: The valiant never taste death, but once." He knocked, this time more gently, and opened the door.

"I apologize for bursting in earlier. I'm irrational where Daniel is concerned."

"I've noticed that." She smiled. "No need to apologize."

"Would you come downstairs and have coffee with me? I need to speak to you." Neither one of them would be comfortable having a lengthy conversation in her bedroom.

Curiosity darkened her gaze, but then she nodded. "Let me grab a robe."

As expected, a pot of freshly brewed coffee waited in the kitchen, prepared by the ever-efficient Edda, who knew his habits.

He poured two cups and set them at a small table the kitchen staff used for breaks. The dining room was too formal for intimate conversation. And he wanted to watch her face when he told her what he'd discovered.

She entered, lowered into the chair across from him, and picked up the cup. "This may keep me up the rest of the night."

"It's decaf." He replaced the carafe and sat back down. "I spoke to your doctor today, about your injury and amnesia."

Her eyes widened. "So you believe me?"

"I accept the possibility you believe you are Mercy Lawrence. With the trauma you've experienced, have you considered that you might actually be Traci Wallace?"

"I don't have all the pieces of my memory." A shadow passed over her eyes. "But I do know who I am. Memories of my early childhood are vague, but when I accepted the position at Sabine Oil, I knew I could do the job, knew I had the training. And I could never have forgotten a husband and son."

He shifted his position and examined her face. Her gaze was steady, and she didn't look away—signals she told the truth.

"Have you done anything with the information I gave you?"

"Yes, I have people working on it. These things take time, especially when it's a foreigner inquiring into the background of an American citizen. I'm not convinced you're Mercy Lawrence, but I'm convinced you think you are."

"I could give you DNA evidence and fingerprints, as I offered in Bermuda."

"Fingerprints would be fairly easy for an expert to check, but DNA would take weeks. That will be the next step. Right now, I'm waiting for basic background information, work history, education, birth records, et cetera."

Exhaustion set in like swimming against the current. The possibility that she wasn't Traci complicated his world beyond his ability to comprehend. He rubbed his hands across the five-o'clock shadow on his face, the sound like sandpaper on wood. "If what you're telling me is true, I have an even greater problem. Not only have I done you a grave injustice, but my son believes you're his mother. I'm not sure he could stand to lose her twice."

"I'm aware of that, Thomas. And I don't have the answer."

"Can I get your promise not to do anything rash until I finish gathering all the information? We'll decide what to do, then."

She pushed the chair back and stood. "I can hardly do anything else."

He couldn't read her expression, unsure whether it was anger or resignation.

Her next words erased all doubt. "You have forced me to come here to this isolated island against my will. Made me homeless and unemployed. Now you want me to obediently sit by while you make up your mind what to do with me?"

Her outburst caught him off guard. "I understand that you're upset, and you have every right to be. But the situation exists, and I can't change that." He ran fingers through his hair. "Granted, I created this mess. But now Daniel is caught in the middle and I don't want him hurt."

Her posture relaxed and she sat back down.

"If you have an easy answer to resolve this, please tell me."

She shook her head.

Silence filled the space for a few minutes. He still needed her help and in her present mood, he doubted he would get any cooperation from her. He removed the spoon from his saucer and stirred the dark brew, stalling. "I need a favor."

She gave him a you-must-be-kidding glare. "From me? What kind of favor?"

"I...we have been invited to a formal affair in Paris

tomorrow night at the American Embassy. My presence is mandatory, and I wondered if you would go with me? Actually, I'm supposed to bring an escort, and since everyone knows we're still married, I can hardly ask someone else." He'd considered the problems with this arrangement on the flight home. Taking her would be risky. If she bolted, it would break Daniel's heart. He lifted the cup to his lips and found it empty. For a moment, he thought she hadn't heard the question, or perhaps considered it too outrageous to respond.

Finally she spoke. "How long would we be away?"

"We'll leave after breakfast tomorrow morning and return when the affair is over. It'll be late."

"You'd be taking a chance. I might try to stay at the embassy. Go back to my life."

"The thought had occurred to me. But as you've reminded me repeatedly, you no longer have a job. I can fix that and your homeless problem when you leave here." He stood and refilled his drink and started to top hers off.

She placed her hand over the cup.

"You might even be able to pull it off. However, the French authorities aren't terribly fond of you after the Concorde fountain episode. If you claim to be someone else, they'll think you're mental." He sat back down. "But I'm hoping you don't want to disillusion Daniel. So how about it? Will you come?"

"All right. Just so we're clear, I'm doing this for Daniel. He doesn't deserve to be hurt anymore than he already has been." She pushed away from the table. "I don't have a passport. Mine is still in Bermuda."

"I took the liberty of getting you a new one earlier

this week."

"It usually takes weeks."

"I just told them you'd lost yours. Replacements are easier than starting from scratch."

"Will Daniel be OK with our absence?"

"He has been in the past. If you need a new gown, you can call some of your...Traci's old connections in Paris. They'll be more than happy to accommodate you on short notice."

She waved a hand towards her room. "I don't think that will be necessary."

"It's your choice. Select your gown and accessories, and Fergus will put them on the plane. You can dress in the stateroom after we land at Orly. We'll have a few hours before time to leave for the embassy."

Mercy drained her cup and returned it to the saucer.

"Then it's settled."

"Yes." She rose, still clearly agitated, and left the room.

He carried the cups and carafe to the sink. Emotions boiled inside him he couldn't describe, even to himself. Bent on bringing Daniel's mother home, had he recklessly kidnapped the wrong woman? How was that possible? How could he have made such a monumental mistake? He needed to talk to someone, someone who could point him in the right direction. But he had pushed God out of his life ages ago.

8

Wallace Island, the Aegean Sea
Saturday, May 20

Mercy rose early and showered quickly. She had to select a dress for this evening and had only given the closet a cursory glance last night—a gown was the last thing on her mind. She'd tossed all night, considering the coffee klatch with Thomas. For the first time since this madness began, she had hope. The comments he made proved he hadn't made up his mind about her identity. At least he was open to discussing it. A major leap forward.

She couldn't deny Paris offered a viable opportunity to get away. To go home. Home to what, was beside the point. She no longer had a job and no place to go. She'd paid her rent only through May. If she didn't return soon, the apartment complex would think she'd abandoned the property and would sell off everything she owned. It wasn't much, but it was all she had. And then there was Paddy. She heaved a deep breath. And she didn't belong here.

Escape in Paris presented obstacles. Big ones. She didn't speak the language. She had no money and no identification. However, she would be at the American Embassy. They assisted stranded tourists. She could repay them once she found a job. She still had some of the insurance money left. Maybe, as a guest, she could speak to the ambassador personally.

But as Thomas reminded her, they might think her mad. She couldn't explain her remarkable resemblance to Traci Wallace. Besides, she'd made a bargain. And, as always, Daniel's face clouded her judgment. How could she hurt him?

She pushed her personal dilemma aside and stood before Traci's closet. She had a decision to make. In another life, she would be ecstatic. Paris was on her bucket list, a place to see and experience before she died. One of Traci's fabulous gowns would make her feel like Cinderella. But Thomas was no Prince Charming, harsh one minute, almost gentle the next. His mercurial behavior made her head spin.

That was a problem for another day. On to the dilemma at hand.

Close examination of Traci's eveningwear revealed her preference for plunging necklines and backless gowns. No way would she appear in public dressed like that. Pity. The lavish money spent on those frocks would feed a family of four for twenty years.

Dare she call one of the designers in Traci's phone directory and ask for something more sedate?

She'd give the closet one last look before calling a designer. Separating the garments one by one, she almost gave up until a white beaded frock in the back came into view. One look told her this was perfect. Simple, elegant, and light as silk.

Decision made, she put her travel wardrobe together, hung it out for Fergus, and then joined the family for breakfast.

As they ate, she refilled Daniel's juice glass. "I'm going away with your father today. But we'll be back in time for church tomorrow."

He gazed down at his plate, but said nothing. No tears, but the look in his gaze spoke volumes.

Their conversation of the other night popped into her mind. He must think she wouldn't come back. How many times had that happened when Traci left and didn't return for months? From the looks of her scrapbook, Traci hadn't spent a lot of time at home.

He finished eating quickly and left the dining room, his head down.

After the boy had gone, she caught Thomas's eye. "Couldn't we take him? It would do him good to get away, see life outside the island."

"We couldn't take him to the embassy. It's an adult affair. There would be no other children there."

"Fergus could come and stay with him while we're away."

He studied her for a moment. She held her breath until he raised his hands in surrender. "Get his clothes packed. Be sure to add some sweaters. It can get chilly for thin-blooded islanders this time of year. Wheels off the ground in thirty minutes."

❧❦

Orly Airport, Paris, France
Saturday, May 20

The flight turned into an unexpected family affair with Daniel and Fergus on board.

Thomas settled down to take care of leftover paperwork from the office.

Fergus and Daniel played checkers in the back, and Traci read a novel she'd brought.

The aircraft was the perfect place to work. With

everyone quiet, it served him well. Often too many interruptions at home and at the office made it difficult to concentrate. Thoughts of the message he'd received Monday made him pull the copy from his inside pocket. He read it again.

----- Original Message -----
From: "Paul Redford" <redford@cia.gov.>
To: "'Thomas Wallace"<twallace@wallaceltd.com>
Subject: Your Eyes Only

Meet me in Paris at the embassy Saturday. Important. Don't say no. You owe me. Something big in the wind. Heim Rosen will join us.

Paul.

In his other life, Thomas had worked with Heim Rosen. The message sounded ominous when he first read it, and it still troubled him. He slid the paper into the shredder and watched it turn into confetti. Whatever Paul's mission, it couldn't be good if it involved Israel and the USA.

After Thomas had finished university, the CIA recruited him. With his American mother and Scottish father, the agency considered him a good candidate. Eager to sow some wild oats, Thomas worked for Paul in a European cell. Six years of chasing bad guys through dark alleys and mosques and trying to stay alive while doing it.

Thomas walked away when his father's health declined, and his dad had asked Thomas to take over at Wallace Limited.

Things were more complicated now. He had a

wife, a son, and no desire to jump back to the dark side. He'd served his time. Unfortunately, as the man stated, he owed him.

Good weather hastened their arrival at Orly, giving them six hours before the party. He unbuckled his seatbelt and stood. "Anybody up for a little sightseeing?"

All gazes turned to him.

He waved a hand towards the window. "There's a big city out there. Where shall we go?"

Fergus shrugged. "I've seen it all, lad."

"I've always wanted to drink coffee at one of the sidewalk cafés," Traci said.

As many times as Traci had been in Paris, and she'd never visited a sidewalk café? He gave a metal shrug. Traci came for the nightlife. She'd probably never been awake during the daytime. Then again, this woman just might not be Traci.

"Great, I know just the place, a little café on Place Saint-Germaine. I should warn you, the coffee is so strong the spoon stands straight up in the cup. Espresso was born in Paris." He laughed. "But it's a little known secret that you can get a cup of tea at a sidewalk café if you ask."

They breezed through customs, only to find a horde of paparazzi waiting. Someone must have tipped them off.

Flashbulbs almost blinded Thomas.

Calls rang out from the crowd of reporters.

"Look this way, Traci."

"Where have you been, love?"

"Things have been dull without you, m*on ami*."

Thomas shouted over the uproar. "Fergus, the boy!"

Fergus sprang for Daniel and loaded him into their hired car.

Thomas took Traci's arm and shepherded her into the back seat behind Fergus.

Daniel, his face as white as his shirt, turned to his father. "Were those bad men, Dad? Did they want to hurt us?"

Traci pulled Daniel in close, her face as pale as her son's. "They meant us no physical harm, but they are not nice people."

"The café is out of the question," Thomas said. "They'll follow us wherever we go. This is the tourist season, and the streets will be crowded. We could be trapped for hours by those bloodhounds."

He hadn't wanted Daniel to have to deal with this.

Fergus turned in the front seat. "What's your game plan, lad? We can always go back to the plane."

Thomas shook his head. "We haven't had lunch. I know a place where the press won't bother us, and we can enjoy a leisurely meal." He gave the driver the name.

"You're sure they won't follow us inside?" Traci asked.

"The hotel won't allow it. We'll rent a suite and have room service. If you haven't been there before, you'll like the atmosphere. It's an Eighteenth Century Renaissance rebuilt in 2001, with Louis XV décor, and high-speed Internet service. Privacy at a price. We'll be safe there. Piece of cake."

She cast him a skeptical glance. "I seem to remember Marie Antoinette saying something similar. Look what happened to her."

❧

It started to rain, and Mercy welcomed the sight of the hotel through the car's streaked windows. Maybe it would dampen the paparazzi's fervor.

Outside the hotel, a Middle-Eastern vendor sold toy puppets under a covered awning. Seeing Daniel, the man stopped and made a red-vested monkey clap and dance. The boy gazed from the vendor to his father.

"Buy it for him," Mercy said.

"It's a cheap toy. He'll break it in a day."

"Then he'll have fun for a day. All his toys are educational. Buy it."

Thomas began a conversation with the vendor in Arabic. Money changed hands, and he handed the toy to Daniel. Looking at her, he asked, "Satisfied?"

She nodded. "How is it that a Scottish businessman speaks Arabic?"

"Actually, it's Farsi, and the answer is simple. I deal in oil equipment. It's the mother tongue of most of my customers."

Cars and motorbikes slammed to the curb behind them, and Thomas herded Mercy and Daniel inside the hotel lobby. The doorman stopped the pack of photographers at the entrance.

Thomas led his family further inside, and they boarded the elevator to the top floor. The doors slid open into the elegant suite. The ornate Louis XV furniture looked too delicate to sit on, but proved comfortable.

Mercy applauded Thomas's decision to have Fergus return to the plane and bring their luggage to the hotel. She'd never experienced anything like the paparazzi. How did celebrities survive such an assault on a regular basis? It must terrify their children.

She had wanted this to be a pleasant outing for Daniel, but he was forced to spend most of his time in a plane and now in a hotel room. Fortunately, he entertained himself with the toy and watching television—a novelty for him.

Now she understood why Thomas kept Daniel on the island. It was the only place the boy could lead a somewhat normal life.

His mother's antics had made his life more complicated than it might have been otherwise. The Wallace fortune would bring him attention over time, but hopefully nothing like what they had faced today.

A glimpse at the clock told her she had to get dressed. After a shower, she used hot rollers on her hair, deciding to wear it down. While the curlers did their job, she applied her makeup, slipped into the gown and surveyed her image in the full-length mirror.

Nervous, a sudden thought jarred her composure. The gown was a full length formal. What if the women wore a simple black dress? This was Paris, after all. Why hadn't she asked? Such a faux pas would be disastrous. Traci would instinctively have known the dress code.

Hands shaking, she picked up her bag and cloak and stepped into the living room.

Already dressed in his tuxedo, Thomas stood at the window, looking out over the City of Lights. He turned when she entered, and something like appreciation flashed into his gaze before he shut it down.

"That's the first time you've worn that gown. What made you choose it?"

Her heart sank. She'd made the wrong choice. "Actually, I chose it because it was the only one with a neckline that didn't plunge to my navel. Please don't tell me it's inappropriate."

Approval returned to his gaze. "It's exactly right. Do you remember where it came from?"

"No. Thomas, I don't know where any of the dresses in Traci's wardrobe came from."

"I bought that dress. The first and only one I ever selected for you...for Traci. When I saw it on the model in the showroom, it seemed to have been designed for Traci."

Mercy stood in the center of the room not knowing how to respond but realized she had pleased him with her selection. He wasn't the kind of man to gush over a woman's appearance, and she was glad. She'd never learned to handle compliments gracefully. She looked around the room. "Where are Fergus and Daniel?"

"Fergus took him to the dining room for dinner to get him out of here for a while."

He walked back into his room and returned with a velvet jewelry box. "I brought these along, just in case they would match your dress. They've been gathering dust in my luggage for a long time."

The case snapped open, revealing a pair of sapphire and diamond earrings and a matching necklace that sparkled like the Paris skyline.

"I bought these after Daniel's birth. When you— Traci ran off to Rome. After Rossellini..." He lifted the necklace. Standing before the mirror, she turned and he fastened it around her neck. The jewels felt cool against her skin.

His hand lingered on her neck for a moment and he caught her glance in the mirror. "They're perfect with your gown."

The telephone rang. Thomas removed his hand and turned to grab the receiver. After a short conversation, he reached for her cloak. "That was the limousine driver from the embassy. He's downstairs in the garage. We won't have to run the gauntlet through the photographers."

That didn't stop flashbulbs from popping like fireworks as the limousine exited to the street. The jackals jumped into cars and followed them.

9

The American Embassy, Paris, France
Saturday, May 20

Inside the embassy gates, the driver dropped them at the entrance.

The attendant accepted her wrap and checked their names off the invitation list.

A crowd had already gathered in the ballroom.

All eyes were on her. The buzz of conversation halted and quiet spread across the room like an oil slick on the sea's surface.

Mercy tried to turn back.

Thomas placed his hand at the small of her back and whispered in her ear. "Hold your head up and smile. They'll get over the initial shock. Your name has been out of the tabloids for a while." A low laugh rumbled in his chest. "But it appears they haven't forgotten your attempt to skinny-dip in their fountain."

Remembering the story from the scrapbook clippings, Mercy could feel heat creep up to her hairline. In a voice so low, only he could hear, she whispered. "This must be how Daniel felt when the guards opened the gate to the lion's den."

A tall, distinguished man with a receding hairline broke away from the pack and hurried to meet them, his hand outstretched. "Thomas, glad you're here."

He introduced himself to her as Paul Redford and

circled his arm around the elegant redhead who had moved from behind him. "This is my wife, Gale. Mrs. Wallace, your photographs don't do you justice."

Gale gave her a sincere smile and clasped her hand. "What a gorgeous dress. Wherever did you find it?"

Mercy's heart left her throat and settled back into her chest. She was going to like this woman. "I truly don't know. Thomas bought it."

Gale smiled at Thomas. "You have excellent taste. Paul would never buy clothes for me." She laughed and winked at her husband. "And if he did I wouldn't wear them."

A white-coated waiter offered drinks.

Thomas took two and handed one to Mercy.

The room atmosphere returned to normal.

Gale took hold of Mercy's arm. "Let's leave these dull men, and I'll introduce you around. You have a son, don't you?"

Mercy let Gale take over. The slightly older woman guided her from group to group, finally stopping to introduce her to the American ambassador and his wife, Mr. and Mrs. Simon Belmont.

Mrs. Belmont was an elegantly plump older woman with a kind face that reminded Mercy of Nanna. "Mrs. Wallace, your wedding photograph on the cover of that magazine was the most beautiful bridal portrait I've ever seen."

Mercy had never seen the cover, and she searched for the right response. "Thank you, it's kind of you to remember."

A French minister's wife standing in the group gave her a disapproving glance. "Yes, they do marvelous work with touchups, don't they?"

Mercy was at a loss for words.

Mrs. Belmont gave the minister's wife a dark look. "I don't think Mrs. Wallace would need help in that department." She turned back to Mercy. "I haven't seen your pictures lately. Have you retired?"

Searching for an explanation, she settled on a half-truth. "My son has been ill and I've stopped working until he is completely recovered."

Concern clouded Mrs. Belmont's eyes. "I'm sorry, I didn't know. Is he doing well?"

Mercy smiled. "Very well, thank you."

They moved back into the crowded room.

Gale placed her hand on Mercy's arm. "Do you have to deal with people like Mrs. Moure often?"

"Mrs. Moure?"

Gale nodded. "The French lady with Mrs. Belmont."

"Actually, this was the first time," Mercy said truthfully.

Feeling a bit like a beached dolphin, she had tried to keep Thomas in her line of vision, but he'd vanished up the side staircase with Paul and another man she hadn't met.

Her experience with cocktail parties was minimal, but she quickly decided they weren't something she enjoyed. She followed Gale's lead, listening to gossip and political rhetoric, smiling, and nodding at the appropriate time.

Gale leaned in close and whispered. "I'm going to the powder room. Want to come?"

Mercy shook her head. "I'll wait for you here."

Gale departed, leaving Mercy alone for the first time all evening.

A familiar prickle at the back of her neck made her

turn. A pair of bold, dark eyes stared into hers.

A man with black hair that curled over his collar stood next to the American ambassador, wearing a black tuxedo. Dazzling white teeth flashed in a dark, handsome face. He nodded at her and raised his glass in a salute. The crooked smile on his face disconcerted her. This man knew Traci. Knew her well.

A cold shiver ran down her back, and she turned away.

Ricco Rossellini—the face from the scrapbook.

She scanned the room again. Neither Gale nor Thomas were anywhere in sight.

Moments later, a hand gripped her arm and a hot breath whispered in her ear. "I've been waiting all evening to catch you alone, *cara mia*. We need to talk."

She tried to pull away, but his hold was too tight. Not wanting to make a scene, she let him propel her across the room and outside into the warm night air.

As soon as they were alone, she jerked her arm away. "We have nothing to talk about...Mr. Rossellini."

He stepped back, his lips twisted into a sardonic smile. "My, aren't we formal. Ricco, please." He folded his arms, his gaze raking over her. "This is a new look for you, *cara mia*. I'm trying to decide whether I like it. Frankly, it seems a little virginal for you."

Heat rose in her cheeks as she turned to leave. "As I said, we have nothing to discuss."

He grabbed her shoulders and turned her around. "Oh, but we do. Give me the photographs. We can forget our disagreement ever happened and take up where we left off." His voice became husky. "Remember those nights on the beach in Naples?"

"I don't remember anything with you."

His hands pinned her arms to her side, pulling her

close, his face lowered to hers. "Let's see if this will refresh your memory."

❧❧

As soon as the secure conference room door closed, Thomas pulled out a chair and plopped down. "OK, Paul. What's this all about?"

The room was small, but plush, like everything else in the embassy. A conference table in the center seated six comfortably. He couldn't see the windows—covered with heavy brocade drapes, and probably bulletproof and soundproof glass.

Heim leaned against the wall to his right. Heim Rosen was a huge bear of a man. He had gained weight since their last meeting, but he carried it well. He moved with cat-like grace, never sitting when he could stand.

Paul pulled out the chair beside Thomas. "You up on what's happening in Iran?"

"You mean that they're pushing forward with their nuclear program and getting ready to start World War III?"

"Correct," Heim said. "And we all know who their first target will be."

Thomas had always found the Israeli agent trustworthy, to a point. But there was never any question that the defense of Israel was his first priority. Thomas couldn't fault him for that.

Paul nodded. "The cell you worked with in Kuwait has a man inside Iran, close to the top. He knows how far along their nuke program is and when they plan to push the button. The problem is getting the information out in time. Our agent is walking a tight wire over an alligator pit. If they get a whiff that he's a spy, he's a dead man. And the information dies with him."

"So where do I come in?"

"There's a meeting of a few members of the oil cartel in Saudi Arabia in a month. Iran is attending the mini-summit. I want you to go into the Magic Kingdom and bring back the launch timeline."

"Paul...I would be in the same position as your man inside. I'd have a target painted on my back."

The CIA chief held up his hand. "Thomas, your company sold oil equipment to Iran in the past—"

"Wallace hasn't sold anything to Iran since 1979, after the religious fanatics seized control. You do remember a little incident called the Iranian hostage crisis? My father refused to sell to that regime or let his people work in a hostile environment. I haven't changed his policy."

"You didn't let me finish," Redford said. "There will be a trade show for all the major drilling equipment suppliers in Riyadh during the conference. It would be simple for your company to go in, set up a sales booth, and show them something new."

"Wallace has already secured a booth for the event. I hadn't planned to attend. You don't think they'll be suspicious if I suddenly show up as a sales rep? And there's the other little matter of the U.S. embargo against Iran."

Paul shook his head. "I don't expect you to sell to them. The Russians and the Chinese will do that. I just need you to be there. Our agent knows you by sight. When he sees you, he'll know you're not there by accident. He'll contact you and pass on the information."

Thomas couldn't keep the sarcasm from his voice. "And this is all to take place in front of hundreds of people?"

Paul waved his hand in a don't-worry-about-it motion. "We'll have the details worked out before you leave." He glared at Thomas. "We do this kind of thing on a routine basis. You should remember that."

"How will the information come? Microdot, CD, flash drive, what?"

Paul's tone turned hostile. "We don't know. We can't contact him. If we could, we wouldn't need you."

Thomas gave him a sideways glance. They'd left that poor devil out there alone for God knows how long. "Pardon me, but I can't help wondering how you let an agent become isolated, without resources to get information in and out? How do you even know he's still alive?"

A flush crept up Paul's collar to his face. Embarrassed he'd lost contact with an asset? Or angry that Thomas had called him on it? "We know because he always travels with the president's entourage when he leaves Iran. Our man is always visible in the background when his boss holds a press conference. He makes sure we can see him. Until recently, he had operatives in place to exchange information. But over the last six months, all of them have been murdered. We'll replace the agents, but that takes time. Time we don't have."

Thomas backed off a little. "So, he won't know who is coming, or any of the procedures we set up. He's flying blind."

Paul gave a tired nod. "Pretty much."

"You don't know what you're asking. I have a family situation. If anything should happen to me..."

Heim walked up and placed a hand on his shoulder. "If you don't get the information, and soon, Thomas, Israel will have to take out Iran's nukes. We can't wait for them to strike first with a weapon of mass destruction." Heim moved back against the wall. "My friend, if Iran starts to launch its nukes, your family situation will be the least of your worries."

Thomas hesitated to ask the next question, knowing once he did, he would be committed to take the assignment. "Who's the contact?"

Paul wrote a name and held it up long enough for Thomas to read it and then dropped the paper into the shredder mounted under the conference table.

Aref Ladifpour. A name from his past.

Aref's Iranian parents had supported the Shah, and they left Iran when religious insurgents led by the Ayatollah Khomeini overthrew the Shah. Aref was dedicated to taking back his country.

Thomas didn't really have a choice.

Iran posed an imminent threat.

If he could help prevent the deaths of thousands, he had a moral duty to stand in the breach. They had to stop Iran's nuclear program before the rogue nation built and armed a bomb. He nodded. "I'm in, but I need another favor."

Paul stood and then sat on the conference table's edge, facing him. "I stuck my neck out pretty far for you already. Heads are rolling in DC these days for using agency resources for non-agency business. What's the favor?"

"Find out everything you can about a woman named Mercy Lawrence. She graduated from Texas A&M. She has an apartment in Houston. Secure her apartment and her belongings." He handed Paul a slip of paper. "Here's the Social Security number. I need everything. Pictures, birth certificate, everything."

Paul took the paper and gave a grudging nod. "When the assignment is completed. Not before."

∂∞∽

Thomas left the two agents and headed downstairs. The task was worse than he imagined. He was not completely convinced Traci or Mercy suffered from amnesia, and if for some reason he failed to come back, she would have control of Daniel and his estate. Fergus and Nanna would protect Daniel, but his mother would have legal control. A nightmare scenario. He'd have to make a new will before he left, naming his father as executor.

Thomas descended to the embassy ballroom. The party was still in high gear. He stopped at the bottom step, his gaze searching the crowd for his wife.

No Traci.

He caught a glimpse of Gale in a cluster of people and headed her way. She stepped back from the group and met him halfway.

He smiled. "The meeting is over. Your husband will be down shortly. Have you seen Traci?"

She glanced away, avoiding his gaze, her brow wrinkled. She inclined her head towards the balcony. "She's outside."

No mistaking the look. He'd seen it a thousand times before. Something was up, something unpleasant concerning his wife.

Fists tight, nails biting into his palms, he strode to the double doors and stepped outside. Moonlight reflected off Traci's white dress. She stood less than twenty feet away, locked in Ricco Rossellini's embrace.

He stood motionless for a moment, wondering if everything she'd told him had been a lie. Was she really Traci, still playing games? A tidal wave of emotions washed over him. Jealousy? Betrayal? Perhaps both. At that moment, it didn't matter.

He launched across the veranda. Before he reached the Italian playboy, Traci stomped the sharp heel of her shoe into Ricco's instep.

He howled, released her, and clutched his foot, cursing. A dark look came over his face, and he stepped towards Traci, his hand raised.

"I wouldn't do that. Not if you want to leave here in one piece." Thomas barreled towards Ricco, unleashed five years of pent up violence, clenched his right fist, and connected solidly with Ricco's jaw. The impact sent the man hurling back against the garden wall. He grimaced as pain shot through his hand.

But Ricco, crumpled on the stone terrace, made the pain worthwhile.

"Don't, Thomas." Traci grasped his arm. "He isn't worth going to jail for. And with his past involvement with Traci, I would have a hard time convincing the authorities the man made improper advances."

Thomas didn't miss the reference to Traci.

He took two deep breaths to decompress, flexed his fingers and guided her back towards the ballroom. Strains of a familiar song drifted across the dance floor, halting him just inside the entrance.

"Do you remember that song?"

She glanced up at him. "Odd you should ask. It's one of my favorites. I have it...had it, as a ring tone on my cell phone."

He shook his head. "The band played it at our...my

wedding."

She would probably think he was nuts considering what just happened on the terrace, but he made the suggestion, anyway. "I think we have time for one dance before we leave, if you're game."

She gave him a wistful smile and nodded. "It would be a shame to waste such beautiful music."

He gathered her into his arms, memories of that day seven years ago flooded his mind. How beautiful Traci had looked. A glorious future seemed to stretch before them, a feeling he could face anything the world threw at him with her at his side. He snapped back to the present and whispered into Mercy's ear. "The tabloids will be filled with speculation tomorrow that we have reconciled."

"Were we separated?"

"I believe that's the word for it."

She leaned in close, the top of her head just under his chin, made to fit. They moved easily to the haunting melody, and he became lost in the moment. The song ended and he returned to reality, reluctant to let her go. "We should leave. I think the party's winding down." His gaze swept the ballroom.

Ricco hadn't returned. He must have left from the terrace.

Thomas found Paul to say good night. The section chief jerked his head towards the French doors leading to the veranda. "What happened out there?"

"I think he had another engagement."

Paul wrinkled his brow in a deep frown, but he let it go. "I'll be in touch."

Thomas tucked Traci's hand in the crook of his arm, and they left the ballroom. On the ride back to the hotel, he glanced over at her. He needed answers, preferably not in Daniel's presence. "Why did you go out on the terrace with Rossellini?"

She twisted in the seat to face him, her eyes glistening in the semi-darkness. "Rather, like you in Bermuda, he didn't ask."

"What did he want, other than the obvious? He took a chance knowing you were here with me."

"He thinks Traci has some photographs he wants."

"What kind of photographs?"

"He didn't elaborate, and I didn't have a chance to ask. I just wanted to get away from him. Do you think you'll be in trouble for hitting him?"

"Ricco won't press charges, if that's what you mean. Not a man with his pride. I think...I owe you an apology, and I accept the fact you quite possibly may be who you claim to be. I brought you away from Bermuda against your will without giving you a chance to explain." He paused before continuing. "Why didn't you run? In your place, I would have."

"I considered it. But people would have thought I was mad, considering all the madcap things Traci did in Paris and elsewhere. And, we made a bargain."

His gaze found hers in the limo's dim lighting. "I have to be away for a while, hopefully not more than a couple of weeks. It's important, or I wouldn't go. I need you to take care of Daniel while I'm away. I'll make it worth your while."

"I would do that without your asking and without your money."

He relaxed against the seat, watching her. If by some strange twist of fate, she told him the truth, and she truly was Mercy Lawrence, he'd have to release her. That would hurt Daniel beyond redemption. And if she was Mercy Lawrence, where was Traci? How had she remained out of sight for so long, without funds?

The worst of it was he would have to begin the search for Traci all over again. Find her for Daniel's sake, and do something about their unraveled marriage. He had to do it soon. He was falling in love with Mercy and that wouldn't do. Despite the obstacles, he didn't want to lose this woman.

She was a better mother to his son than Traci had ever been.

∂∘∾

Ricco Rossellini rubbed his jaw and headed to his Ferrari. He climbed inside and slammed the door with vicious force, ignoring the pain in his jaw. How dare she attack him! Treat him like a common pervert. Pretend not to know him. Juvenile.

For what reason? Because her husband was there? Thomas Wallace had to have known about their affair for years. The tabloids had made it an open secret.

What he couldn't fathom was why she failed to turn over the photographs to the authorities. Had she lost her patriotic fervor and had a last-minute change of heart? Planning to blackmail him? Sell to the highest bidder? That was more like the Traci of old. If so, she overestimated her charm.

Whatever the scheme, he was finished with her—and her interfering husband. He'd take care of Thomas Wallace personally. But that was another matter for another day. He punched a number into his cell phone. "Have you found the pictures, yet?"

"No," Lorenz answered. "My island contact searched her room—everywhere. They're not at the villa. She must have stashed them somewhere. Could have put it in a safety deposit box in Naples, sent it into cyberspace, who knows? We may never find them."

"Forget about the pictures, for now. I want Traci Wallace dead."

10

Wallace Island, the Aegean Sea
Sunday, May 21

Exhaustion settled over Mercy as the jet touched down on the island runway and came to a stop. The flight home was quiet, but she was too restless to nap. The scene at the hotel and at the embassy rewound and replayed in an endless mind-loop. She picked up the book she'd brought along, hoping to distract her thoughts. But it didn't work.

The whole Paris experience, her encounter with Rossellini, Doubting Thomas's near u-turn, from grim accuser to sensitive protector, left her with more questions than answers. The emotions she felt while they danced made her realize her precarious position — desperately attracted to a married man.

Thomas had been charming at the hotel, admiring the gown she selected. He'd given her the exquisite jewelry to wear, not to keep, but to compliment the dress. At the embassy, he stood beside her, a gallant defender in front of a disapproving crowd, making her feel secure in his presence. It was a new experience. No one had ever made her feel safe until that moment.

When he stalked onto the balcony and saw her in Ricco's arms, she caught a flash of not just anger, but jealousy. She didn't kid herself. The jealousy was for Traci, not her. Somehow, it didn't matter.

Throughout the flight home, Thomas and Fergus huddled in a corner of the aircraft cabin, speaking in low voices, their faces grim.

Whatever the topic, both men were disturbed about something, apparently having to do with the trip Thomas planned. He hadn't told her why he was leaving, or his destination, but she'd overheard "unarmed" and "Saudi Arabia" in hushed tones. This wasn't his usual business trip. Of that, she was certain.

The request that she stay with Daniel was a mere formality. She couldn't leave the island if she wanted to. That he asked, rather than demanded, made her feel better. Taking care of Daniel wasn't a chore; it was a pleasure.

ه‍ک‍ه

Wallace Island, the Aegean Sea
Thursday, May 25

Thomas's mood appeared bleak after their return from Paris, and he went out of his way to avoid her. Their paths crossed only at mealtime, and then he closed himself in his office or worked out with Fergus in the basement gym as if training for a marathon. Any spare time, he spent with Daniel, swimming or playing catch on the beach.

His distance stung.

She'd considered the attraction mutual, but apparently it was one-sided. Hers alone. She told herself Thomas had chosen the wisest course of action. There could be nothing between them. He was married. But that didn't keep it from hurting.

She awoke next morning at loose ends, tired of

reading, unused to the lady-of-leisure role foisted upon her. With Thomas spending so much time with Daniel, the minutes and hours dragged.

After breakfast, she went upstairs and changed into running shorts and a T-shirt. Exercise might revive her spirits. A hot wind blew in off the sea. The clouds vanished, leaving the sky a crystal blue canvas above.

Tennis shoes pounding the sand, she ran two miles on the beach and then returned to the villa. She showered and changed into a swimsuit. One of Traci's. A one-piece, but with a French cut that left little to the imagination. At least it came with a matching beach robe. The pool water was cool, and she swam half a dozen laps, climbed from the pool, and fell into a lounge chair. Eyes closed, she lay on her stomach letting the sun's ray warm her skin. After a while, her back felt hot, and she applied a thin layer of sunscreen.

Laughter coming from the path that led to the pool made her look up. Thomas and Daniel approached from the villa. Daniel skipped along in front of his father. As they reached the pool, he squealed and did a cannonball into the water spraying the deck with fine droplets.

Thomas pulled up a chair beside her. "How's the water?"

She twisted to her side and rose up on one elbow. "The temperature is perfect. I highly recommend it." She adjusted the lounge chair to a sitting position "When will you be leaving?"

His gaze ran the length of her body in the wet suit, came back, and then settled on her face.

Uncomfortable, she slipped into the robe.

He diverted his attention to Daniel. "Can't say for sure. I'm waiting to hear from Paul. Could be any time now." He removed his shirt and joined his son in the pool.

After a few laps, he returned to the chair, water dripping from his hair.

She tossed him a towel. "When will you be back?"

He toweled his hair and leaned back. "I don't know. I'm not trying to be evasive. I truly don't know."

She nodded towards Daniel. "He's an amazing swimmer. Have you worked with him?"

"Yes." He gave an embarrassed laugh. "I was on the U.K. Olympic Swim Team my sophomore year at university."

"I'm impressed."

He grinned. "Don't be. I didn't win an individual medal, but our team won silver in the relay."

"Still, it's quite an accomplishment just to make the team and bring home a medal. You must have spent a lot of time training."

He grinned and nodded. "Endless hours in the pool. I thought I'd grow fins."

Footsteps on the path made them turn.

Fergus cleared his throat. "Thomas, ye have a phone call."

❧❦

With a slight nod to Mercy, Thomas rose and went into the villa. Under normal circumstances, his mentor would have brought the phone to him, but Fergus understood Thomas would want to take this call in private.

He hurried into the office and picked up the phone.

"Thomas, Paul here. You ready to roll?"

"I've just been waiting for your call. When and where do you want me?"

"Leave Sunday. A plane will pick you up at Heathrow in London and bring you to North Carolina. We have three weeks before the oil summit. I want you to spend some time getting in shape. You looked a little soft in Paris."

"I'm not soft. And I'm not going into battle, just taking a package from an agent."

"You know my philosophy; expect the best, prepare for the worst."

"Yeah, yeah. You going to be in North Carolina?"

"Yes. We'll finalize the plans once your training is finished."

Fergus waited by the door until Thomas disconnected. "Yer're leaving?"

Thomas nodded.

Minutes later, he returned to the pool area and reclaimed the chair he'd vacated. He inclined his head towards the villa. "That was the call I've been waiting for. I'll be leaving Sunday. But tomorrow, Daniel has a scheduled checkup with his surgeon."

ॐॐ

Wallace Island, the Aegean Sea
Friday, May 26

Mercy grabbed her bag and Daniel's hand and then hurried to the upstairs landing.

"You ready for a visit to see your doctor, Danny?"

His face scrunched into a frown, and he shot her a wide-eyed look.

She squeezed his hand. "It'll be OK. He only wants

to make sure you're healing well after the surgery. I'll hold your hand all the way."

"No shots?"

"I can't promise, but there shouldn't be. It's only a checkup."

Thomas stood in the downstairs entryway, pointedly glancing at his watch. "I thought I'd have to come and get you two."

When Daniel skipped ahead with Fergus, Mercy leaned close to Thomas. "He's getting very independent. He wanted to pick out his clothes. Doesn't he look adorable?"

And he did, in navy shorts, striped turtleneck, and a white sweater with the family crest on the pocket. Knee-high socks and black loafers completed the outfit.

"He did select more than one outfit, right? We'll be gone overnight. Raincoat and umbrella? That's required equipment in London."

She preceded him up the stairs into the aircraft. With a glance over her shoulder, she smiled. "Don't worry. It's all taken care of. He's good to go."

෴

London, England
Friday, May 26

They arrived at the surgeon's suite promptly at two o'clock and the nurse ushered them right into his office.

Mercy and Thomas waited in the doctor's office while he gave Daniel a thorough examination.

When he finished, he brought Daniel into the room and sat on the edge of his desk while he read the test results. Dr. Able Abrams was in his early fifties, tall and slim, with a receding hairline. Dark eyes peered through steel-rimmed glasses, and a well-trimmed salt and pepper beard covered the lower half of his face. He folded the report, looked up, and extended his hand to Mercy. "You must be Daniel's mother. I'm happy to finally meet you, Mrs. Wallace."

Mercy sensed an underlying reprimand in the comment, and heat warmed her cheeks. "How is he doing?"

"Excellent. Vast improvement since his last visit." He lifted his glasses, massaged the bridge of his nose, and then gazed directly into her eyes. "I don't know if your husband told you, but I was concerned about Daniel after the operation. His health was good, but his mental outlook wasn't. I told your husband he needed to fix whatever was troubling the boy. Looks like he did just that." Dr. Abrams thumbed through the report again and gave them a confident grin. "The incision is completely healed, and the X-rays indicate his physician did an outstanding bit of surgery."

Thomas laughed and shook the surgeon's hand. "I couldn't agree more."

It was almost five o'clock when they checked into the hotel overlooking Hyde Park.

After they'd settled in their suite, Thomas pulled her aside. "How would you like to go out to dinner, just the two of us? I could use some decompression time."

She'd enjoy a night out in this famous old city, but her resemblance to Traci made public appearances hazardous. "Sounds like fun. But what about the reporters and flashbulbs?"

"The good news is that Traci is not that well

known in London. Which isn't to say you might not be recognized, but it's much better than Paris and Rome. And I discovered a little known restaurant that serves fantastic seafood with a small dance floor. "

"Should I change?"

"It isn't formal, but you can if you wish. I have an appointment I need to take care of, first. Shouldn't be more than an hour. I'll pick you up at seven o'clock."

ॐॐ

Thomas strode into Heathrow Airport terminal and into the coffee shop. A big man wearing a ball cap sat at a booth near the back. Chip Nelson, the appointment he told Mercy he had to keep.

Chip had been a star linebacker for his university and first round draft choice for the pros before he came to the agency. Couldn't hack pro-football, joined the Navy, and went on to become a SEAL. Now he ran a CIA supply depot out of London, and organized clean-up crews when needed. A native of Austin, Texas, Chip usually dressed in western boots, but today he wore field boots.

Chip stood and stuck out his hand. "Hey, Wallace, I thought you were too smart to get sucked back into this business."

Thomas shook his hand. "I guess you overestimated my intelligence." He motioned towards Chip's footwear. "What happened to the western gear?"

"European ladies don't go for the cowboy look." He grinned. "I roll with the flow. You back for good?"

Thomas shook his head. "No, just this one gig. You bring the stuff I asked for?"

Chip patted the dark backpack in the seat beside him. "Black ops spy kit 101, minus the P-229 Sig weapon you usually carry. Redford said to give you whatever you wanted. Why no weapon?"

"Can't take it where I'm going." In fact, he would have to send the kit into Riyadh with the Wallace freight for the showroom setup.

"Then why do you need the other gear?"

"You know Redford. He's a stickler for being prepared for anything."

"Whatever."

A slim, redheaded waitress walked over to take their order. "Would you like to order now, sir?"

"Just coffee and whatever my friend would like."

Chip winked at her. "I'd like to have your phone number."

"My husband doesn't like me to give it out. He's cranky that way. Is there anything else you want?"

"Guess I'll just have to get a refill on the java." He turned his attention back to Thomas. "You still married to that gorgeous model?"

Thomas nodded, not wanting to expound on the subject.

"I would love to live your life for about six months."

Thomas picked up the coffee cup and took a long sip. "Be careful what you wish for, my friend."

ॐ♥ॐ

Mercy slipped into a black silk suit and heels while she waited for Thomas's return.

He arrived promptly at seven.

"What will Daniel do while we're away?"

Thomas held out her lightweight coat. "Fergus is the best babysitter you'll ever meet. He's had loads of practice with me." He laughed, leaned in, and whispered in her ear. "And it didn't stop when I was out of short pants."

From the outside, the restaurant looked like an 18th Century pub, with rustic wooden siding and lanterns. Inside, it was small, with discreet tables in alcoves looking out over the river. Table candles and a live band in the corner near the postage-stamp dance floor added a subdued ambience to the occasion.

Thomas ordered the chef's special for both of them, a taster's platter of all the restaurant's signature seafood entrées. Enough food for four people, but he managed to put away half. When he finished his last bite, he shifted back in his chair. "After that, I need some exercise. Shall we dance?" He led her onto the dance floor.

Two other couples moved to the haunting strains of a romantic ballad. He pulled her close and spoke into her ear. "Tell me about your life, Mercy. I know next to nothing about you. My life is an open book."

"It's boring. You'd fall asleep."

"Try me."

"My grades were good, but not good enough for a scholarship. I went to college on student loans, which covered tuition and books. You've heard the story a thousand times. I worked to pay for housing and food. No time for anything but study, and work."

"That does sound dreary. Weren't all the college jocks chasing you?"

"Hardly. Those guys don't hang out in the library. The ones who did find me, I didn't have time for."

"We'll have to do something about your boring

life."

She couldn't suppress a laugh. "I think you already have."

"I walked right into that one, didn't I?"

She became lost in the moment with the woodsy scent of his nearness, coupled with the romantic atmosphere and music, until the song ended.

He took her hand and led her back to the table. "Come on. Let's quench our thirst." His fingers trailed down her arm as he held out her chair.

"Traci, is that you?" A dark man, obviously drunk, staggered across the dance floor towards her. "I told Clive that was you." He stumbled, almost fell, and then righted himself. As he drew closer, he hiccupped and put his hand over his mouth. "Oops, I see you're with your hubby. Too bad." He turned around and staggered away. "Call me. You still have my number?"

❧❦

The spell was broken.

"Come on. I'll pay the check, and we can leave." Thomas' jaw tightened. He settled the bill and held her coat.

The two drunks waved as they left.

He always avoided going out with his wife for just this reason. She had enjoyed the celebrity.

But Mercy obviously didn't. Her back had stiffened when the drunk approached, and she leaned closer to him as if seeking protection.

When they were in the taxi, he gave their destination.

"I apologize. Perhaps I should have known better than to risk dinner in a public place."

"Don't apologize. It couldn't be helped, and I enjoyed the evening until..."

At the hotel, Fergus had already put Daniel to bed and retired himself.

Thomas said a reluctant good night and went to bed, still feeling Mercy in his arms, seeing her smile, the scent of sandalwood and vanilla in her hair, as he slipped into a restless sleep. As he drifted between awareness and sleep, he realized. He was beginning to think of her as Mercy.

A sharp clap of thunder startled him awake. He glanced at his watch. Two AM. Over the storm's intensity, he heard moans coming from Mercy's room.

He threw back the cover, not stopping to grab his robe, and opened the door to her bedroom. In the light filtering through the half-open drapes, he could see she was alone. Her head made agitated movements from side to side on the pillow, whimpers escaped her lips.

A nightmare.

He crossed the room and sat on the side of the bed, shaking her gently. "Mercy, wake up. You're having a bad dream."

Her eyelids opened. She sat up abruptly and then pressed her head against his bare chest. "Don't let him touch me. Make him go away." She trembled, and he felt her heart beat against his own, racing like a wild animal in flight. He held her until the tremors stopped, speaking soothing words in her ear as he would to a frightened child.

Her arms went around his neck, and she tilted her head upward. "Thomas, help me. I'm so frightened."

The invitation was too much to resist. His mouth covered hers, and the kiss deepened. She responded with an awakening passion. With a quick jerk, she broke away, breathing hard. "Thomas...I can't...I'm not Traci."

"I never thought you were."

She lay back against the pillows.

He pulled the cover up under her chin and felt her gaze follow him as he left her room.

He came away with one conclusion. The woman in that room was Mercy Lawrence. The passion he felt for her was certainly physical, but more than that, emotional, and something deeper he couldn't find the words to describe. He crawled back into bed, and watched the lightening flash through the drapes. It was a long while before he fell asleep.

る∞め

London, England
Saturday, May 27

The following morning Thomas ordered room service and was on his second up of coffee when Mercy emerged dressed and ready to leave. Thomas watched her face as she sat down at the breakfast nook.

"It's my turn to apologize," she said softly. "I'm sorry about last night."

He waved it off. "Does that happen often, what happened last night?"

"Which part?"

"You know what I'm talking about. The nightmares."

She shook her head and glanced out the window at the cloudy, gray day. "No, not too often. But they're always horrible."

"Did you tell your doctor in Houston about the

dreams?"

"It didn't occur to me."

Fergus and Daniel came into the room.

Daniel picked up a piece of toast.

Fergus grabbed a cup of coffee. "Ye ready to leave, lad?" he asked Thomas.

"Have you both had breakfast?"

The Scot nodded. "An hour ago. The boy's a bottomless pit these days."

"Then let's head out." He wasn't finished with this discussion with Mercy, but it would have to wait until he returned from Saudi Arabia.

11

Wallace Island, the Aegean Sea
Sunday, May 28

Sunday afternoon, Thomas came downstairs with his bags.

Mercy and Daniel waited in the entryway.

Mercy placed her hand on Daniel's shoulder. "Say good-bye to your father. He's going to be away for a while."

Daniel jumped into his arms and gave him a long hug. "Bye, Daddy."

He gave his son a tight, lingering squeeze. "Take care, and be a good boy." He turned to Mercy. "I'll send the plane back. You'll need it for supplies and in case of emergencies. Fergus will look after you both. He'll keep me posted."

She gave him a wavering smile. "Strange. For some reason I want to tell you to be careful."

He put the boy down. "I always am."

Somehow, a good-bye kiss seemed appropriate. He leaned down and touched her lips with his own, soft and pliant. The excitement was still there, only better.

She didn't pull away.

That surprised him.

Her sapphire gaze stared into his, as if looking for answers. Answers he didn't have. All they had between them were questions. If she wasn't his wife, where did they go from here?

Aboard the plane, Thomas took his seat by the window, buckled up, and gazed through the window. His family stood on the terrace, Daniel bouncing like a rubber ball and waving with abandonment. The taste of the kiss lingered on his lips, and it would haunt his dreams.

Odd that she picked up on the dangerous aspects of this trip. Something Traci would never have done. This woman was an enigma. More evidence Mercy was who she claimed to be.

After the plane took off, Thomas released his seatbelt, stood, and removed his jacket. Smoothing his shirt over his abs, he examined his waistline for love handles and found none.

Soft, huh? Paul Redford needed his eyes checked.

❧

After Thomas's plane lifted off, Daniel wandered back inside.

Mercy watched the plane disappear into the setting sun. Knots of tension squeezed her stomach. A successful executive, he shouldn't have to worry about anything more dangerous than a paper cut. But instinct warned her that Thomas headed into danger, as certainly as the evening sun would soon disappear into the sea. Her concerns were merely conjecture at this point. She could only guess why his destination was Saudi Arabia and didn't know how long he would be away. But the premonition of impending danger lingered.

She stepped inside to join Daniel and Nanna in the

dining room.

Dinner that evening consisted of shrimp scampi, baked potatoes with all the trimmings, and cauliflower with cheese sauce. Not a green vegetable anywhere on the horizon.

Mercy shuddered when dessert arrived. Bread pudding loaded with butter, sugar and heavy cream. She could feel her arteries clogging.

Edda's meal planning had too much fat. It wasn't healthy for anyone over a long period, especially anyone Nanna's age, and Daniel had just had heart surgery.

Mercy passed on the dessert and folded her napkin. Everyone considered her mistress of Wallace Island, and beginning tomorrow, she would act like it. She would assume responsibility for menu planning— add lean meat, vegetables, and fruit to their meals. It wouldn't endear her to the kitchen staff, who still held grudges over Traci's past antics. Like it or not, she still carried the mantle of Traci's sins. However, the job needed doing.

If Edda resented her intrusion, so be it. She would just have to get over it.

∂∽⧸

Wallace Island, the Aegean Sea
Monday, May 29

The next morning, Mercy proceeded with meal changes as planned. She called Edda into Thomas's office after breakfast.

In her early forties, Edda was pretty, blonde hair,

blue eyes, nice tan, and trim figure. But there was harshness in her countenance. She seldom smiled and seemed to prickle whenever Mercy was near. Only Thomas seemed able to coax a light into her icy gaze.

"Have a seat, Edda. I wanted to speak to you about menu planning."

Edda lowered into the chair, her mouth drawn into a grim straight line.

"I've decided we need to go to healthier meals, more fish and lean meat, vegetables and fruit. Nanna and Daniel need less fats and carbohydrates in their diets, as I'm sure we all do." She waited for a response from the housekeeper, and when none came, she continued, "I've planned meals for this week, beginning with lunch today. I kept it simple." Mercy handed Edda the packet of menus. "I'll give you each week's meal plans a week in advance after this week. I apologize for the short notice."

"There have never been any complaints before. Mr. Wallace always complimented me on their excellence."

"Our meals have been delicious, Edda, and I'm sure they will continue to be. But they should also be good for us. If you have any questions, I'll be happy to answer them."

Edda's back stiffened. "I'm not sure we have the produce—"

"I took the liberty of checking with cook to make sure the food supplies were available."

Edda huffed away without a word, her glare could have lit a match.

Mercy approached lunch with trepidation. She shouldn't have worried. Lunch consisted of the cold baked chicken, Caesar salad, and fresh strawberries she'd requested. She must remember to thank Edda.

Traci had burned a lot of bridges, and it was up to Mercy to forge some kind of working relationship with the housekeeper and the staff.

She should have felt a boost of self-confidence, having won a minor skirmish, but she didn't. The solemn expression on Thomas's face as he boarded the plane and the wrinkled frown on Fergus's craggy brow constantly ran through her thoughts.

Nanna caught Mercy's gaze across the table. "What's gotten into Edda? She looked like a thundercloud earlier."

"Probably just stress. Managing a house this size is a big responsibility."

Daniel looked across the table at her. "Mummy, does Edda think you have magical powers?"

"I don't think so, Danny. Why do you ask?"

His tiny brow wrinkled. "I heard her tell Cook the princess witch thought she could wave a wand and turn the kitchen upside down. Stella asked Edda if she meant you and she said yes."

Mercy almost snorted water through her nose. Time for a change of subject. "Nanna, have you or Fergus heard from Thomas?"

"No," Nanna said. "But he usually only calls twice a week to check in, unless something important comes up."

Daniel tugged on her sleeve. "Mummy, may I be excused? Fergus is taking me exploring."

"Sure. Just be careful." Probably an unnecessary caution. The island was one of the safest places in this hemisphere, and he would be in Fergus's charge.

As Daniel left the dining room, Nanna glanced at Mercy. "Speaking of Fergus, the man has had permanent frown lines embedded in his brow since Thomas left. I can't help but wonder if Thomas is on some mission for the Americans again."

Mercy halted her fork in midair. "What do you mean, mission?"

"Surely, you knew your husband was in the CIA before you were married."

Was that what the meeting in Paris had been about? The thought that Thomas would confide in Nanna, rather than in her, hurt. "No. Did Thomas tell you?"

Nanna took a sip of water and relaxed against the chair's back. "Fergus told me about it right after I moved here. Fergus was a commander in the Royal Regiment of Scotland's Black Watch unit. The elder Wallace hired him when Thomas was small, a kind of bodyguard, companion, and mentor all rolled into one."

Mercy let what Nanna had said sink in. Thomas with the CIA? Apparently, before he married Traci. That explained his caginess about where he would be going and for how long. That first day in Bermuda, he'd had a dangerous look about him, and she thought he might be FBI. So why not CIA? But why would he suddenly accept an assignment now?

Fergus's background didn't surprise Mercy. His military bearing and watchfulness flagged him as more than a chauffeur. A pent-up bundle of energy ready to spring in an instant, despite his age.

"I believe you've solved the puzzle, Nanna. Thomas is on a mission, a dangerous one." Whatever the assignment, it involved Paul Redford, and the meeting in Paris.

Mercy could only imagine what Thomas might

face. The visions that flashed through her mind did nothing to quiet her unease. She'd asked Father Joseph to dinner that evening and looked forward to entertaining a guest. His lively wit would take her mind off Thomas.

Father Joseph arrived promptly at six thirty, handsome in a black polo and slacks. As a non-Catholic, she hadn't realized priests dressed in casual clothes.

They sat on the terrace waiting for Edda to announce dinner.

The sun lowered into the sea leaving behind a breathtaking purple horizon. Cool breezes floated in from the water. Only the soothing sounds of waves caressing the sand filled the night air.

Nanna broke the spell. "Have you heard from Father Paul since his return to Rome?"

Father Joseph pulled his gaze from the view. "Yes. He is undergoing tests. He was in renal failure. Unfortunately, he had to go on dialysis. That is hard on anyone, and especially someone his age. It was kind of Mr. Wallace to offer to take him on the plane." The priest's voice was as soothing as hot tea and honey. "It made the trip easier on the good father in his frail condition. He won't be returning to the island."

"I'm sure Thomas was glad to help. I'm sorry about the diagnosis. Does this mean you'll be staying on as pastor?"

"I'm awaiting word from the Church. If not me, then they'll send a replacement. Although, men surrendering to the priesthood are fewer every year."

She glimpsed the sadness in Father Joe's eyes and wondered if it had anything to do with his posting on the island becoming permanent. "If there is anything we can do for Father Paul, let us know."

"Thank you. Everything that can be done is being done. His age precludes his getting placed on a kidney donor list."

"If you need to travel to see him, I'm sure we can help," Mercy said. "I know there are few travel accommodations off the island."

"That's kind of you. I may take you up on your offer." His gaze roamed over the garden and the ocean view. "You truly have a paradise, here, Mrs. Wallace. The garden is beautiful."

"Please, call me Mer...er...Traci. It is lovely, isn't it?" Mercy's gaze traveled over the imposing arches and the intricate architectural details of the villa. It must have taken years to build. Just shipping in materials and workers represented an engineering miracle on a Mediterranean island.

"How long have the Wallaces lived on the island?"

Nanna gave him a thoughtful glance. "Since the 1930s, as I understand it. Thomas's grandfather built the villa back when prices were much lower. His son Edward, Thomas's father, hated the isolation and never lived here. Thomas however, loved it. When he became of age, he moved in. It has been his primary residence ever since.

"Thomas's mother didn't like living here year round. But she often came for vacations before her death four years ago. She doted on Daniel."

The priest turned his attention to Mercy. "Nanna tells me your husband is not a religious man."

Mercy smiled over her glass of chilled juice. "My husband and I don't discuss his religion. You'll have to ask him. However, he'll be away for a while. We're not sure how long. I would appreciate your prayers for his safe return."

"Of course. I'll light a candle for him in the chapel. Is he away on business?"

A maid entered the terrace through the archway and announced dinner, saving Mercy from having to tell the priest she didn't know where her husband had gone or what he was doing.

12

CIA Training Camp, North Carolina
Monday, May 29

Duffle bag in hand, Thomas stood on the steamy black tarmac of a private airstrip, carved out in the middle of a forest of fifty-foot pines. He hadn't packed much. He wouldn't need much. Running shoes, underwear, and shaving kit would suffice. The facility provided training gear.

He leaned against the aircraft stairs, waiting for his ride. The pilot stood nearby, smoking his third cigarette, anxious to get back into the air. They'd exhausted the topic of American sports teams, which Thomas had little knowledge of.

Insects dive-bombed the aircraft lights in an ancient ritual of suicidal frenzy, their noise loud in his ears. This historic ground spoke to his American heritage. Here in this dense forest of soaring pines, Indian wars, the American Revolution, and the Civil War had been fought.

He'd spent many summers with his maternal grandparents near Charlotte. His grandfather, a history buff, instilled in Thomas the proud heritage of his American ancestors. Gramps led him through famous battlefields, reciting the bravery and tenacity of an untrained revolutionary army, outgunned and outmanned, who had fought against the best-trained military force in the world at that time, and the ragtag band had prevailed. It still inspired Thomas.

A faint glow in the distance heralded the arrival of his driver. Minutes late, a camouflaged vehicle pulled up next to the plane.

A grim-faced driver in black jeans and T-shirt exited and marched to where Thomas stood. "Wallace?" he asked, in a voice like rolling thunder.

Thomas nodded and threw his bag into the back seat.

Enroute to the camp, he clenched his teeth to keep them from clattering as the heavy vehicle bounced on the rutted gravel road. The darkness would have been impenetrable had it not been for the vehicle's wide-view headlights. The forest lent a sense of security. A man could disappear in the trees and ground cover and live off the land indefinitely, unlike his Middle Eastern destination, where he'd have to dig a hole in the sand to find a place to hide.

He wasn't convinced that only he could undertake this assignment. There must be hundreds of operatives who could do the job—a simple hand-off of information. Paul was holding out on him. He'd learned spooks were not always trustworthy.

A premonition of unpleasant things to come settled on the back of his neck and stayed there.

The driver entered a code into the security gate, and they drove into the compound. A weatherworn cabin appeared in a distant clearing, the outline hazy through the dust-streaked windshield. Two long, low frame buildings sat approximately twenty-five yards on each side of the shack, probably housing for the trainees and a mess hall. One of those bunks would be his new home for the next three weeks.

Thomas's experience with training camps had never been pleasant. Usually in the middle of some deserted area in a bare-necessities facility and run by strict leaders who seemed to think pushing the trainees to their limits and beyond was a good thing. So far, this one seemed right on target.

The vehicle came to a halt in front of the cabin, and Paul Redford strode forward to meet him. Dressed in khakis and a yellow polo, he looked cool and calm despite the sweltering heat and humidity. "Come on inside. I want you to meet the head man. Then you can get settled in."

Thomas went into a large room with heavy, masculine furniture surrounding a massive stone fireplace. An oak bar sat tucked neatly in the corner.

A balding man with massive arms and slim hips stood to greet them.

"Thomas, meet Clint Monroe, head of this unit. Clint, this is Thomas Wallace."

Instead of reaching out to shake hands, the trainer-in-chief sent a tight-fisted punch towards Thomas's gut. A split second before the blow landed, Thomas blocked the assault and succeeded in deflecting some of the blow's force. Otherwise, he would have been on his knees gasping for air.

Before the man pulled his arm back, Thomas grabbed it, brought it up behind Monroe's back, and then gave the unit chief a forceful shove.

Thomas straightened and glared at Monroe. "You greet all your trainees this way?"

Monroe turned around, straightened his shirt, and smoothed the sides of his hair. "It saves time. Lets me know how much work I have to do."

Maybe Paul was right. He had gotten soft. Seven

years ago, he would have seen that blow coming while it was still a thought in Monroe's mind.

❧❧

CIA Training Camp, North Carolina
Tuesday, May 30

Thomas had forgotten how brutal training could be. Sleep eluded him the first night. Heat, insects, an uncomfortable bed, and the snoring of his fellow trainees made it impossible to sleep.

When early morning came, the drill instructors cared not at all about his sleepless night. Rousted from his bunk before daylight, he and his comrades had only minutes to get dressed and into formation outside the barracks.

Thomas glanced at his watch before putting it in his kit. Four thirty. The Army gray T-shirt and shorts he'd been issued were insufficient against the early morning chill. Probably sixty-five degrees, but island living had made him sensitive to cooler weather. That would soon change. Late May in North Carolina meant high temperatures and high humidity. Both would kick his backside before the day ended.

Ground fog hovered around their ankles as he and his eleven barracks-buddies fell into line. The drill instructor, Sergeant Booker, smiled.

Thomas cringed. He was in for a long day.

Over the next hour, Booker called into question the group's lack of character, IQ, and manhood, all in colorful language. Comforting to know drill instructors hadn't learned any new profanity since his first experience with training camp. Booker ran through his entire repertoire before the real fun began.

"You girls hit the dirt. I want one-hundred push-ups, one hundred sit-ups, and then we'll finish up with a five-mile run before breakfast."

By the time they returned to the mess hall, Thomas was too tired to eat, but he stuffed down every carbohydrate he could manage in the time allotted, something he'd learned at his first boot camp. He'd need every calorie before the day ended.

"Hey, grandpa," a young man about Thomas's size, with close-cropped blond hair, called out from the end of the table. "What're you doing out here? We didn't know they were recruiting senior citizens for us to carry."

Thomas threw him a dark look and returned to his food.

A recruit to Thomas's left yelled at the big mouth. "You'd better try to make friends with the new guy, Reid. Maybe if you get in trouble, he'll help you. Cause none of us are coming to your aid."

"Shut your pie hole, Redwing. I won't need anybody's help."

Why was it that every group of men had at least one loud-mouthed bully needing to be taught a lesson? It never failed.

"Just remember, old man. If you fall out, you can just lay there. I'm not helping you."

Thomas shook his head at the arrogance of youth.

One of the men in his barracks identified the blowhard as Brad Reid, supposedly the son of a Washington power player. When Reid failed to get a response from Thomas, he moved on to harassing the youngest member of the group, cursing and bullying the kid named Cory at every opportunity.

At thirty-four, Thomas was hardly ready for retirement, but he had at least ten years on most of the other men in the group. The kid didn't worry him. He could handle the jerk when the time came. But it was a distraction he didn't need. He'd barely swallowed his last bite before the DI blew a whistle, and they were back on their feet to repeat the morning's performance.

The afternoon sessions came easier, but not easy. He was getting into the rhythm. The calisthenics were torture, no question, but he was motivated to finish and get on to the job at hand. Finishing the training was as much about mental toughness as physical strength. The human body had a miraculous ability to take profound abuse but a stubborn will not to give up was also required.

He ran and swam for miles at home on the island and had done so since leaving the Company. And he worked out weekly with a martial arts trainer in Edinburgh. The reflexes weren't as sharp as they once were, but that would come back quickly.

Thomas couldn't fail the course even if he fell on his face. Redford would see to that. But to Thomas it was as much a contest against himself as it was against what was thrown at him. He would finish, and he would finish well. For him there had never been any other option.

ళ~ఌ

CIA Training Camp, North Carolina
Friday, June 2

The fourth day they gathered after dinner for the final exercise drills. Thomas was last in line and closest to the building.

"Wallace, get my clipboard. I left it in my office," the DI yelled.

Thomas double-timed it to building two. He found the clipboard and headed out the door when a movement on his bunk caught his eye.

Putting a grass snake in your roommate's bed was a juvenile summer-camp trick. Booker was waiting, and he didn't have time for this, but he couldn't wait until the recruits turned in for the night. With three quick steps, he reached his bunk, jerked back the army-green blanket, and quickly back-peddled.

It wasn't a grass snake. It was a water moccasin.

Before the snake could coil, Thomas took a carefully aimed whack at its head with the clipboard. The first blow killed the viper, but he added six more just to be sure. If a thing was worth doing, it was worth doing well. Almost killing a snake wouldn't cut it.

Thomas wiped snake guts off the board, cleaned up the mess, and then hurried back to the drill line.

"What took you so long? Have to use the little girl's room?"

"Had to find the clipboard. It was under the desk. Must have fallen off."

An hour later, drills ended and they all hit the showers.

Brad paid particular attention to Thomas.

It confirmed Thomas's suspicion. Shower over, Thomas stowed his gear and slid into bed.

His gaze on Thomas, Reid climbed into his own bunk.

The man let out a scream that rattled the rafters and tumbled out of bed, trying to stand and run at the same time. "S-Snake! There's a snake..." He dashed to the barracks door and ran into Booker coming in.

The DI flipped on the lights. "What's going on, Reid? You lost your mind?"

"O-One of these guys put a snake in my bed," Reid said.

Laughter rumbled through the building and Reid's face flushed red.

Booker marched to the bunk and jerked back the cover. The dead water moccasin lay coiled on the sheet.

Booker picked the snake up by the tail, looked at Reid and then at Wallace. "This isn't a joke. A moccasin can kill. That's no laughing matter. If I find out who did this, you're out of this unit."

Booker wasn't stupid. He suspected Reid brought the snake into the barracks. He also probably knew Thomas had put the dead snake in Reid's bed. Booker sent Thomas a look, obviously realizing why it had taken him so long to retrieve the clipboard earlier. But Booker wouldn't mess with the son of a Washington powerbroker. The DI took the trophy with him and switched off the lights.

Redwing called out in the darkness. "Reid, you scream like a girl."

13

Wallace Island, the Aegean Sea
Friday, June 2

With Thomas away, days on the island fell into a slow, easy rhythm. While Daniel studied in the classroom, Mercy spent her mornings planning meals and visiting some of the island families.

With the children making regular visits to the villa for playtime with Daniel, the islanders seemed to be thawing towards her. Mothers often came with their children and stayed for refreshments, sharing a part of their lives with her. Her favorite was Rita Garrett, Frank's wife.

Idleness wasn't part of Mercy's gene pool. And there were things that needed improvement, even in this idyllic setting.

An idea tickled the back of her mind. She caught Fergus at lunch in the kitchen and pulled up a chair to run the proposal past him. Thomas appeared to have a lot of faith in the old Scot's opinion.

"Fergus, what would you think about having a clinic set up here on the island to take care of minor emergencies?"

He looked unsure, probably suspecting she had an ulterior motive. "Why would we need that? We've done fine without one."

She poured a glass of iced tea from the

refrigerator, and sat back down. "Minor broken bones, burns, and cuts happen here all the time. Things that really don't need a hospital, or even a doctor. Something a nurse could handle. Not to mention all the time it takes to fly into Izmir to the hospital. Something minor could become serious in that length of time."

"And where would you find this nurse, lass?" Over the past weeks, Fergus had become more relaxed around her, a gradual shift from cold disdain to tolerance.

"Are you kidding? We'd advertise. With the beauty of this place, we'd have people standing in line for the position."

"Aye, I can see it might be a good idea. But that's a decision you'll have to wait for Thomas to make when he returns."

"Good. I thought as much, but I can lay out my concept in the meantime. Thanks, Fergus. I value your opinion."

She could swear the old Scot's chest expanded a couple of inches.

On the fun side, she and Nanna brainstormed for a staff picnic tentatively scheduled for the first Monday in September, Labor Day in the states. She would be gone by then, but they could carry on without her.

"Nanna, we need to put together a menu. What are your thoughts?"

"My dear, you're talking to an Englishwoman. I know nothing about American food." She gave Mercy a stern nod. "You're in charge of the menu. I'll take care of decorations."

"You've never been to America?"

"Once to Washington D.C. During the winter. It was lovely. Snow covered everything and with the stately buildings and monuments lighted for the holiday, it looked like a Currier and Ives Christmas card."

"How long have you lived on the island?"

The old woman's brow came together, and then her expression cleared. "Thomas told me you had an accident and lost some of your memory. You should have told me." She took a deep breath. "I came here after you and Thomas were married. You lived in my family home in London before your wedding. Thomas didn't want to leave me alone there, so he invited me to live here. I sold the estate and moved. The family home was much too big for an old woman and you would never have lived there. I've been on the island a little over seven years now."

"Are you happy here, Nanna? Do you ever miss London?"

"Yes. I sometimes miss the seasons, but this climate is much better for my arthritis. Winters there can be brutal."

Mercy reached over and hugged the old woman. "I'm glad you're here, Nanna. You've been a good influence on Daniel."

Nanna smiled and patted her hand. "I'm also glad, my dear."

అం

Wallace Island, the Aegean Sea
Saturday, June 3

The following morning, Mercy left her room and met one of the maids at the landing. "Hi, Lily. Do you know where I might find Nanna?"

"Yes, ma'am. I believe she went to her room after breakfast."

"Thank you." Mercy followed the corridor to Nanna's suite. The door was open, and she knocked on the door. "Nanna, may I come in?"

Nanna walked into the sitting room and waved her in. "Of course. Come on back to the sunroom. I was just doing my Bible study for the day." Nanna wore white slacks and a blue silk blouse the exact color of her eyes, every hair in place in a neat chignon.

"How do you always manage to look so majestic and well groomed?"

Nanna gave a throaty chuckle. "You make me sound like a well preserved mausoleum. It takes years of practice and hard work."

"This is my first visit back here. It's lovely," Mercy said. Her gaze roamed around the suite decorated in Nanna's favorite colors of pastels, lavender, blue, and seashell pink. Half of the sunroom's roof and two walls were glass. Heavy wicker furniture with a sofa and two chairs formed a seating area. One wall was devoted to family portraits.

Mercy stood in the doorway. "Don't let me disturb you. I was just looking for some company. Daniel is doing his exercises with Fergus, and I was at loose ends."

Nanna placed a marker in her Bible and closed it. "You're not disturbing me at all. I can always pick up where I left off. I ordered tea about ten minutes ago. I'd love for you to join me."

"I'd like that. Do you mind if I look at your family photos?"

"Not at all. They're your family, too. And although you may not remember them, you've seen them many times." Nanna stood and joined her beside the portrait gallery.

"This was your mother and father on their wedding day." Christopher Montgomery was a handsome man, a male version of his mother. Dorothy Montgomery was blonde and beautiful, as expected.

Nanna pointed to the next picture. "And this was mine and your grandfather's wedding portrait."

Mercy's gaze zeroed in on Nanna in her wedding dress with its long train. This could be Traci in the vintage bridal gown. "This looks just like—"

"You?" Nanna said. "Yes, everyone says that. And I'm always flattered."

A couple of hours later, Mercy and Daniel dived into the pool and swam laps, with Daniel beating her handily.

Fergus kept watch over them from close range these days, occupying a chair nearby.

Laughing and exhausted, she and Daniel climbed out of the water and grabbed their beach towels.

"Get down!" Fergus shouted.

A body slammed into Mercy, knocking her and Daniel to the deck, landing on top of them as a sound like angry bees whizzed by her head and smacked into the nearest palm tree.

Fergus grunted and jumped to his feet faster than Mercy thought possible. "Quick, lass. You and the boy get behind that large urn. Hurry! The shooter has a laser sight rifle."

Another whiz and rocks sprayed into the air just inches away. "Run, lass, unless you have a death wish."

Grabbing Daniel's hand, she shoved him behind the plant and squatted down, keeping their heads behind the cover of the urn.

Daniel was pale and trembling, but he didn't cry.

Fergus took cover behind another urn, his left arm limp and bleeding at his side. He pulled a two-way radio from his pocket. "Frank, grab some men and get up to the villa. Someone's taking shots at us from the north bluff overlooking the pool. Hurry!"

Static crackled and then Frank's voice sounded. "I didn't hear shots."

Fergus's face wrinkled with pain. "He's using a silencer. Get moving, man."

In five minutes, Frank, Mac, and two other men she didn't know stormed the area. "Fergus, where are you?"

The old Scot waved him over with his good hand.

"Whoever the man was," the pilot said, helping Fergus into a chair. "He's gone, now. I found spent cartridges in the sand. Looked like he used an M24, fitted with a silencer, like you figured. That's why we didn't hear the shots. I sent two of the men to follow his tracks. If he's on the island, we'll find him."

Mercy scrambled from behind the urn, her scraped knees and hands stung. She looked down at Daniel. "Are you all right?"

He nodded without speaking.

She squeezed his shoulder and then hurried to Fergus's side. "You're hurt."

"It's just a flesh wound," he said, shaking his head. "But it smarts a wee bit." He looked down at the wound. "This what you had in mind, lass, when you said we needed a clinic?"

Mercy pressed a white beach towel against the wound to stanch the blood flow. "I think a bullet wound requires a doctor. How did you know someone was shooting at us?"

"He used a laser sight. I saw the red dot on the back of yer head. Another second and ye'd have been playing the harp in a heavenly band."

Her hand shook as she added more pressure to the old Scot's wound. She turned to the pilot. "How fast can you get the plane ready?"

14

Izmir Hospital, Izmir, Turkey
Saturday, June 3

Mercy, Nanna, and Daniel waited in the emergency room lobby as hospital personnel attended to Fergus's injury. He hadn't wanted them to come, but Mercy insisted.

Black-and-white photos of what she assumed were local attractions hung on the pristine white walls. The waiting room furniture was worn, but clean. Other people scattered around the room waited, their faces anxious, speaking in a language she didn't understand.

Fergus had taken a bullet for her. No doubt, as Traci's stand-in, she'd been the shooter's target. Someone wanted Traci dead. Ricco Rossellini? No evidence supported Mercy's supposition. Apparently, his desire for her death outweighed his need for whatever he thought Traci had.

Visions of escaping back to her old life tracked through her mind. Just her presence on the island put everyone else in danger. What if the bullet had hit Daniel? Or killed Fergus?

She studied Daniel as he stood at the second-floor window, watching the traffic below. A blond lock of hair hung over the boy's brow, above his astonishing blue eyes. What an amazingly beautiful child he was, and so sweet. And the reason she couldn't leave.

She made the decision to ride this out, to let Thomas prove himself wrong. A very vulnerable child stood in the center of this monumental mess. She wouldn't be responsible for causing him more pain. And somehow, she had to protect him from whoever had her in their sights.

These were good people. Thomas was overbearing, but not evil. He had good reasons for his actions, misguided though they were. After he'd gathered proof of her real identity, perhaps together they could work out a plan that wouldn't hurt Daniel.

She glanced at her watch. "Nanna, would you like to take Daniel to the cafeteria for tea and sandwiches? I'll wait here for Fergus. It shouldn't be too long since the wound didn't require surgery."

"That sounds like a fine idea, doesn't it, Daniel?" Nanna reached for his hand. "We might even find some nice scones to go with our tea." Nanna took the boy's hand and headed to the elevators.

"You can see him now." A nurse came out and motioned for Mercy to follow.

Heavy white bandages covered Fergus's left arm. He sat up in bed, fully awake, his usual feisty self. "I'm ready to leave this place, lass." He held up a sheaf of papers in his right hand. "The lady just handed me my walking papers."

"Sure you're up to it? A gunshot wound is not to be taken lightly. Especially at your age."

"Aye. Never more sure of anything in my life. I've had worse than this playing football as a lad." He cocked a shaggy eyebrow. "Are ye trying to say I'm old, lass?"

She held up both hands. "I'm only pointing out that you're not a *lad*, anymore."

His face tightened, and he mumbled under his breath. "Just hand me my boots."

Too late, she realized she'd challenged his manhood. "Fine, but let me get Nanna and Daniel before you go storming out. I'll call Frank and have him bring the car to the front entrance. I'll come back for you."

Ten minutes later, Frank picked up the small group and headed to the airport. They hit the afternoon rush-hour traffic.

A store on the corner at a traffic light caught Mercy's attention. "Frank, pull over, please."

"What's up, lass?" Fergus turned in the seat and looked at her.

"The pet store. I want to let Daniel pick out a puppy."

Speechless and wide-eyed, Daniel gazed at her. "Really, Mummy? I can have a puppy?" He clapped his hands and bounced on the car seat.

"Absolutely."

"Good idea. After what happened, a guard dog makes sense."

"This is a pet for Daniel. He gets to choose."

Fergus didn't look pleased. Nevertheless, he got out and followed them inside the pet shop.

Spreading her arms wide, Mercy looked down at the boy. "Go find your pet, Danny."

Thomas might kill her, but every boy needed a dog.

A few minutes later, Daniel pointed out a sad-eyed little beagle who watched from the corner of a cage.

Mercy turned to the clerk. "Looks like we'll take that one. Oh, and we'll need a carrier, puppy pads and food." Realization suddenly struck her. Embarrassed, she turned to Fergus. "I don't have any money. Can you...until Thomas returns?"

He pulled out his wallet and scowled at her. "Where are yer credit cards?"

"In the bungalow in Bermuda, with the rest of my things." A thought suddenly occurred to her. "By the way, what happened to my property?"

"Thomas had your things in Bermuda stored. Would ye like me to have them shipped to the island?"

"Just leave them there. For now." She didn't have much, but it was all that really belonged to her. Bringing her possessions to the island would be pointless. She'd just have to pack and move them again when she left.

❧❧

Fergus took his seat in the plane's cabin, running details of today's shooting through his mind, planning ways to tighten security on the island.

Daniel and the puppy he named Pal played in the bedroom.

Mercy and Nanna settled across the aisle from him for the trip home.

They'd only been in the air thirty minutes when the satellite phone rang. Fergus pushed the call button and moved to the back of the cabin.

"Fergus, it's Thomas. I'm almost finished with training camp. Then I leave for London, and then on to Saudi Arabia. Is everything all right?"

"Aye. Everything's fine, lad. Ye surviving the re-indoctrination?"

"No problem. Is Daniel around?"

"No, he's down for a nap. By the way, we have a

new member of the family." He winced at his lie.

"Did I hear you correctly?"

"Aye. His name is Pal, and he's a six-week old beagle."

"Whose idea was that?'

"Ye know me well enough to know it wasn't mine."

Hearty laughter sounded through the connection. "I won't ask. Is Traci behaving herself? Is she treating Daniel well?"

"Aye. The two get along like the best of friends. I never thought ye would hear me say this, but I think she's good for the boy."

"Great. That takes a load off my mind. I'll check back later if I get a chance."

Fergus snapped off the connection. Deliberately lying to Thomas was something Fergus had never done. It wasn't an outright lie, but it certainly was a lie of omission. If he'd spoken to the boy, Daniel would have mentioned the shooting.

Thomas would take off his Scottish hide if anything happened to Daniel or Traci. Especially when he discovered Fergus deliberately kept the shooting from him. The lad had enough on his plate. He'd need to keep his wits about him on this assignment. And he couldn't do that and worry about his family.

Despite Thomas's assurance this was a routine mission, Fergus had played the game long enough to know better. Nothing in the Middle East was routine.

Daniel bounced out of the stateroom. "Fergus, look what Pal found under the bed. What is it?"

Fergus took the small torn package with Thomas's name on the outside. "Looks like something your dad left behind."

Mercy rose from her seat and took Daniel's hand. "Come, we'll put this in the work station. Pal was very smart to find it. It could be important."

Fergus gazed out the porthole. A fine mist obscured the gray sky.

The aircraft's intercom buzzed, and Frank's voice sounded. "Fergus, you folks need to fasten your seat belts. We're headed into a storm. I'll try to climb above it."

Fergus didn't worry. Frank was one of the best.

On the way to the hospital and back home, Fergus had a lot of time to process the shots at the pool. The island men had searched every square inch of sand. The shooter had disappeared. Probably had a speedboat waiting, headed who-knows-where.

While Traci was in the bedroom with Daniel, Fergus sat beside Nanna. "I'm bringing in some of my friends from my old unit. There's none better to have around for security. At least, until we find out who set up a duck shoot on the island, and why."

She gave him a wise nod. "Thomas has always trusted you to handle such things. Do what you think is needed."

"Aye, the lad knows I'll care for his family while he's away. Frank will fly to Edinburgh and pick up the men after he drops us off, weather permitting."

෨෬

Wallace Island, the Aegean Sea

The jet landed on the runway in the midst of a full-blown gale and taxied to a stop near the hanger.

Fergus decided to wait a few minutes before

allowing the women and child out in the elements. They would be drenched getting to the villa, and the storm might move on quickly.

Mercy joined him. "Was that Thomas who called earlier?"

"Aye."

"Did you tell him what happened?"

Fergus shook his head.

"Good. We can handle this. He doesn't need the worry right now. And we're all OK."

Fergus scanned her face for signs of irony, but found none. He no longer knew this woman. She had been the worst spoiled brat he'd ever encountered. Since coming home from Bermuda, he had watched her every move—her gentleness with the boy, her kindness to Nanna, and even her attitude towards him, which had always been hostile.

Something happened to Traci while she was away, something that brought about a major change in her attitude.

The assassin was playing for keeps. She must have gotten herself into a mess of trouble and made a very dangerous enemy.

᠉

CIA Training Camp, North Carolina
Tuesday, June 13

The next ten days were do-overs of the first one. Too tired to think, Thomas pushed his family to the recesses of his brain. Making it through each day became his singular focus. His head hit the pillow at day's end, and he crashed. Thomas stayed in the middle of the pack, behind Reid, keeping distance between Cory and his tormentor.

The DIs added the obstacle course and the shooting range to the daily workout. Thomas lost control of his place in line, when the instructor sent him out on the course first. It had been a while since he'd scaled a fifteen-foot wall, navigated moving logs, and crawled under barbed wire. Surprisingly, it all came back.

The DI held the group at the end until everyone made it through the course.

Finally, all but one of the twelve-man unit finished. Everyone, except Cory.

Thomas moved next to the man who came in last, Michael Redwing. "What happened to Cory?"

Redwing cast a dark look at Brad Reid and uttered a few choice words. "I didn't see what happened, but just before Cory started his initial run at the course, I think Reid gave the kid a kidney punch. I'd asked the instructor a question, and when we turned around, Cory was on his knees moaning. I'm not sure, but I think the jerk had a rock in his fist. I saw him toss something into the brush. The DI pulled Cory out of the line. Not sure where they took him from there. It was my turn to hit the wall."

"The instructors didn't pull Reid?"

"Couldn't. No witnesses. Just suppositions. And Cory wouldn't tell what happened."

Reid stood about six feet away, a smirk on his face. He moved closer to Thomas and spoke loud enough for Thomas to hear, but too low to catch the instructor's attention. "Too bad you weren't there to protect your little boy, old man."

Thomas moved into Reid's personal space. "I'm

going to pretend what you did to Cory wasn't personal—it was just a practical joke gone wrong."

"What makes you think it wasn't personal, gramps? Ever hear of something called the survival of the fittest?"

"That kid posed no threat to you. This is supposed to be team building, not a contest. You may need these guys someday, and if you keep this up, they'll pull back and leave your sorry tail behind."

"Everything's a contest, grandpa. When the training is over, I intend to be top dog."

"A word of warning, Reid. Don't let it happen again."

The unit double-timed it back to the compound for lunch, the mood somber. Thick pines along the trail blocked the sun, offering some relief from the heat. For once, the torturous terrain and fatigue didn't dominate Thomas's mind—his body was on autopilot.

Unless someone stopped him, Reid would move on to the next victim.

Reid was first in line in the mess hall. He filled his plate and sat at the end of the table, a pariah to his teammates. Peer pressure wouldn't change a man like him.

Thomas couldn't talk sense into the man, he'd tried.

Redwing sat his tray down beside Thomas and nodded at Reid. "The man doesn't belong in this unit. He's a sadistic misfit."

"Makes you wonder how he made it past the psych tests. Either he had connections, or the analysts were asleep at the wheel."

"Right the first time," Redwing said. "He's a junior, as in, the son of U. S. Congressman Bradford

Reid."

After he'd finished, Thomas patted Redwing's shoulder. "Watch your back."

The recruit nodded.

Thomas would have to wait until the end of the course for a shot at Reid in hand-to-hand combat, one on one. He would never work with these men again. He'd move out soon. The Company didn't need a ticking time bomb like Reid in the field.

Another round of body-numbing calisthenics followed lunch and then they moved on to the shooting range. Push-button flexible cables sent and pulled in targets.

Shooting was a gift that came naturally to Thomas. He could hit the kill zones, head and heart, empty his clip and leave only a small circle in the target. He avoided first place. Finish this assignment, and then he was out of the black ops business and back home. Medals and ribbons wouldn't impress the enemy.

15

CIA Training Camp, North Carolina
Saturday, June 17

The last day at camp arrived, and Thomas wasn't unhappy to see it end.

Clint Monroe hadn't approached Thomas since that first day. He caught an occasional glimpse of the camp's head honcho watching from the cabin balcony that overlooked the campsite, his gaze seeming to focus on Thomas.

Something about Monroe bothered Thomas, and it didn't wholly have to do with their volatile first meeting. Six years in the field had honed his ability to appraise men. In the CIA, like organizations everywhere, the cream didn't always rise to the top. Observation told him Monroe most likely made it by tenure rather than leadership skills. A good camp commander would have washed Reid out long ago.

Thomas learned from the DI that Cory had suffered a ruptured kidney. The young recruit was out of the program until he recovered—if he recovered well enough for action in the field.

As anticipated, Reid picked someone else to bully, the next weakest member of the team. Leaving nothing to chance, Thomas stayed between Reid and his new victim.

After breakfast that morning, individual combat

lessons were in progress, and Reid stood across the mat, breathing hard. Reid wasn't all talk. He had defeated five men previously, and did it without dirty tricks.

Today's contest consisted of elimination rounds. Each time a trainee defeated an opponent, he moved on to the next man. The last man standing—was the winner.

Through the process of elimination, it had come down to the final two, him and Reid.

Hand-to-hand combat had only one rule. You could take down your opponent using boxing, mixed martial arts, whatever it took, but mortal blows to injure a teammate were forbidden. Any man who wanted to end a bout had only to tap out.

For the past few days, this contest had dominated Thomas's thoughts. He didn't want to kill or maim this kid. He just wanted to teach him a lesson. Trouble was, he didn't know how to accomplish the task, because he didn't know what to expect from Reid.

Pride and overconfidence were Reid's biggest handicaps. He would do everything possible to keep from losing to "the old man."

Thomas's knowledge of men of Reid's caliber warned him not to expect a tap-out. Reid's ego wouldn't allow it.

Reid took a position across from Thomas. "Hey, grandpa. I'm coming after you. Gonna teach you to respect your betters."

They circled each other for a few seconds.

Reid dove for Thomas's feet, exactly what he expected after watching Reid's other bouts.

Thomas stepped aside easily, and delivered a stunning chop between the kid's shoulders as he sailed by.

Reid recovered quickly, anger flushing his face. His hot temper made him more vulnerable. Rather than planning his next move, he reacted. He made another rush at Thomas, who once again stepped aside and then landed a haymaker to the side of Reid's head.

Reid shook off the stunning blow, stood, and launched a drop kick at Thomas's throat that would have crushed his larynx or broken his neck if it had landed.

Enough.

Thomas swept Reid's legs, knocking him off his feet. He reached down and jerked the kid upright. Left arm across his opponent's neck in a classic chokehold, Thomas tightened the vise by grabbing the kids shoulder. Reid struggled, but to no avail. Within seconds, he was unconscious. Out, but unharmed.

The bout lasted less than a minute and Thomas wasn't even breathing hard.

He could feel the eyes of the other recruits following him as he left the mat.

If Reid didn't wash out, hereafter, he wouldn't cast such a long shadow. His teammates had seen him beaten. They knew he could be taken.

∂∘⊰

Paul Redford watched the bout from a window on the second floor above the arena. He turned to Clint Monroe. "Is he ready?"

"I would say so. I'm surprised he could take Reid. The kid has been first in everything since he arrived."

The agency chief turned from the window, moved to the coffee bar, and poured a cup of the lethal looking brew. "You don't read men very well, do you, Clint? If you did, you'd know Thomas Wallace has been right where he wanted to be since he arrived. I'm not sure even he knows what he's capable of. He speaks half a dozen Middle Eastern dialects fluently. He's one of the finest marksmen I have ever seen, and he has one of the best analytical minds I've come across. Indisputably, the best agent I ever put into the field. It killed me when he retired." Paul sipped the hot liquid carefully. He gazed at Monroe over the rim of his cup. "Send Wallace to see me at the shack. We need to talk before he leaves."

Twenty minutes later, a knock sounded and Wallace entered, his hair still wet from his after-match shower. He strode across the room and extended his hand. "You wanted to see me?"

Paul grasped his hand solidly and pointed to the bar.

Wallace shook his head.

"You ready to leave?" he asked.

"Whenever you say. Have you got the details worked out on your end?"

Paul tapped a folder on the table. "We're set. You'll fly in on a commercial airline. We don't have a set time for the Iranians to arrive at the show, but we have confirmed Aref Latifpour is included in the entourage. You'll need to be at the showroom every minute until he hands off the information. He'll have only one shot. He can't hang around your sales booth. After he makes the transfer, stay around for a day afterward to avoid looking suspicious."

"How will he pass the data?"

"We don't know exactly. My guess is, it will be a flash drive. As far as we know, he doesn't have access to microdot technology. He went in with a couple of USB drives that look like money clips." Paul set his empty cup on the counter. "The driver who picked you up at the airport will arrive at 7:00 AM tomorrow. He'll take you to Charlotte Douglas International. A company plane will take you on to London. You're on your own from there. Emergency numbers and funds are in the folder. You know the drill. Memorize the numbers, and then destroy them."

Thomas stood. "A word of advice. Get rid of Brad Reid."

"Not sure I can afford to. He has powerful connections in the Capitol."

"He's sadistic and baits the men in his unit. He'll never be a team player. You can't afford *not* to lose him."

"I'll see what I can do." He cleared his throat. "Thomas, I wouldn't be sending you on this assignment, but you are the only operative with a legitimate excuse to be at that trade show. That, and Aref knows you. Be careful. It's a very hostile environment and if anyone suspects your real purpose there...I don't have to tell you what you'll be facing."

"I knew that when I accepted the job."

Paul extended his hand. "I'm comforted knowing you are qualified to get in, get out, and come back alive."

Thomas gave a sarcastic chuckle. "Do me a favor and don't tell the bad guys how much trouble they're in."

৵৵৽

Wallace Island, the Aegean Sea

Monday, June19

Excitement on the island diminished for Mercy after their return.

Frank had brought back four soldiers from Fergus's old regiment. They took turns on sentry duty, patrolling outside the villa and the surrounding bluffs and hills. The men were a pleasant distraction, a rowdy bunch, but friendly and respectful.

Fergus joined in their wild tales and teasing, his inhibitions lost around his war buddies.

Evenings on the terrace were filled with the sounds of Hamish's bagpipe playing Scottish ballads.

Daniel was mesmerized. He slipped into the center of the group whenever the opportunity arose. The Scots often lifted him onto their shoulders, riding him around the island, and tantalizing him with embellished tales of their exploits. A diminutive mascot, they gave him a taste of his Highland heritage.

Impromptu dances sprang up on the terrace, with all the ladies bid to dance by the light-footed warriors. Even Nanna joined in for a waltz or two, still as graceful as a sixteen-year-old.

After such an occasion, Mercy leaned over and whispered to Nanna, "I'm going to put Daniel to bed and turn in myself. I'll see you in the morning."

"You look a little pale. Are you all right?"

"It's just a headache, nothing serious." A throbbing pain in her temples and an upset stomach had plagued Mercy for the past few days. A good night's rest would put her back to normal.

She read to Daniel and then tucked him into bed.

In her room, she swallowed a couple of aspirin, succumbed to the persistent ache in her head, and went down for the night.

Wallace Island, the Aegean Sea
Tuesday, June 20

Morning came and Mercy's headache hadn't diminished.

From across the breakfast table, Nanna's gaze followed her as she picked at the food on her plate. "Still not feeling well? Have you taken anything? Perhaps you should see a doctor before the headache gets out of hand. Frank can fly you to Izmir."

"It's nothing, really. It'll be gone in a couple of days."

Mercy left the dining room table and joined Daniel at the pool. A little sun would make her feel better. She moved a deck chair into the sunlight and sat down, suddenly exhausted from the exertion.

A light breeze from the sea ruffled the branches of the palm trees at the pool's edge, bringing on a slight chill.

What was wrong with her? A virus didn't normally get to her this fast. Head resting against the lounge chair, she inhaled a few deep breaths and felt better.

Edda entered the pool area with a tray of drinks. She smiled and handed Mercy a tall glass of ginger ale. "Nanna sent this to you. She thought it might make you feel better."

"Thank you, Edda. I appreciate it. It should help settle my stomach."

But it didn't. Dizziness and a bout of nausea washed over her when she finished the drink. She almost didn't make it back to her room before losing what little breakfast she'd consumed. Stomach empty, she sprawled across the bed, face warm, her skin clammy. Suddenly cold, she pulled the comforter up under her chin.

Paddy snuggled in close, curling into her body, his purr loud in the room's silence.

అలఠ

The little girl, about ten years old, stood near a grave, crying.

A pretty woman lingered nearby, her face frozen into a stone mask. The scene changed and the little girl became a pre-teen, standing beside a casket that held the pretty lady.

Ominous figures moved around the child, and a harsh-faced woman led the girl from a large house surrounded by trees and flowers, to a sterile, cold building with rude, jeering children.

Loneliness and fear enveloped her, but she found no comfort, no one to hold her. And no place to hide from the hands that reached for her in the night. Hands that cause her pain. But she knew she could not give up—couldn't let them win. She tucked the horrible memory back into its hiding place.

Mercy awoke, startled and frightened, reliving the images. Chilled by a cold sweat, she pulled the cover tight under her chin, staring at the carved ceiling above her bed.

It hadn't been a dream. It was a memory.

Hand shaking, she picked up the phone and asked Lily to bring her some extra blankets. "Would you warm them, please? I'm having a chill."

Lily soon arrived with the warm cover which

brought a measure of comfort.

Confusion filled her thoughts. Whatever was wrong with her? Tossing in the damp, tangled sheets, the feverish dream returned.

She was back in college and graduate school. The stress, the outsider, the loner. No time to make friends, join in the campus parties. Four years of cramming, working, and worrying about her financial problems— barely enough to cover the tuition and books. Watching every penny to pay for rent and food. Never enough. The pressure inside was mounting until she wanted to scream.

16

Riyadh, Saudi Arabia
Wednesday, June 21

Thomas buckled his seatbelt for landing at King Khalid International Airport. His plane arrived on schedule and pulled into terminal two, designated for the flight.

He'd flown first class to avoid the chitchat necessary in coach, not wanting to answer questions about his purpose for visiting Saudi Arabia. He'd have to deal with that at customs.

Deplaning with the other first class passengers, he stepped into the architectural splendor of the airport. Thomas had flown here many times on business and was always amazed by the lush landscaping in and around the terminal.

His father served here during the first Gulf War as an administrator in the British Army's General Evacuation Hospital. The United States Air Force had used the airport as an airbase for aerial refueling tankers.

A mosque occupied the center of the passenger terminal. Thomas collected his luggage and walked around the temple with loud speakers that called the faithful to prayer five times a day.

Outside the terminal, heat seared his face as he moved to a waiting taxi and gave the name of his hotel.

Thirty-five minutes later, he checked into his suite, dropped off his bags, and went directly to the trade center.

Trade shows were the same everywhere in the world. And this one was no different, except for the white *thobes*, and red and white-checked *ghutras*, worn by some of the customers. And, of course, the fact that several times a day while the trade show was open, the place almost emptied for Muslims to stop for prayer.

The show room was massive. Every major drilling equipment manufacturer in the world had a booth. Wallace Limited secured a large space near the main entrance, giving Thomas an unobstructed view of the incoming crowd.

⊰•⊱

Riyadh, Saudi Arabia
Thursday, June 22

The next day, the Iranian contingent was a no-show, but that didn't surprise him. The oil producers' meetings were still underway and the big guns wouldn't make a showing until they had set the price of oil in an attempt to manipulate the world economy.

Thomas scheduled lunch and bathroom breaks in conjunction with the prayer times, which left the showroom nearly vacant.

⊰•⊱

Aref Latifpour assembled in the lobby with the rest of the Iranian entourage. Something was wrong. He'd felt it last night when members of the team began to avoid him. He would join a group, and it would slowly disperse, leaving him to stand alone.

He couldn't ignore his paranoia. Too many of his contacts had disappeared over the last six months. He was in double jeopardy. Being a Christian in Iran was worse than being a spy.

Anxious to get started, Aref moved ahead of his friends to the hotel entrance. Two black limousines slid silently under the entrance portico, and the group piled in, Aref in the lead car with his boss. The vehicles drove the short distance and parked at the curb in front of the trade center. Double glass doors hissed cold air as Aref and the group entered the showroom.

Thomas Wallace was the first person he saw inside the showroom. His handlers had sent help. He stuck close to the president whenever there was a photo op. But he had no way to know when, where, and how his people would contact him. His camera exposure had worked. They knew he was alive.

But the president strrode past the Wallace booth and Aref had no choice but to follow.

৵৽৻

Thomas had returned to the sales booth after lunch and spotted the Iranians coming through the entrance, and behind them, Aref Latifpour. He hadn't seen his old friend in eight years, but there was no mistaking his slight frame and intelligent, dark gaze.

Aref made casual eye contact, but the group moved on inside the exhibit hall.

Now what?

Chasing Aref through the showroom wasn't an option.

Chill.

If Aref realized why Thomas was there, he would ensure his group stopped by the Wallace display before the Iranians left.

Putting on his sales face, Thomas dealt with customers, answering questions and handing out product information brochures. In preparation for his eventual takeover of the business, his father had made him work in every aspect of the business, from maintenance, to personnel, and finally to sales.

A few hours later, the Iranian group approached, minus the president. He must have stopped elsewhere. Even better.

He caught Aref's gaze and spoke in Arabic. "May I help you find something?"

Aref moved to the counter and shook his head. "I'm not a buyer, but I am looking for any new technology you have."

"Great," Thomas said as he reached under the counter and brought out a packet containing brochures and a CD. "We've recently developed something we're excited about."

A few others in the group moved closer to listen. "I'm sure you know, water seepage into oil wells is a common problem. Removing the liquid is an energy intensive, costly process. Wallace has developed a new system that cuts the water accumulation as much as seventy percent at minimal cost."

"I would be very interested to see this."

Thomas handed the packet to Aref. "This explains the entire process."

Aref pulled out his money clip and offered it to Thomas. "I will buy this information."

Thomas put his hand over the clip and laughed.

"No, it's free. You don't need to pay."

Aref removed his money from the clip under the cover of the CD, and Thomas palmed it. The spy returned the cash to his pocket. "Thank you. You have been most helpful."

As the group turned away, Thomas called, "Share the information with your buyer. I'm sure he'll be interested."

It was almost too easy. In a matter of minutes, he had the timetable for the Iranian nuclear program. Now all he had to do was get out of Saudi Arabia with the information—alive.

⯍⯌

Wallace Island, the Aegean Sea
Thursday, June 22

Thursday morning sunlight startled Mercy awake. The brightness hurt, sending sharp pains through her temples. Where was she? Certainly not her apartment. Much too elegant.

Paddy stood by her pillow, his hazel eyes gazing into hers. He leaned down and touched her nose with his own. Her hand came out from under the cover and stroked his fur. "Hey, Paddy, you still hanging in there?"

It all came rushing back. Wallace Island, Thomas, and Daniel.

She closed her eyes and pushed the other memories away. Repressed memory. That's what the doctor called it. Were the dark, lonely years after the death of her parents, the anguish of the orphanage, and the stress of college what she'd suppressed?

A cool hand rested on her brow.

"Traci, are you all right? I heard you moaning." It was Nanna's calm voice. She had pulled a chair close to the bed.

Mercy sat up and smoothed her hair from her face. "Only a bad dream, Nanna. I'm fine. Just need to find something I can keep in my stomach."

"You must go to the doctor, child. You know this is not normal."

"If I'm not better in a couple of days, I'll go. I promise."

Dizziness and a sick stomach overcame her again. She jumped out of bed and hurried to the bathroom. But there was nothing left to lose.

Nanna waited until she returned to bed. She heaved a deep sigh and stood to leave. "Traci, you haven't done anything stupid, have you? Like your grandfather, Thomas Wallace is a one-woman man. Do you know how rare that is?"

Mercy tried to shake off the fog in her mind. "I don't understand..."

"I've watched your husband since your return. He's falling in love with you again. I hope you haven't done anything to destroy..." Nanna crossed to the door. "I'll have Edda send up some soup and ginger ale. Perhaps that will help."

After Nanna left, Mercy fumbled her way into the bathroom again and tried to vomit, but couldn't. She turned on the shower as hot as she could stand to chase away the chill. She sat on the bench, letting the heat soak into her body.

What was Nanna worried about? She'd done nothing to hurt Thomas. She leaned against the shower tile, too sick to piece it all together. Wrapped in a large white towel, she glimpsed her reflection in the bathroom mirror. A gray face with sunken, bruised eyes stared back at her. Stumbling back into the bedroom, she slipped into a fresh nightgown and fell into bed.

❧⚜

Nanna left Traci's room, deep in thought. She made her way to the terrace. Even the fragance and loveliness of the flowers didn't calm her spirit. Her granddaughter was seriously ill, and she couldn't stand by and do nothing.

Fergus approached and pulled up a chair beside her. "Where's Traci? Haven't seen her in a couple of days. Fortunately, Daniel is occupied with Pal."

"Traci isn't feeling well. And she refuses to go to the doctor."

"Why is that?"

"She says she's fine, but she isn't. She looks terrible."

The two old friends sat in silence, gazing out at the sea.

"You don't think she could be expecting, do you?"

"I don't know. That's what's worrying me. She has all the symptoms. She's my grandchild, and I love her dearly, but I also know she has been unfaithful to Thomas on more than one occasion. Perhaps she's afraid to find out."

"Aye. That would explain the change in her behavior. If that low-life Rossellini left her with child, she would have no one to turn to, except Thomas. And she's afraid of what he'll do when he finds out."

Nanna gave a solemn nod. "Exactly."

❧❧

Fergus rose to his feet. "We have to know. Call Frank. Tell him to get the plane ready. We're going back to Izmir." Fergus stormed up the stairs and into Traci's room without knocking. He strode across the room, and grabbed a robe from her closet. Pulling back the cover, he tossed her the robe. 'Put this on."

She peered at him through weak, bloodshot eyes, so pale it evoked a pang of sympathy in spite of himself.

"Fergus...what are you doing?"

After she put on the dressing gown, he lifted her into his arms. "Come on, lass. Ye have a doctor's appointment in Izmir."

❧❧

Izmir, Turkey
Thursday, June 22

Mercy arrived in the hospital emergency room too weak to care what happened to her. All she wanted was to curl into a little ball away from the headache and queasiness.

In minutes, technicians surrounded her, taking copious amounts of blood and then sending her to the bathroom for a urine sample. Later they came back and removed a few strains of hair.

Nurses who spoke no English wandered in and out, faces scrunched into long frowns, and communicating in sign language.

Mercy wondered if it was their usual demeanor or if they were concerned about her health. After receiving medication for her head and nausea, she felt almost human again and stopped worrying about it, grateful just to feel better. She tried to sleep, but the bed was too narrow, and the lights and noise around her made it impossible.

Finally, a dark-skinned man in a white smock stepped into the cubicle, followed by Fergus.

The doctor spoke in very precise English. "Mrs. Wallace, I asked your father to step in while I go over my diagnosis." He pointed Fergus to a chair. "You came into the hospital just in time to prevent acute arsenic poisoning."

"Poison?" she and Fergus echoed.

The physician gave a solemn nod. "I'm afraid so. All the tests were positive. I'm putting you on a low dose of dimercaptosuccinic. That is normally used in acute cases, but I want to take all necessary precautions."

The doctor inclined his head towards Fergus. "Your father thought you might be pregnant, but I'm happy to report you are not. Arsenic poisoning during pregnancy would be devastating to the fetus."

Mercy made a conscious effort to keep her mouth from dropping open. So that's why he and Nanna acted so strange and disapproving. She cooled her temper with the realization their suspicions had saved her life. Still, it was humiliating. Her anger refueled— tired of the bullying and being treated like a six-year-old with no mind or will of her own. Why didn't they just ask her outright? But if she had denied their suspicions, they wouldn't have believed her.

The old curmudgeon would probably have been a

good father, if he wasn't so stubborn and such a determined bachelor.

She put on a serene mask and looked from the doctor to Fergus. "Yes, Dad is always looking out for me."

Fergus's face turned a subtle shade of red, and he suddenly found his shoes of great interest.

The doctor ripped off a sheet from a pad on his clipboard. "Here's the prescription. I'd also like you to pick up garlic extract and take the pills as directed. Garlic has proven very successful in treating arsenic poisoning."

Mercy admired Fergus's nerve as he pushed off his embarrassment and went into security mode. "Doctor, can ye recommend a good home-care nurse? I'd need someone to live in while my daughter recovers. Someone who can cook her meals and make sure she stays well."

"I'll get you a list of names to choose from."

"Preferably, someone who speaks English," Fergus added.

"That will shorten the list considerably, but I think we can accommodate you."

When the doctor had gone, Mercy cast a cold glance at Fergus. "This will never happen again, Fergus. I'm tired of being pushed around like a pawn on a chessboard. Thomas snatched me away from Bermuda; you charged into my room and brought me to a hospital. Both actions without my consent. Admittedly, you most likely saved my life, but for the wrong reason. Do you understand me?"

He looked into her eyes without anger. "Aye, lass." Fergus stepped off a few paces to make several phone calls while they waited for Frank.

Mercy couldn't overhear but assumed he arranged for a nurse.

"Yer in luck, lass. I found a nurse, an American. She'll meet us at the airport."

Once in the car, Fergus turned to her, his face solemn. "Yer right, lass. I owe ye an apology. It'll not happen again."

The physical and emotional rollercoaster she'd been on since leaving Bermuda left her weak and depressed. She glanced out the window, not looking at him. "It doesn't matter. This probably falls under your job description."

"Aye, it does matter. I should have given ye the benefit of the doubt, especially after the shooting. I won't make that mistake again, ye can be sure."

Mercy rested her head against the back of the car seat and didn't respond, her thoughts clouded with the dilemma she faced. Her illness, her situation here on the island, and her doomed-to-fail attachment to Daniel.

Minor issues by comparison to her present predicament. Someone at the villa wanted her dead. It was too much pressure to shoulder in her weakened condition. Righteous anger bubbled up. "What were you planning to do, if I had been pregnant? Leave me at the nearest airport with a ticket home?"

The old man dropped his head. "No, lass. Thomas would never allow that. Ye are, after all, the mother of his son. He will always see to yer welfare. That's the kind of man Thomas Wallace is. Aye, I've met none nobler."

She found herself wishing for Thomas's return, remembering his kindness in London. But she had no claim on his protection. No right to expect anything from him. He was married She must keep reminding herself of that fact.

There was a long silence before Fergus spoke again. "Until we find out who's responsible for this bit of mischief, ye're to accept nothing that isn't delivered by the nurse, Nanna, or me. No one else. Understand? I don't know who yer've angered, lass, but whoever it is seems determined to take yer life, one way or another."

A short while later, Mercy watched through the open stateroom door as the nurse boarded the plane and headed straight for her. She was medium height, medium build, with wispy auburn hair and an infectious grin. "Hi, Missy. I'm Katy Martin, and I'm gonna take good care of you." Her gaze roamed over the well-appointed stateroom. "Although it looks like somebody's already taking good care of you."

"You're a Texan. Where?"

"And here I thought I'd lost my Texas twang. Guilty as charged. San Antonio's my home base. You?"

Tears stung the back of Mercy's eyes. "Houston. You can't imagine how good it is to hear your voice."

17

Riyadh, Saudi Arabia
Thursday, June 22

Thomas secured his cash in the money clip Aref passed to him. Using the clip openly should alleviate suspicion about its real purpose. The afternoon was busy, keeping him occupied until closing time. He accompanied a group of Wallace salesmen to a nearby Lebanese restaurant.

He spotted the tail almost as soon as he left the showroom. Was he being paranoid? He was always suspicious when on a mission. It had helped him stay one step ahead of the Grim Reaper.

These two men were not figments of his over-active imagination.

During dinner, he pulled his sales manager aside. "Josh, when dinner is over, go to the hotel and reserve a room under the name of James Jameson. Charge it to the company account. Get the key-card and bring it back to me here when you're finished. I'll stay and socialize until you return."

"You got it." A puzzled expression crossed Josh's face, but he didn't ask questions. He placed his napkin on the table and pushed his chair back. "This shouldn't take more than twenty minutes." Josh returned and slipped Thomas the new room key.

Thomas paid the restaurant tab and then shook

Josh's hand. "See you in the morning."

Outside the restaurant, he stepped into the hot night air. The pungent smell of onions, garlic, and cumin followed him outside.

The night was too warm for the six-block walk to the hotel, but Thomas wanted a closer look at the men following him.

Both were most likely connected to a local terrorist cell. They were big, at least six feet, dressed in western clothing, rather than native garb, and they weren't pros.

He'd spotted them too quickly.

The big question was, why were they targeting him? Had someone witnessed the exchange at the showroom? Were they on to Aref? If so, he was probably in a torture chamber somewhere, where they would bleed all the information in his head before killing him. Information about Thomas and the money clip.

He called the hotel and asked if Aref was still registered and was told he'd checked out. Further questioning revealed that the Iranian entourage was still registered. No question. They were on to Aref.

In his room, Thomas went straight to his laptop and uploaded the data from the clip onto two small USB disks. One he inserted into a tiny slot in his watch, the second he would attach to the video equipment in the sales booth that would go back to Wallace Limited in Edinburgh. Task completed, he started a program that destroyed all data on the laptop, and then returned the money clip to his pants pocket.

He pulled the SAT-phone from his luggage and punched in the number Paul had him memorize. His message was brief. "Package received, but delivery vehicle is missing. Send mechanics ASAP. May need repair." His first priority was to get the data in safe hands.

Then he would come back to find Aref if Redford didn't send help before he left.

Thomas packed and took his luggage to the room reserved for James Jameson. Changing rooms wouldn't ensure his safety, but it would take the tail a while to find him. If whoever was shadowing him crashed into his room, he would be defenseless without a weapon, the downside of taking a mission in a country that didn't allow visitors to bring in weapons.

As he tossed and punched his pillow into submission, Daniel's face ran through his thoughts. Death was one of the risks that came with the job, and something he had never worried much about. But he wanted to see his son grow into manhood, to guide him over the rough spots. Try to keep the son from repeating his father's mistakes.

Mercy, too, absorbed his thoughts. As much as he'd tried to avoid it, she had awakened old longings. Seeing her in the kitchen without makeup, and the quiet, glamorous beauty at the embassy, were sides of her personality he wanted to know better.

But his most vivid memory was of her standing in the moonlight on the balcony. And the surge of warmth as his lips touched hers in London, and the day he left the island. She was totally fascinating and infinitely desirable. She wasn't Traci.

His every instinct confirmed that. And he was a married man. That put her off limits. He'd loved only one woman in his lifetime.

She had broken his heart and almost crushed his spirit. He could face a band of terrorists without fear, but a small woman had brought him to his knees. He didn't think he could bear that much pain again.

He'd left the agency before his marriage because marriage was a handicap to an agent. Families were a distraction he couldn't afford. Not in the middle of an operation. When this was finished, it would be his last assignment.

Lying awake, he punched the pillow again and forced his thoughts to his next move. Before the showroom opened to the public tomorrow, he would hide the USB drive in the slide-projector and then head for the airport.

A car rental would be safest. He didn't want to put his people in danger by asking them to drive him to the airport. With luck, he would make his scheduled flight out. The sooner he left Saudi Arabia, the better.

ॐॐ

Riyadh, Saudi Arabia
Friday, June 23

He awoke the next morning, his eyes gritty from lack of sleep, deciding to skip breakfast. Best not to alert the hotel to his room change.

Pulling the satellite phone from the night stand, he dialed Fergus's number. "I'm headed home today. I'll call when I reach London so you can send Frank to pick me up."

"Did everything go all right?" Fergus asked.

Thomas couldn't explain. Anyone could be listening. "There...may be complications. I'll fill you in when I get back." He punched end and placed the phone in his briefcase.

Dressed in casual jeans and a long-sleeved polo, he walked the six blocks to the trade center. Heat radiated from the early morning sidewalk like a furnace on full blast. Through the mirrored surface of buildings along the route, he confirmed he still had his escort service.

The two men followed him to the showroom and stopped outside. They couldn't come inside until the conference opened, and then they'd need a badge. Whoever these people were, they wouldn't strike in the open. The Saudis wouldn't knowingly sanction an open murder or kidnapping on their streets.

The conference center was almost empty, except for a few early birds getting ready for the day's exhibits. Thomas taped the UBS drive in the projector case. Before leaving the showroom, he peered through the sliding doors, scanning the sidewalk.

The two-man surveillance team was nowhere in sight.

Thomas hailed a cab, directed the driver to the hotel for his luggage, and then to the car rental agency. After the paperwork was finished he headed to the car he'd rented.

King Khalid International lay thirty-five kilometers outside Riyadh, a well-traveled thoroughfare.

He couldn't shake the feeling he'd missed something—the internal warning bell that always signaled a mission was about to blow up clanged loudly.

After a stop at the airport rental depot to leave the car, he strode into the terminal. He filled his lungs with air and released it slowly. It seemed his paranoia was working overtime. He hadn't even spotted a tail on the trip to the airport. Just a few more steps to the terminal. Once on board his flight, he would be home free.

Thomas headed into a short hallway just inside the terminal. The corridor in the busy airport was empty, and it registered too late.

Two men in black appeared, and although he didn't look back, he knew there were others behind him. The men in front charged forward, cutting off his path into the terminal.

He dropped his luggage and laptop, and landed a blow on the first man to reach him. A sharp pain at the back of his head stopped him cold, and a dark tunnel opened up and swallowed him.

ॐॐ

CIA Headquarters, Washington, DC
Friday, June 23

Paul Redford paced his office and re-read the Air France passenger list. He hadn't overlooked it. Thomas Wallace wasn't on the flight. That meant trouble. That, and Thomas's message that Aref was missing.

His phone buzzed and he snatched it up. "Heim, thanks for getting back to me so quickly. Thomas missed the plane."

"I know. I checked the passenger list, also. Do you know if he and Aref made the transfer?"

"Yes, they made the transfer. Thomas called after the exchange was made. He also said Aref was missing."

"If his missed flight means what I think it does," Heim said, "the terrorists know Aref passed the timetable to Thomas. Which means they will change the strike date. But the data on the progress of the nuclear program should be good. We'll at least know when they project to have a bomb ready to launch."

"Aref may have passed on other useful intelligence. Can you do anything on your end to find out what happened? Where they've taken them?"

"I'm already on it. I'll contact you when I know something."

"Heim, do whatever it takes. We both know what happens to Thomas and Aref from here. You have my backing, men, and resources, anything you need. I want both men home. Alive."

18

Riyadh, Saudi Arabia
Friday, June 23

Thomas opened his eyes in almost total darkness, relieved only by rust holes that sent tiny shafts of sunlight into the trunk of the moving car. His large frame was folded into a fetal position and stuffed into the cramped quarters.

No limousine. Whatever the model, the car traveled at high speed, forcing dirt and sand into the small space.

He tried to shift position to relieve cramped muscles. The airport. The deserted corridor. Four men attacked him, two in front, two behind him. They pinned his arms to his sides, but he'd managed to take one man down before he was overpowered. That was the last thing he remembered.

What happened next would follow one of two scenarios. They would take him to a cellar somewhere, strip, torture, and then kill him. Or, they would give him a very public execution, getting as much mileage as possible for kidnapping and killing the Wallace heir. Either way, he wound up dead. He couldn't allow that to happen. If they got him into a building, it would be all over. There would be no escape.

He had one chance, and it was slim.

When they opened the trunk, he had to be ready.

He'd be outmanned and outgunned. A quick death was preferable to a slow, public one. Despite the cramped quarters and pain, he flexed the muscles in his arms and legs. Mind over matter.

Heat waves from the car's exterior permeated the trunk. His throat felt like sandpaper. Sweat soaked his clothes—his shirt was stuck like a second skin on his back.

A sudden jolt slammed him against the un-padded seat back and announced they'd reached their destination.

Thomas braced for the attack. Opening the trunk would bring immediate brightness. He would be temporarily blinded. No way to prepare for that. They didn't want to kill him now. Not yet. Otherwise, they would have done so in the airport corridor.

Men would die, and he was OK with that.

God made allowances for self-defense.

He twisted in the tight quarters, drew his knees to his chest, and placed them towards the opening. If things went as he hoped, he could brace himself against the back of the seat, giving him the momentum he needed to land on his feet. Silently he thanked Paul Redford for the training he'd insisted on. It just might save his life.

Arabic chatter sounded outside, and the trunk popped open.

He squinted against the glare but forced himself to focus.

Four men stood around the trunk, weapons drawn, the closest about two feet to his right.

He sprang forward and landed on his feet, unsteady for a brief moment. He whipped right and caught the man closest to him with a lethal kick to the neck. The terrorist went down without a sound.

Someone grabbed him from behind and pinned his arms to his side. Thomas smashed his head backwards into the terrorist's face. The man howled and his grip loosened. Thomas sent a fierce blow to the side of the man's skull, snapping his neck.

Two down, two to go.

Arabic curses filled the air, and the remaining two men advanced, forgetting any instructions not to kill him.

The shorter, thinner one rushed him, knife drawn.

Thomas sidestepped but the blade sliced into his left arm.

The terrorist grinned and plunged forward again.

Thomas was ready. He pivoted and swept the man off his feet, and then rushed to the prone form. He stomped his chest, stopping his heart.

The last man took a step forward and raised the AK-47 in his hand.

An almost inaudible pop sounded and the man dropped to his knees, and then fell face first into the dust.

Shock registered in Thomas's brain, and he glanced up, searching for the angel of mercy.

Two big men, the two who tailed him in Riyadh, rushed forward, silenced weapons drawn.

The man who reached him first, said in English, "Wallace, stop! Heim Rosen sent us."

Thomas shook his head to clear the cobwebs. The adrenalin rush had numbed his arm, but now the pain seared towards his shoulder and blood saturated his shirtsleeve. "You're Mossad?"

"Yes." The agent stuck out his hand. "Moshe Baum. We let you see us following you, so you'd know you had backup."

Thomas shook his head. "I didn't read it that way. I thought you were just amateurs."

The Israeli grinned. "I'm offended. Amateurs, indeed." He inclined his head towards his partner. "Shaul Lobel."

Moshe had the look of a warrior, thick shoulders and a taut frame, a man one wouldn't want to tangle with if it was avoidable. Strength and stubbornness was chiseled into a firm chin. He moved with quick, purposeful strides, his gaze taking in everything at once.

His partner, Shaul, was tall, rugged, and sleek as a panther, with movie-star good looks and the same dark, brooding eyes.

Thomas lowered his voice and shook hands with both men. "I've never been happier to see anyone. You guys have been watching me since I arrived in Riyadh?"

Moshe nodded.

"Why didn't you stop the kidnapping, just let me get on the plane?"

"They had Aref. We needed them to lead us to him. We couldn't leave him in their hands. He knows too much about Mossad agents. About your agents."

The sun hung high, baking the earth as the small group stood in a narrow alley between two dust-covered cement-block buildings in the middle of a date palm grove. An ancient British vehicle sat beside the old sedan Thomas had arrived in. The arid soil swallowed the blood spilled beside the dusty car, leaving only reddish-brown stains in the sand.

Thomas reached down and snatched the Russian-made assault rifle, three magazines, and a knife from the dead men's bodies.

Moshe waved him forward. "No time for a discussion. We don't know how many more are inside the buildings."

Shaul moved closer to Thomas and handed him a handkerchief. "Tie this above the wound. We have medical supplies in the van."

"It's just a scratch. The knife only grazed me."

Moshe pointed towards the building on the right.

Shaul took the house on the left.

Thomas and Moshe moved to the entrance. It was an arched opening, no door.

Moshe stuck his head around the corner, scanning the premises and then waved Thomas forward. The structure had three levels. Moshe took the ground floor and the roof. Thomas darted to the basement.

The assault rifle wasn't his first choice. The noise would rouse everyone in the place. He'd have to use the knife or his bare hands.

On quiet feet, he moved to the bottom of the stairs. The stench of open sewage and other smells he didn't want to put a name to almost made him gag. He moved down the wide corridor and checked the first room on the right.

Empty.

The unmistakable scent of cigarette smoke made him stop and step into an alcove. A door closed, and footsteps headed towards him. As the man passed, Thomas pulled him close with a right-handed chokehold, tightening the grip until the terrorist blacked out. Using the butt of the rifle, he delivered a sharp blow to the man's head to keep him unconscious a little longer.

Mossad would have killed him, but Thomas had

other plans. If Aref wasn't here, this man could tell them where to find him. Moving quickly to the door the terrorist just left, Thomas eased it open. No one was in the room except Aref.

His friend sat naked, bound to a chair with duct tape, his chin resting on his chest.

Thomas pressed his fingers to Aref's carotid artery. He was alive, but the pulse was weak. Thomas shook him. "Aref, it's Thomas. Can you hear me?"

The man lifted his head and opened his eyes. He gave a slight nod before his head slumped back to his chest.

A noise behind him made Thomas whirl and raise his weapon.

Moshe and Shaul slipped into the room.

"The building next door and the other floors are cleared," Moshe said. "Is Aref all right?"

Thomas began to cut the tape from Aref's hands and feet. "In a manner of speaking. He's alive. You and Shaul check the other rooms down here while I untie him."

The two agents left.

Thomas lowered Aref to the floor. He dragged the dead terrorist from the hallway and stripped his clothes. The man had a bullet through his heart. One of the Mossad agents' handiwork.

He quickly dressed Aref and hoisted him to his shoulder. In the hallway, he met the two Israelis with two more victims. These were on their feet, wounded, but able to walk.

Shaul handed the men a set of keys and said in Arabic. "Get out of here as fast as you can. Take the Land Rover outside."

The men helped each other up the stairs and

disappeared.

A grim expression passed over Moshe's face, and he nodded towards Aref. "What are you going to do with him?"

"I'm taking him out of here."

"He will be a major handicap. He's wounded. I don't think he's going to make it."

"You came here to find him. Now you want to do what? Put a bullet in his brain and leave him behind?"

"I thought we could get him out alive. He probably has a treasure trove of information in his head about Iran's nukes, but we have to get out of here with what we have. He could get us all captured."

Thomas headed towards the stairs. "I'm not leaving him. Period."

Moshe threw his hands up. He waved his gun at Shaul. "Gather all the extra ammunition you can find."

Moshe wheeled back to Thomas. "OK, but if we run into trouble, I'm leaving you both behind." He paused. "And I want the money clip."

Thomas nodded. "I can live with that."

As they moved outside, the distant roar of approaching vehicles sounded in the quiet desert air.

Moshe cast a see-what-I-mean look at Thomas and motioned them back inside. "Sounds like the rats are returning to the sewer."

"What now?" Shaul asked.

"We hope for the element of surprise and shoot as soon as they come into range."

"We don't know how many of them there are," Shaul said.

Moshe leaned forward, almost in Shaul's face. "Thanks for stating the obvious. You have a better idea?"

Shaul's brow creased, and he shook his head.

Thomas gently dropped Aref onto the floor. "Give me the rifle. I'll cover you from the roof."

Moshe threw Thomas the rifle.

He caught it in mid-air and raced for the stairs. He popped the door that led to the roof and scurried behind a low wall, about two and a half feet high, that surrounded the roof. On hands and knees, he crawled to the rampart and peered over the wall.

In the distance, two vehicles approached from the south. He didn't take time to count, but guessed there were ten, maybe twelve, bad guys.

He braced the rifle against his shoulder. As the vehicles drew closer, he sighted on the two drivers, taking them out with a single shot each.

The passengers jumped from the vehicles and scattered into the date groves, raining gunfire around him, pinging against the cement balustrade. Men in the second vehicle peppered the ground floor when the two Mossad agents returned fire.

Thomas waited for a pause in the gunfire, darted a glance towards the shooter, and fired two shots. The barraged of bullets stopped and he was able to keep the targets pinned down while Moshe and Shaul split up and moved to get behind them.

Realizing what was happening, the terrorists tried to change positions, but each time they showed themselves, Thomas picked them off.

Once the two Israelis were in place, the firefight was over. They quickly dispatched the remainder of the group.

Thomas met the men downstairs. He picked up his Iranian friend and placed him over his shoulder.

"Nice shooting." Moshe slapped him on the arm.

"We've better get out of here before the rest of the family comes home."

∂∾⸙

Thomas made Aref as comfortable as possible in the back of the Mossad van. He opened Aref's shirt and examined his chest. Thomas winced at the fierce burns at the contact points, apparently from electrical shocks received during his interrogation. He opened the well-stocked first-aid kit and cleaned the wounds with alcohol wipes, glad the man was still unconscious. Then he applied an antibiotic ointment. When finished, he dressed the wounds with gauze and tape. He would have to repeat this process daily until the wounds healed. Infection could kill Aref.

When Aref awakened, he'd give him an antibiotic capsules and pain reliever. Perhaps some of the morphine, if the pain was too intense. The Iranian was in good physical condition and depending on the severity of the burn, he should heal quickly.

Thomas threw a couple of blankets over Aref to help prevent shock. He turned his attention to his own injury. He cleaned and dressed the cut and downed two of the antibiotic capsules. "Where are we headed?"

"To a Kurd camp about fifty kilometers down the road. They're Iraqi refugees, reverting to the nomadic life of their Bedouin ancestors."

"Can they be trusted?" Thomas asked.

"We've used them in the past. They hate everybody after Bloody Friday. Saddam dropped cluster bombs filled with gas on Halabja back in the eighties. Killed thousands of Kurds, mostly women and children. We give them food, medicine, and firearms, so they're willing to help occasionally."

Shaul turned around in the front seat. "There's native garb in the back. You and Aref need to put those on before we reach the camp. Your dark coloring should help you pass as a Kurd, and Aref will have no trouble."

"Then what?"

"We make our way with these nomads to Jordan and from there, to Israel. Once we reach Jordan, we should be able to contact Heim to bring us out."

"You guys have a Sat-phone?"

Moshe nodded. "Yeah. Heim knows where we are. He won't risk sending in help unless the situation is critical. You?"

Thomas shook his head. "Lost it at the airport. Can you get him to contact Paul Redford?"

"He already has. Paul agreed we should work our way out. They don't want to risk ticking off the Saudis. They wouldn't like us running a covert operation on their turf without letting them know."

Thomas didn't like it, but he knew that was the right course of action. The perfect outcome would be for Heim or Paul to send in a chopper now, but that wasn't going to happen.

The Saudis were American allies, but they had no love for Israel, or for that matter, Americans. They wouldn't give diplomatic clearance for such an undertaking, and any covert team would run the risk of being shot down as soon as they crossed the border.

Thomas changed into one of the *thobes* and a white *ghutra*. "Sounds like a plan."

"Should work. Unless another group of our terrorist friends put in an appearance." Moshe added.

Thomas was under no illusions about Mossad's

goal in this operation. If they got into a losing firefight with terrorists, the Israelis would shoot Aref and perhaps him, as well. It wouldn't be their first choice. But their objective was to get the information back to Israel.

He could appreciate their dilemma. He certainly didn't agree with it. He'd cross that quagmire when the time came.

The thumb drive data was already at Langley. He'd forwarded it before erasing his computer's hard drive at the hotel. The extra drives were just backup.

19

Saudi Arabia near the Jordanian Border
Sunday, June 25

The Rekani family were hospitable, but kept their distance. Distinguished in his tribal robes, the patriarch, Abdul, and his two sons, instructed them in the care and feeding of goats, sheep, and camels, finally leaving them to their jobs. Three silent females and four children moved about the camp. The women brought food twice a day and then disappeared like silent ghosts.

Thomas's aspirations never included herding goats in the desert, but like it or not, he had led the smelly animals to grass and water for the past two days. That, and praying five times a day. He prayed not to Allah, but to the God of Abraham, Isaac, and Jacob.

For the first time since his life blew up in his face, Thomas found himself seeking God in the quiet solitude of the sand, and the simple life around him. Near here, Moses found the burning bush, walked on holy ground, and surrendered to God's will.

In the darkness, with an unbelievable canopy of stars above him, Thomas had come to understand he had blamed God for all the evil he encountered in his personal life and on black ops missions. He'd blamed God for Traci's infidelity, and the pain it caused him and Daniel.

The awareness was humbling.

Thomas wandered back to the tent he shared with Aref and the two Mossad agents. The three of them were responsible for taking down their dwelling and resurrecting it as the camp inched its way to the Jordanian border.

When he entered their tent, Aref was alert for the first time.

Thomas handed him a bowl of goat meat and rice. "Think you can eat this?"

Hands shaking, Aref accepted the bowl. "Where are we?"

"Enjoying the hospitality of a Kurd family, the Rekanis. Trying to work our way into Jordan."

Aref took a bite of the food. "Rekani is probably the name of their tribe. Kurds inherit their surnames from the tribes of which their families are members. How long have we been here?"

"Three days. I don't know how close we are to Jordan. We have a couple of Mossad agents guiding the way."

The sound of approaching voices made Thomas look up.

Moshe and Shaul entered. They grabbed the bowls of food left for them.

"I see our man is awake," Moshe said. "How are you feeling?"

"Drained," Aref replied. "But it's been worse. Much worse."

"How far are we from Jordan?" Thomas asked.

Moshe scooped the food into his mouth like a seasoned Kurd. "Two, three days, if all goes well." He cast a glance at Aref. "Do you think you'll be on your feet by then?"

Aref nodded and took a few more bites. He sat the bowl down and pushed it away. "Thank you for finding me, Thomas. I thought I'd bought the farm."

Laughter exploded from Thomas's throat. "Where did you pick up that expression?"

Aref grinned and leaned back on the cushions behind him. "From some of your countrymen."

Thomas nodded at the two Israelis. "These are the men you need to thank. They saved both our lives."

Aref reached out and shook their hands.

"How did they get on to you? Someone in your group see you pass the money clip?" Thomas asked.

Aref shook his head. "No, someone tipped them off. They'd been acting strange ever since we left Tehran. When I returned to the hotel after we met, they were waiting for me."

⮞⮜

Wallace Island, the Aegean Sea
Sunday, June 25

Recovery was taking longer than Mercy liked.

Katy bustled in with a breakfast tray, set it down on the bed, and put her hands on her hips. "It isn't fair that a woman can look like you do in the morning after a near death experience." She fluffed Mercy's pillows and gave her a stern look. "Now eat every last bite or I'll have to put a stronger dose of arsenic in it tomorrow."

Mercy laughed. "How did you wind up in Turkey, Katy? Your patients run you out of the states?"

"Don't be impertinent. My patients loved me." She

sat on the side of the bed. "Actually, I came here looking for adventure and a husband. Pickings were slim for women my age back in Texas." She gave a deep chuckle, put a hand to her auburn hair, and leaned over, speaking in a stage whisper. "Now tell me, is that Mr. Fergus married? He's a handsome figure of a man. I keep imagining what he would look like in a kilt."

Mercy couldn't contain her smile. The woman's wit was better medicine than the pills she pushed. "No, he's not married. You go get 'im, Katy. I'll help you all I can."

Katy turned to the door. "Enough fun and frivolity. I'll be back in half an hour to give you a bath."

"Oh, no, you won't. I'll take my own shower."

"Then I'll be back in an hour to give you a massage."

"Now, that I'll gladly accept."

The nurse eyed Paddy, curled up beside Mercy. "Where did you get that scruffy looking cat?"

"Paddy isn't scruffy looking. He's a sweetheart." She picked him up and held him to her chest. His purr resonated against her ribs.

"I'll take your word for it. By the way, I don't like your housekeeper. If you ask me, she's the one who tried to poison you. In Texas, we'd call her shifty." She placed a finger to her temple and tapped. "Never trust anyone who can't smile."

Katy had put words to Mercy's own suspicions. She knew Edda didn't like her, but poison seemed a little extreme. Changing the household diet was hardly grounds for murder, even for a psychopath.

After a shower and a skin tingling massage, Mercy

felt ready to get out of bed and back to life.

Daniel bounced into her room with Pal in his arms.

Paddy hadn't totally accepted Pal, but he didn't bow his back in the puppy's presence. Still, he kept a watchful eye on him.

Pal, however, was curious about this strange looking creature and wanted to play.

Mercy placed Paddy on the floor, and he wandered off to the balcony, with Pal at his heels.

Daniel sat on the bed. "You still sick, Mummy?"

"No, I'm much better. Want to take a swim this afternoon?"

His head bobbed up and down.

"Lesson's going well with Mac?"

"Uh huh. He's teaching me about evil King Edward I who killed Sir William Wallace."

Mercy laughed. "That would be a subject dear to Mac's heart."

Gathering Pal into his arms, Daniel walked to the door and waved. "Bye, Mummy."

"See you later, Danny."

A knock sounded at the door. Not waiting for Mercy to answer, Katy backed into the room, a lunch tray in her hand. "Here you go, Missy." She set the tray on the nightstand and lifted the dish covers.

Mercy wrinkled her nose at the liver, spinach, and carrots. She grinned at the irascible nurse. "Let me guess, you weren't hired for your culinary skills."

"You must be feeling better. You're getting a smart mouth." She smoothed her uniform over her hips with both hands. "My clients hired me for my charm and exceptional good looks." Katy picked up the tray, set it on Mercy's lap, and pointed at the food. "Eat. You keep complaining and I'll let that shifty blonde make your meals."

"You know, you have a mean streak."

Katy moved to the door and wiggled her eyebrows. "So I've been told. Doesn't hurt my feelings a bit. "

At six o'clock, Mercy felt well enough to join the family for dinner, which brightened her evening. Casting aside the invalid role greatly improved her mood.

The nurse cleared the move with Fergus. He told Katy whoever was responsible for Mercy's illness, probably wouldn't poison the entire family just to get at her.

Fergus informed Mercy that he and his men had searched the house. They'd removed all the rat poison, and garden products, and then locked them away in the gardener's shed. He'd stopped short of searching the staff's private residence — that was, in essence, their home.

Katy joined the family for dinner that evening. She brought in a large glass of mixed fruit juice, set it by Mercy's plate, and winked at her. "I made this myself. Why doesn't Mr. Fergus eat in the dining room?"

Mercy had wondered about that herself.

"He doesn't like the formality," Nanna said. "He prefers the kitchen but usually joins us on holidays."

Before dessert arrived, Fergus appeared in the doorway. "Traci, may I speak to ye for a wee bit?"His expression revealed nothing.

Mercy felt her stomach knot as she followed him down the hallway and into Thomas's office.

"Close the door, lass."

He moved to the window, not turning to look at

her. For a long moment he stood silent, his back straight. He drew in a deep breath, his voice unsteady. "I just had a call from Paul Redford. Thomas is missing."

❧◦❧

Saudi Arabia, Near the Jordanian Border
Tuesday, June 27

By the fifth day of their journey, Aref was making short forays to help tend the goat herds and camels. They'd kept to the desert's edge for grass and water, which meant they took a circuitous route to their destination.

Thomas was getting antsy.

If Aref was right and someone had compromised the mission, they were still in imminent danger. He wanted to trust the Mossad agents. They'd had multiple chances to kill him and Aref.

Perhaps someone in Redford's camp leaked the information accidentally.

One thing Thomas knew. They didn't need to be out here wandering around in the desert like lost sheep. He sat on a grassy knoll overlooking the animals.

Aref squatted beside him. "There's a caravan headed this way. Moshe has been watching it all morning. He and the Rekani men went out to meet them about thirty minutes ago." He slapped Thomas's back. "We'll eat well tonight, my friend. No more goat and rice."

An hour later, Moshe and Shaul joined them on the knoll.

Moshe stared into the distance in the direction the caravan had gone. "The merchants in the caravan said two days ago men in military vehicles were looking for you and Aref. They didn't use names. Just gave a vague description. We may have company soon."

"If they come, couldn't we take their cars and drive on into Jordan?" Aref asked.

Moshe shook his head. "We would have trouble crossing the border in a vehicle. You don't have papers. As part of the Kurdish tribe we can pass through without notice."

Aref shrugged. "So what do we do when, and if, they show up?"

Moshe didn't blink. "We kill them."

Thomas listened to the exchange. If the hunters came looking for them, it would be up to him and the two Israelis to deal with whatever trouble came their way. The Rekanis wouldn't get involved, and Aref was still too weak to help.

"I agree with Aref." Thomas said. "We take their means of transportation and identification, and then cross the border. Heim and Paul Redford can pick us up. The longer we stay in Saudi Arabia, the greater the chance of running into something we can't handle."

Moshe shrugged thoughtfully. "It's worth a try." He turned to Shaul. "What do you think?"

"I think Wallace is right. This is taking longer than we anticipated. We needed to be out of this desert yesterday."

Moshe gazed at his partner and then back to Thomas. "We would have the element of surprise since we blend in with the family." He plopped down on the ground. "Looks like we're agreed. We wait for the hunters to show up and fall into the trap."

20

CIA Headquarters, Washington, DC
Tuesday, June 27

Heim Rosen waited in the lobby outside Paul Redford's office. There was a stark contrast to this building and his headquarters in Israel. Where Mossad was high energy and less structured, Langley was a conventional, well-oiled machine that turned out cookie-cutter agents.

Thomas Wallace had been the exception. The agency had been crazy to let him walk away.

After a few minutes, a blonde, big-haired secretary led Heim into Paul Redford's office. "Mr. Rosen's here to see you, sir." He nodded, and she closed the door.

Redford's expression turned serious as he stared at a television on the wall. The news channel was running the lead story of the day, featuring a Jewish American male captured by al-Qaeda. The terrorists had just released a tape of the victim pleading for his life.

Heim turned to Redford. "Will you deal with them?"

Frustration etched furrows into Redford's face. "Would you?"

"No," Heim said. "If you meet their demands, they'll kill him, anyway. If he isn't already dead. They could have filmed that clip when they first captured him. He was a dead man the minute they grabbed him."

"We have agents looking for him in Pakistan—trying to find the location. That's the best we can do." Redford lifted the remote and muted the sound. He turned his chair around to face Heim.

Heim took a chair. It made the CIA chief crazy when Heim paced.

"Have you heard anything more on Thomas?" Redford asked.

"No. We know both he and Aref are alive, but you already know that. Have you heard anything?"

"We have to assume they're still OK. If Thomas Wallace had been killed, it wouldn't be kept secret."

Heim knew almost the exact location of Thomas Wallace. He couldn't let his counterpart know this, however. He hadn't told Redford he'd sent agents in.

Every fanatic regime in the Middle East had Israel in its crosshairs. It wasn't the USA that faced annihilation if Iran dropped a nuke in Israel's lap. Protecting his country was his first priority. He'd share information on a need to know basis. Not before. He wanted a chance to pick Aref's brain before his handlers shuffled him somewhere out of reach.

"What brings you to D.C., Heim?"

"I flew in to the embassy yesterday. Wanted to check in with you while I was here." He nodded towards the TV screen. "We have an ear to the ground for any leads on that guy. He's also one of ours." Heim stood before the huge window, his back to Redford. The view overlooked the Mall.

People hurried to their appointed tasks like ants in an active anthill.

"Who in your agency knew about this operation besides you, me, and Thomas?" Heim asked.

"No one. My people made the travel arrangements, but they didn't know the purpose. Why do you ask?"

Heim moved back to watching the newscast that still ran the al-Qaeda reel. "It crossed my mind that someone tipped off the terrorists. I'm speculating that the cell didn't confirm Aref's deception until shortly after he passed the data to Thomas. Otherwise, the exchange would never have taken place." He nodded at the screen. "We need a plan to prevent Thomas and Aref from meeting the same fate as that poor devil."

ॐ∽

Wallace Island, the Aegean Sea
Tuesday, June 27

Legs suddenly weak, Mercy felt behind her for the chair arms and eased down on the cushioned seat. "What does it mean? Is he..."

"It means they don't know where he is or what happened," Fergus said. "Redford has deployed people to find him but nothing so far."

Her hand went to her brow as she tried to absorb the news. Thomas could be dead or seriously wounded. *Please God, not Thomas.* "What do we tell Daniel?"

"Nothing, for the time being. Not until we know for sure what's happened."

ॐ∽

Saudi Arabian Desert, Near the Jordanian Border
Wednesday, June 28

Thomas had just swallowed the last bite of the evening meal when the roar of engines and automatic gunfire announced the arrival of the guests they'd been waiting for. The commotion rousted everyone in camp.

He grabbed one of the AK-47s and magazines and motioned to Aref to stay put.

Moshe and Shaul were already half out the tent flap, automatic weapons and rifles in hand.

"Leave me a weapon," Aref called.

He threw Aref the assault rifle and a magazines.

Thomas caught up with the two Israelis. "If they know we're here it's stupid to announce their arrival, don't you think?

"They don't know we're here," Moshe said. "It's a form of intimidation when they come into a camp. Lets the occupants know they're armed and ready for a fight." He turned to Shaul. "Tell the Rekanis to stay out of sight."

Shaul disappeared for five minutes. When he returned, they scurried behind a sand dune.

Field glasses in hand, Moshe scanned the approaching vehicles. "Looks like they're about a mile out, maybe more. It's impossible to judge in all the sand. How many are there?" He passed the glasses to Thomas.

"I count three vehicles." Thomas replied. "Four men in each."

Shaul nodded. "That's what I counted."

"Give me a rifle. I'll draw them away from the Rekani tents." Thomas said. "Goat skin won't repel bullets."

Moshe tossed him a rifle and grinned. "Be careful. Sand doesn't stop bullets, either."

Crouching low, Thomas moved away from the camp and towards the approaching vehicles. A nearby dune looked like a good place to wait until they came into range. He took his position at the top of the knoll and examined Moshe's rifle.

It was a Swiss B&T with scope and silencer. He'd never used this model. The gun was fitted with a night scope, but they could end this in the two hours left of daylight.

Thomas muttered under his breath.

The desert was the worst possible place for a gunfight. No cover to speak of, and moving through sand was like walking with weights on one's ankles.

Within minutes, the first vehicle came over a rise and down at a forty-five degree incline to the shallow dip below.

Thomas sighted on the driver and squeezed the trigger.

A scream echoed in the silent sand, and the driver spilled out. The vehicle turned on its side, dumping the other occupants. Panicked, the terrorists scrambled in the dirt shouting curses.

Because of the rifle's silencer and the roar of the engines, the two remaining vehicles weren't aware of the ambush until they crested the rise. The driver tried to avoid the downed vehicle and men scrambling for cover, and failed. He rammed into the first one, bounced back, and tipped over.

Thomas had the high-ground advantage and there was no cover from his bullets. He picked off the third vehicle's driver and it became part of the wreckage. He zeroed in on two more men before the remaining terrorists dived for cover.

Wild gunfire sprayed the sand in all directions, but

nothing came near him.

Fifty yards away, Moshe and Shaul inched into position, and began firing on full automatic, sending a hail of bullets over and under the wreckage.

Two men escaped the carnage and made for the closest sand hill.

Thomas downed both before they reached their destination.

Grunts and screams, and then silence.

"Thomas, you OK?" Moshe yelled.

"Yeah, you guys?"

"We're good," Moshe called back across the distance. He and Shaul checked the bodies for survivors and found none. The two men scrambled over the hilltop and trudged towards him.

Thomas met them in the middle. The next order of business was to find papers and clothing that would fit. No time or need to bury the dead. The desert had its own eco-system.

They made their way back to the camp in silence, Thomas running the events through his mind. Over the past few days, he developed a grudging respect for Moshe and Shaul. Hard men. Patriots to the core. They shared that in common.

At an oasis near the campsite, they washed the clothing and let them dry overnight.

Aref peppered them with questions, wanting details of the firefight. His curiosity finally sated, they tried to catch some sleep for the next, and hopefully last, phase of this operation.

The following morning, they discarded the *throbes* and *ghutras* and dressed in the terrorists' wardrobes. Thomas's pants proved a little short, but he tucked the bottoms into his boots to conceal the fashion faux pas.

The Rekanis packed up early to get away from the area before authorities discovered the bodies.

Before the family left, Thomas sought out Abdul. "Thank you, sir, for your hospitality. We are much in your debt." They shook hands, and Thomas rejoined his friends.

The four of them loaded into the vehicle and pointed its nose towards Jordan.

21

Wallace Island, the Aegean Sea
Thursday, June 29

Katy Martin went in search of Fergus and found him outside with the Black Watch soldiers. "Mr. Fergus, may I speak to you for a moment?"

Fergus left the group and came towards her. "There's no mister in front of my name, Katy. Is something wrong with Traci?"

Katy kept her face serious. The matter she wanted to discuss had troubled her for days. "No, Traci's fine, for the present. I was wondering if you had any further word on who was responsible for the arsenic in her food."

His eyes narrowed. His face became tight. "No, but that's no concern of yers. Yer only job is to see that Traci stays healthy."

"I won't stand for your rudeness, *Mister* Fergus." She put her hands on her hips. "It was a simple question and deserved a polite answer. And my job, as you put it, is to see that no more poison gets into her food. Your job, I'm told, is security, and if you would open your eyes and stop standing around telling jokes and laughing with your friends, we might find the person responsible."

He stepped forward, his six-foot four frame towering over her five-foot five stature. His face flushed with anger. "We? Are ye telling me how to do my job?"

"Don't think you can intimidate me. Did you ever consider installing nanny cams in the kitchen and setting a trap for this would-be murderer? Next time it might not be poison. I like that young woman. I don't want to see her harmed."

Fergus rubbed both hands over his face. "What's a nanny cam?"

"It's a small camera you hide in a strategic place to watch people you don't trust, or people you do trust, to prove them innocent. They're available in most electronic stores."

He looked beyond her and gave an almost imperceptible nod. "I know what ye mean. Just never heard it called a nanny cam. I'll check it out. But I don't want ye playing detective. Most of the staff has been with the family for years. Don't be interfering with the smooth running of this household. Do ye understand me, woman?"

"Perfectly clear, *Mister* Fergus. And my name isn't woman. It's Katy Martin. You can call me Katy or Miss Martin, but not woman."

She turned her back to him and stalked away. This romance was going fine, indeed. She wouldn't take any guff off a rough-around-the-edges Scotsman.

ॐॐ

Back on her feet, Mercy resumed her household duties, which consisted of planning menus and spending time with Daniel.

Katy graciously volunteered to work with Father Joseph to get the island children up to date on their inoculations and see to the other inhabitants' medical needs. They'd set up a first aid station on the terrace, with Mercy and Father Joseph acting as Katy's assistants, handing the nurse syringes, alcohol swabs, and whatever else she needed.

The busy-work kept Mercy from dwelling on Thomas. Each day that passed without word, she feared the worst.

The last islander walked away after being treated, and Katy expelled a deep breath, breaking Mercy's introspection. "Well, that's the last one."

"So it is. Nice work, Katy."

Lily dropped a tray of tea and sandwiches on a table nearby.

"I think our three-person triage unit has won the day. Time for a break," Mercy said.

"Words dear to my heart," Father Joseph said. "Then I must return to the chapel. God's work is never done."

"I'll drink to that." Katy raised her teacup.

After the priest left, Mercy and Katy remained on the terrace sipping their drinks in silence.

"You know, I really don't need a nurse any longer."

"I know. I've been expecting to get my discharge notice for the past few days."

"Would you consider staying here, running a clinic on the island?"

Katy's eyes widened and laughter bubbled from her throat. "Would I? Who in their right mind wouldn't want to work here? Where do I sign?"

"I'll have to clear it with Thomas, but I think I can swing it. We need a clinic here for minor emergencies, and I'd love to have you stay. Not to change the subject, but what's going on between you and Fergus? When you two are in the same room the temperature drops twenty degrees."

"Have you noticed that our Mister Fergus is a bit of a chauvinist? He seems to think a woman should stay in her place, but he's not sure what her place is."

"That character flaw hasn't escaped my attention. But he's a lamb once you set the ground rules."

"Well, I set the ground rules a few days ago, and he hasn't yet shown me his lamb side." She glanced around and lowered her voice. "I suggested he put in a few nanny cameras in the kitchen. Edda hanging around while I'm preparing your food unnerves me. I feel that when I leave, whoever is trying to harm you will pick up where they left off."

"Did he take your suggestion?"

"Yes, although somewhat reluctantly. He sent one of his army buddies shopping. The kilt brigade is going to install them Sunday on the staff's day off."

"That was clever of you, Katy."

"We Texas gals have to stick together. There's more than one way to skin an armadillo. Or in this instance to catch a wannabe killer." Katy took a long sip of tea and gazed at Mercy over the rim. "Tell me, what is your husband like?"

The question caught Mercy off guard. She gave a slight shrug. "He's handsome, wealthy, and intelligent."

"I know that from reading the tabloids and magazines. What is he like as a man, as a husband?"

Mercy couldn't hold back the slight smile as Thomas's face eased into her mind. "He's very charming when he wants to be. I think he's a good man, an honorable human being, but very strong-minded."

"You think? After seven years of marriage, you're not sure?"

"We've been separated until just recently." She looked into the nurse's eyes. "He's missing, Katy. I'm terribly worried about him."

"Well, we will pray for him." Katy stood, as if she sensed she couldn't ask any more questions. She picked up the tray. "I'll take this back to the kitchen."

Mercy returned to her room and called up the menu file on the computer, but her mind refused to concentrate on meal planning.

Katy's questions brought Thomas to the forefront of her thoughts.

What would she do if he never returned? Stay here and raise his son? She couldn't help wondering about the real Traci Wallace. What if she came back? Would she, if something happened to Thomas? It was her rightful place as Daniel's mother and Thomas's wife.

Paddy jumped into her lap, nuzzling against her chest. She stroked his fur and scratched behind his ear.

Thomas had to return safely, and not just for her protection. Doomed as their relationship was, the kiss he'd placed on her lips when he left held promises she'd never dared consider. But she couldn't let her thoughts go there.

How had she ever allowed herself to become so deeply entangled in Thomas Wallace's life?

❧◦❧

Saudi Arabia/Jordan Border
Thursday, June 29

They'd taken turns driving until they neared the Jordanian border. Then Moshe took the wheel. Since the Sheikh Hussein Border Crossing was closest, that's where Moshe suggested they cross, mixing with the heavy mid-morning tourist traffic.

Harried border guards wouldn't pay too much attention to their papers.

After crossing the border, they could contact Paul Redford and Heim and get transportation to Israel.

As the line of cars inched forward, an overpowering hunger for home hit Thomas.

Smells and senses of the island swept over him. The fragrance of the lemon trees, the beauty of the purple water lilies were almost tangible. Ocean breezes soothed his skin, and the sound of the waves washing ashore calmed his spirit. One phone call and Fergus would pick him up. He could chuck the assignment and be home for dinner. Home to Mercy and Daniel. Nice dream, but it couldn't happen. Not now.

Debriefing had to come first. And there was still the matter of a mole inside the agency. The worst kind of traitor, hiding behind patriotism while sending real patriots to their death. Selling men's lives for money. An informant who had gotten Aref's contacts in Iran killed. And almost succeed in eliminating him and Aref. He must find the mole before other good men lost their lives.

The vehicle halted, and the Jordanian border guard approached. "Your papers please," he said in Arabic.

Moshe and Shaul had also taken papers from the terrorists as insurance. Most Arab countries refused entry to passports bearing an Israeli stamp.

The guards gave the documents a cursory glance.

"Any weapons?"

"No," Moshe said.

They'd ditched the automatic weapons just before reaching the border.

"Will you be staying long?"

"We're just passing through to Amman to meet friends."

"If you decide to stay, you'll need to renew your visas."

Moshe nodded. "We understand."

The guard handed them their visas and waved them through.

A collective sigh and nervous laughter filled the vehicle once they were on Jordanian soil.

Moshe stopped at the first café he sighted. He and Shaul ordered *mansaf.*

"Guess I'll have the same," Thomas said, "although I have no idea what it is."

Aref concurred, making it unanimous.

After they'd ordered, Moshe stepped outside to contact Heim and get the small band transported to Israel. When the agent returned, the wrinkles in the corners of his eyes had disappeared and the tense muscles around his mouth relaxed.

The food arrived and it was quite good—lamb cooked in a dried yogurt sauce, served over rice.

Over coffee, Moshe explained the plan. "Heim is sending a private plane for us to Queen Alia Airport in Zyzia. That's about thirty-two kilometers from Amman."

"How far to Amman?" Thomas asked.

"About ninety kilometers. We have a total of one hundred, twenty-two kilometers to go. Heim says the plane should be there by fourteen hundred hours.

They'll standby until we arrive."

Thomas finished the last dregs of his coffee. "I need to contact my boss. May I borrow your phone?"

Moshe handed him the phone. "Heim said he'd notify Redford. He's been waiting in Tel Aviv for news about you."

≈≪⁘≫≈

Zyzia, Jordan
Thursday, June 29

Two hours later, Thomas parked the stolen vehicle in the airport parking lot and left the keys in the ignition.

Just inside terminal one, Heim stepped forward. A huge smile spread across his rugged face when he caught sight of their ragged band. He greeted Moshe and Shaul with hearty hugs and Thomas and Aref with an enthusiastic handshake. He stepped back and scanned their apparel. "I'm so glad to see you men safe I'll overlook your atrocious wardrobes. I want to hear everything as soon as we're aboard the plane."

The agency chief led them through the terminal to the unmarked jet waiting on the tarmac. As they stepped into the heat, noise from construction crews and heavy equipment fought for dominance over the roar of incoming and departing flights. No jetport here for the private plane, which was just as well. They were less noticeable this way.

Thomas and his three friends followed Heim up the flight steps. Thomas was the last to board, feeling truly safe for the first time since he'd left home.

Inside the aircraft, the four men ahead of him

jammed the entrance, despite the fact they had no luggage to store.

Heim, Moshe, and Shaul moved to the back.

Aref took the first seat on the left.

Thomas slipped into the seat beside him.

When he glanced to his left, Paul Redford sat in the seat across the aisle. Next to Paul was Clint Monroe.

22

Wallace Island, the Aegean Sea
Monday, July 3

The security installations had taken place on Sunday as scheduled. Fergus set up two monitors in Thomas's office, with recording equipment to save the data on disks. He and his buddies spaced four cameras throughout the kitchen and butler's pantry.

Despite the protection around her, Mercy didn't feel safe.

The reason someone was trying to kill Traci Wallace was still unknown. If Ricco Rossellini wanted the photographs, how could he get them with her dead? Another possibility was that Traci had other dark secrets and enemies no one knew about.

At breakfast, Katy seemed giddy with excitement, waiting for the security cameras to solve the crime. She and Fergus appeared to have called a temporary truce, huddling in corners discussing who-knew-what.

Mercy was more concerned that she hadn't received any further word about Thomas. Every day her fear escalated. After lunch, she returned to her room to rest.

A short while later, a faint tap sounded at her door and Katy slipped in.

"Do you want to be on hand for the fireworks?"

"What are you talking about?"

"Ever since the cameras were installed, I've been leaving your juice unattended while I went to get your medicine." Katy sat on the bed. "As I told you, Edda always hangs around in the background when I'm preparing anything for you. Today, she took the bait. Come downstairs and I'll show you."

Mercy slipped her shoes on and followed the nurse to Thomas's office.

Fergus sat watching the two screens. When he saw Mercy, he nodded.

"Rewind the recording please, Fergus." Katy requested.

On screen, Edda entered the butler's pantry. She glanced around, leaned over, and dumped something into the juice that sat on a silver tray. She gave the liquid a quick stir, returned the bottle to her pocket, and left.

"So it *was* Edda," Mercy said.

"Yep, and we have her dirty deed on camera."

"What now?"

"You go out to the terrace and wait." Katy walked her to the door.

As instructed, Mercy took a lounge chair overlooking the garden.

Ten minutes later, Edda walked towards her. "Katy asked me to bring you your juice and medication, Mrs. Wallace." She waited for Mercy to take the glass from her hand.

"I think ye should drink it, Edda." Fergus stepped from the shadows before Edda.

"I-I don't understand, Mr. Fergus."

"I think ye do. Drink it."

Fear flashed into the woman's gaze. She lifted the glass, but instead of drinking it, she splashed half the liquid on the terrace stones.

Fergus spoke through clenched teeth. "We've taken the liberty of packing yer bags, Edda. Everything ye did we recorded on CD. The disk, along with the contents of this glass, will buy ye a wee bit of time in a Turkish prison. Who paid ye to try to kill Traci?"

Edda's shoulders slumped. She seemed to wilt before their eyes. "It doesn't matter who. It won't help me, now."

"I hope whoever hired ye can get ye a good lawyer. The prisons in Turkey are a nasty business."

All the color drained from Edda's face, but she didn't confess.

Sympathy rose inside Mercy. She could have died a very unpleasant death if the poisoning hadn't been discovered in time. Turkish prison would be a horrendous price to pay for Edda's actions. Mercy offered a silent prayer for the woman.

Dejected, the housekeeper stood before them, her head down.

Two of the men took her arms and escorted her to the boat. They would drop her off at the nearest police station on the Turkish coast.

At dinner, Fergus entered the dining room, the satellite phone in his hand. "Traci, ye have a phone call."

"For me?"

He nodded, his eyes misting.

A spark of hope flashed inside her as she accepted the phone from Fergus's hand. "Hello."

"Mercy." Thomas's welcome voice sounded in her ear. "I'll see you soon. I've got a few days of debriefing, and then I'm coming home."

Her throat tightened so that she could barely

speak. A weight had lifted. He was alive and unharmed. "Thomas, I-I'm...so glad you're safe."

It wasn't until hours later she realized he'd call her by her own name.

౭∘ఄ

Tel Aviv, Israel
Tuesday, July 4

Thomas emerged from his first day of debriefing determined to find Paul and Heim. He found the two head spooks in Heim's office. Heim kicked a chair towards him. "Have a seat. What's on your mind?"

"You guys know yet who outed Aref to the Iranians?"

Heim waved a hand at Paul, giving him the floor.

Paul broke eye contact and shifted his position in the chair. "Not really. Since knowledge of the mission was closely contained, I'm thinking someone saw the transfer." Paul was hiding something.

"That won't fly, Paul. Aref said they were acting funny after they arrived in Riyadh. And they were waiting for him ten minutes later when he returned to the hotel after the exchange. There wouldn't have been time to set that up. Face it, Paul, you have a leak. Tell me, what was Clint Monroe doing here? I thought his job was training recruits."

"Wait a minute, Thomas," Paul said. "I know you don't like Monroe, but you have no reason to think he's a traitor."

"I didn't make an accusation. I just asked a question." Thomas walked to the door. "You'll have to forgive me. But when someone paints a target on my back and passes out ammunition to the bad guys, I take it personally."

"Monroe came to escort four graduates to their new assignment. Nothing more."

"I'll accept that for the time being," Thomas said.

Creases formed on Paul's brow and he looked directly into Thomas's eyes. "Don't think I'm not taking this seriously. I'm giving it my full attention. The last thing I want is to put our operatives in danger. It's my job to protect them."

Thomas returned to his hotel room. Before he could settle in, a knock sounded at the door. He swung it open and Heim, Moshe, and Shaul stood outside.

"Grab your jacket. We're going to show a *goy* how to have a good time."

Thomas laughed and slipped into his coat. "Is that me?"

Heim slapped his back. "Well, it isn't one of us."

Thomas flipped off the lights and closed the door. "Where are you taking me? I'm not sure I'm old enough to party with you guys."

Heim put his arm around Thomas's shoulder. "I'm taking you to one of our finest restaurants. We'll feed you asparagus with chestnut, smoked sirloin, and ply you with wine. Tonight, my friend, you will forget all your troubles."

The evening turned out to be everything Heim promised.

Thomas found himself laughing and applauding as his three Hebrew friends provided an impromptu floorshow. Heim grabbed a guitar from one of the musicians and sang while Moshe and Shaul, arms extended, danced, movements of hands and feet passed down through the ages.

Although the song was in Hebrew, Thomas understood the meaning. They celebrated another victory over their enemy. They rejoiced to live to fight another day. Shouts of *L'chayim*, to life, rang out from restaurant patrons and the staff alike followed by wild applause.

Thomas's heart swelled with admiration for these proud, courageous people, surrounded on all sides by enemies dedicated to their destruction, yet they fought on, holding onto life with both hands.

A salty, warm breeze tossed Thomas's hair as he exited the restaurant with his friends. It was late and there were only a few cars left in the parking lot.

When they reached Heim's car, Shaul stepped in front of Thomas, laughing. "Wait, Wallace. I know you're not used to opening your own car doors, not without a chauffeur to do it for you."

Thomas laughed as Shaul opened the rear door.

Almost simultaneously, a light flashed from the rooftop across the street and a whiz singed the air.

Thomas recognized the sound immediately.

The bullet caught Shaul in the back and he fell into Thomas's arms.

Thomas caught him before he hit the ground and felt the warm wetness of blood on his hands.

Time and sound stopped.

There was no blast of gunfire.

There was no sound from Shaul.

An awful slow motion encompassed Thomas as he dived to the cement, wrestling his gun from the shoulder holster with one hand, holding on to Shaul's body with the other. His movements were like swimming in molasses.

Sound exploded around him. Shouts and angry

bursts of gunfire broke the silence.

Thomas focused on the warehouse roof across the street where the shot came from. He pumped off two shots, but the shooter had gone.

The few patrons left, streamed from the restaurant scattering in all directions, away from the gunshots. A siren sounded in the distance. Someone had called for an ambulance.

Thomas eased Shaul's body to the pavement and leaned against the car. Unfamiliar wetness on his face made him touch his cheek. He wiped blood with the back of his hand, bringing away a red smear.

Shaul had taken a bullet meant for him.

A man in a dark suit shoved Thomas aside. "I'm a doctor. I'll do what I can until the ambulance arrives."

Thomas raced towards the warehouse, Moshe right behind him. They found the unlocked door leading to the roof. Thomas stormed up, taking the steps two at a time. He stopped at the top to catch his breath. He eased the door open, waved Moshe to one side. No need to take chances. He threw the door open and stepped to the side, his weapon in hand, but the rooftop was empty. He moved to the parapet and looked down below.

The shot had come from this position. The assassin had removed the shell, leaving nothing behind. A professional. Probably used a drag bag to lay on while waiting for the four men to emerge from the restaurant.

Tel Aviv's crime scene people would scour the area for evidence, but it didn't look promising.

Below, cops and agents stood in silence, faces grim, as an ambulance drove away. They would continue to search the area, but they all knew it was wasted time. Still, it had to be done.

Whoever pulled the trigger hadn't planned to hang around. He left the scene within minutes of the assassination.

23

Wallace Island, the Aegean Sea
Tuesday, July 4

Mercy gazed around the breakfast table. "Anyone want to go shopping? Daniel and I are accompanying Fergus to pick up supplies in Naples. It's farther than Izmir...but I want to take Daniel to a carnival and do a little sightseeing."

"No, thank you," Nanna said. "I've reached the age where carnivals are no longer appealing."

Katy's mouth turned down. "I'd love to go, but I have three patients today. Just my cotton-pickin' luck to miss out on the fun."

"I'm sorry," Mercy said. "We'll bring you back some cotton candy, if they have such things at an Italian carnival."

"Yeah, that helps a lot." Katy snorted. "I miss an opportunity to get Fergus to myself for a day, and you offer me cotton candy as a consolation prize." She grinned. "It's my own fault, so I shouldn't complain."

"Poor Katy." Mercy patted her hand. "Next time I'll give you advance notice. Don't work too hard. We'll be home rather late."

On the two-hour flight to Naples, Daniel bounced in his seat asking questions about the rides.

The changes she encountered since Thomas Wallace charged into her life boggled the mind. Until she arrived on Wallace Island, the trip to Bermuda was her first time outside the states. Since then, she was becoming a world traveler, with a private jet at her disposal. Unbelievable.

Fergus demanded she let one of the soldiers accompany them, insisting that though they'd caught Edda, didn't mean the threats to her life were no longer in play. Whoever hired Edda was still a mystery.

Mercy couldn't argue with Fergus's reasoning. The hulking presence of Hamish, a very nice man, screamed bodyguard and drew attention she preferred not to have. A bodyguard was overkill, but she couldn't risk putting Daniel in jeopardy.

She wanted Daniel to experience a small fair near the bay, with rides, games, and fireworks. But she also thought they should see a little bit of Naples, first.

Fergus left to take care of the shopping list. "Give me a call when yer ready to leave. I'll pick ye up at the carnival entrance. Do ye have cash and yer cell phone?"

With a mock salute, she said, "Yes, Dad. We'll be ready after the fireworks are over." She took Daniel's hand.

Hamish waved a taxi to the curb.

Mercy leaned into the window. "Do you speak English?"

"*Si, signora.*"

"We want to see the local sights. Can you do that?"

He gave a smiling, vigorous nod. "Si, si, signora."

While the taxi waited nearby, they visited the dock at Castel Nuovo, one of the symbols of Naples.

Daniel skipped along beside her, holding her hand, Hamish trailing behind.

Later they joined a small tour group to visit the city's palaces and churches. She couldn't help but gape at the architecture of the century-old buildings.

When the tour ended, they strolled to the *Piazza del Plebiscito*, where they ordered authentic pizza at a waterfront restaurant. The Pompeii ruins were on her bucket list but not today.

By five o'clock, they'd finished sightseeing and returned to the carnival to watch the fireworks. Confetti rained down as they passed through the crowded fairway, much of the crowd in masks. Excited children pulled their parents to the next ride or the next game.

She and Daniel strolled unhurried through the maze, enjoying the smells of popcorn mixed with exhaust from the rides.

After sunset, they found seats in the stands to watch the fireworks—brilliant splashes of colored rockets exploding to music. The bursts of light, with their beauty and excitement, kept Daniel popping up and down in his seat, clapping his hands, and pointing. When the last flash of color drifted from the sky, Daniel leaned against her, exhausted.

Mercy lost sight of Hamish in the crush of the crowd after the fireworks. She and Daniel made their way to the front entrance to wait for Fergus and give Hamish a chance to catch up. Her gaze searched the cars parked out front, but there was no sign of either man when they stepped onto the sidewalk.

Mercy reached for her cell phone, and a firm grip clamped on her arm, taking the phone from her hand. "Don't cause a scene, Traci. I wouldn't want to have to hurt the boy."

She twisted away, trying to loosen the hold on her

arm.

Ricco Rossellini's grasp tightened. His steel grip cut off the circulation in her arm. "My car's this way."

∂∞∽

Tel Aviv, Israel
Tuesday, July 4

By the time Thomas and Moshe came back to the parking lot, most of the police and agents had gone. Crime scene specialists were still there with cameras and tape measures. A few police were still questioning witnesses from the restaurant and taking down license numbers in the parking lot and nearby streets.

Heim was on the phone with the hospital.

Thomas caught his attention. "Shaul...?

The Mossad chief shook his head.

Heim and Moshe returned with Thomas to his hotel room, and he ordered coffee from room service.

Moshe paced, almost incoherent with grief and anger.

Room service arrived and they sat at a small table near the window, curtains drawn.

Guilt haunted Thomas. Except for happenstance, he would be dead, and a good agent would still be alive. He sensed no blame aimed at him from Heim and Moshe, only grief for their loss. That didn't relieve Thomas's feeling of responsibility. He poured the coffee, passed the cups around, and looked directly at Heim. "You know the shot was meant for me."

Heim nodded.

"I'm assuming the same person or persons were responsible for tipping off the terrorists about Aref.

Would you agree?"

"What does your gut tell you, Thomas? Who in your organization would do that?" Heim asked.

Thomas had a moment of clarity, a moment of pure, perfect, knowledge. Part experience, part a student of human nature. "Before I answer, what four agents did Clint Monroe bring with him to Tel Aviv?"

"Four recruits is all I know. I was introduced to them, but I don't remember their names."

"Was one of them a blond kid named Brad Reid?"

Heim nodded. "Yeah, I remember him. Cocky, smart-mouthed little snot."

Facts were what agents relied on, but Thomas also respected his instincts. They'd proven correct more times than not. He looked across the table at Moshe. "I think Clint Monroe and Brad Reid are the leaks, and they're perhaps involved up to their eyeballs in this, but I have no proof. They were staying at this hotel. Let's see if they're still registered."

After a short conversation with the concierge, Thomas turned to Heim. "They checked out tonight." He handed the phone to Heim. "Can you see if the plane is still in Tel Aviv and if so, have the authorities hold it?"

Heim brushed away the house phone and pulled out his own, punching in numbers as he disappeared into the bedroom. He returned a few minutes later. "I think you're on to something, Thomas. They left about an hour ago, giving them plenty of time to shoot Shaul and get to the airport. They're long gone from Israeli airspace, so I can't turn them back."

"We can always locate them when we need to. I was hoping to find the rifle in their procession. There are a few things we need to verify, in the meantime."

"Do we bring Paul onboard? Let him know what we suspect?" Heim asked.

"I think we have to." Thomas stood and paced across the room. "We'll check Monroe's finances. Paul can do that quickly. He has people at Langley who can find the needle in the haystack."

"And if he doesn't find anything?" Moshe asked, his face grim and lined.

"Then we look elsewhere for the leak. However, I'm confident we'll find a money trail. If Monroe is our guy, he strikes me as more muscle than brains."

Heim sat back down at the table. "There are video cameras throughout the city. My people are already checking the videos for suspicious characters in the area. We may be able to track one or both of them to the restaurant, or at least put them in the area."

Once again, Thomas picked up the house phone, this time he punched in Paul Redford's room number.

Paul Redford didn't want to believe Clint Monroe was involved in the compromised mission, but after the death of Shaul Lobel, he couldn't afford to be wrong. He and Clint went back a long way. As young recruits, they went undercover in Venezuela before and after the Granada invasion and later in the Middle East before the first Gulf War. They'd been forced to learn fast. That was the only way they'd survived.

Clint had been adamant about keeping Brad Reid.

Aware of Clint's shortcomings, Paul knew the man's ruthlessness and materialism. He wore only designer labels, drove a high-end automobile, and lived in a house above his pay scale. His wife came from Boston old money, which could explain Clint's expensive lifestyle. Now, Paul had to wonder if the wife's wealth accounted for Clint living beyond his means. And there were rumors the Monroes' marriage was on the brink of divorce.

Paul hadn't told Thomas that this wasn't the first mission compromised in the last year. It was one of the reasons he brought Thomas on board for this assignment and tried to contain who knew the details.

Clint knew Thomas was headed out on an assignment because of the training camp recertification. But Clint couldn't have known Thomas's destination, or about Aref. Monroe wasn't privy to any list of agents on foreign soil. It was the closest held secret at Langley. Men's lives depended on it remaining that way.

He decided to let Thomas and Mossad handle the investigation for the present. If the FBI became involved, everything would go on public record. He didn't want that. Once he knew what evidence they had against Monroe, he would decide to call in the FBI. Or not.

Mossad wanted a scalp to hang on the wall for Shaul Lobel's death. If it turned out to be Clint, God help him. Paul couldn't hold back Heim Rosen if he tried. And he wouldn't try. Not to protect a traitor.

Clint's fate hung on what his financial records revealed.

With a resigned breath, Paul picked up the secure phone and asked for the head computer geek at Langley.

☙❦

What was left of the morning hours for sleep Thomas spent tossing fitfully, trying to dull the guilt. He should have seen it coming, have taken steps to prevent it. But that was part of the covert world. One never knew when and where the kill shot would come.

He finally gave up on sleep and went to Mossad headquarters. The debriefing had come to a halt after the agent's death.

Thomas and Moshe hung out in Heim's office to await word from Paul.

When Thomas could no longer stand the confinement, he grabbed his jacket. "I'm going for a walk. Call me when you have news."

Pedestrians crowded the streets of Tel Aviv, reminding Thomas of New York City, minus the skyscrapers that eclipsed the sun. It also lacked the high stress, hustle-bustle of the Big Apple.

As he walked, Thomas's thoughts were of Shaul. He'd been a good agent, and seeing him last night open and carefree, revealed a side of the Israeli far from the serious-natured agent Thomas had come to know.

Now Shaul was dead. He had no wife and children, but he left behind parents and seven siblings, Shaul the youngest.

Jewish custom dictated the burial service be held as soon as possible, and the funeral was set for tomorrow morning. The service would take place at the gravesite.

A Hebrew friend once explained their burial customs. Jewish families didn't use traditional funeral homes. They had something called *chevra kadisha,* a burial society that prepared the body according to Jewish customs.

Caskets had no embellishments, just a sheet used to cover the body after it had been prepared. Soil from Israel was sprinkled on the body and the casket closed. It would remain closed during the funeral service.

After burial, the family set aside a week for sitting *shiva*, their period of mourning.

But it would take more time than that for Thomas to forget Shaul Lobel's sacrifice. His phone buzzed and he read the text message.

Return to office. p r has info u wanted. It is as u suspected.

Videos placed Brad Reid in the area of Shaul's shooting before and after. And Monroe's financial information revealed large cash deposits that ran a tortuous route back to several known terrorist bank accounts.

24

Naples, Italy
Tuesday, July 4

Mercy and Daniel sat in the backseat of the Rolls-Royce between Ricco and a tall henchman who looked more like an executive than a kidnapper.

She put a protective arm around Daniel and pulled him close.

He hadn't yet realized the danger they faced.

Clouds formed overhead and rain splattered the vehicle's tinted window, blurring the trees and vendors along the narrow roadway.

Fear settled over Mercy like a cold blanket of snow, freezing her reflexes and numbing her mind. Not for herself. For Daniel. Even when Thomas had taken her from Bermuda, it hadn't taken long to realize he intended no physical harm.

Not so with Ricco Rossellini. Hidden behind a handsome face and charming smile, his eyes held the same black, merciless depths as a shark.

Mercy would willingly turn over anything to protect her son...her son. Funny, she had begun to think of Daniel that way. His very life depended on her now. Most frightening of all, she felt certain that whether she could give Ricco the information, or not, he would kill them both.

"Mummy, where's Fergus?"

"He's probably still shopping. We'll catch him later."

Daniel accepted her explanation without question.

The car moved easily through the streets of Naples, which was crowded with cars and people. Yet she couldn't scream or call attention to her plight because of Daniel. "What did you do to Hamish?"

Rossellini looked puzzled.

"The bodyguard."

"He's well enough. Probably just waking up with a bad headache."

"What do you want, Ricco?"

"You know what I want. I want the photographs you took."

"What If I told you I don't have any photos and don't know where they are?"

"I wouldn't believe you, of course."

"Where are you taking us?"

Ricco placed his finger under her chin and turned her face to him. "We're going on a long, lovely cruise, *cara mia*. You do remember our cruises, don't you?"

She jerked her head away. "Take the boy back. I'll go with you wherever you want."

He leaned close and whispered in her ear, his breath hot on her neck. "You'll go with me whether I take the boy back or not."

"You don't need him, Ricco. Let him go."

"Ah, but I do need him for leverage. To keep you in line, *cara mia*. You've proven to be most untrustworthy."

The sleek car pulled to the dock, and the driver got out with an umbrella, holding it while Ricco pulled her from the backseat.

She reached for Daniel.

Ricco pushed her hand away. "Lorenz, bring the boy to the launch."

Daniel's tiny brow scrunched into a frown.

She smiled and nodded to him. "It's OK."

His expression cleared, and he flashed a weak smile.

The thug beside him pulled an umbrella from a rack and lifted the child into his arms.

A covered launch waited at the end of the pier.

Still holding her arm, Ricco shoved her onboard.

Lorenz sat Daniel beside her.

Wind whipped drops of rain under the covering as they pulled away from the dock, dampening their clothes with a fine mist.

Mercy pulled Daniel close, trying to shield him from the worst of the spray. Chills surged through her body, not entirely caused by the weather. She noted the yacht's name as they stepped onboard the *Fleeting Fortune*.

She and Daniel followed Ricco below deck. He opened a compartment door and stood beside it.

"Make yourselves comfortable. You'll find a few clothing items you left behind in the closet. I have nothing to fit the boy. Have him remove his things and we can dry them in the ship's laundry. I'll have hot drinks sent down for you."

She gritted her teeth.

The perfect host.

The cabin was a two-room suite, a bedroom and sitting room, plus a nice size bath with a dressing table, rather than the usual tiny shower and toilet. The sofa and chairs were cream-colored with bright yellow pillows. Seascape paintings formed a collage over the sofa. A large vase of yellow roses sat on a nearby table, and a flat-screen TV was mounted on the wall opposite the couch.

In the second room, a yellow floral comforter with white lace pillows and bed skirt covered the queen-sized bed. An overstuffed chair and reading lamp stood in the corner. All furniture was bolted to the floor. Under different circumstances, the cabin would have been cheery.

Mercy sent Daniel in to get out of his wet clothes and turned on a hot shower. While he bathed, she slipped into jeans and a sweatshirt that presumably belonged to Traci Wallace. When Daniel came out wrapped in a large white towel, she gathered his damp clothes and placed them outside the door.

A knock sounded, and a white-uniformed steward entered, his jacket brilliant against his dark skin. His dark eyes seemed to absorb light rather than reflect it. He bore a tray with tea, hot cocoa, and sandwiches.

She handed Daniel the hot drink and fluffed pillows around him in front of the television. The cartoons were in Italian, but he didn't seem to mind. A thought suddenly occurred to her.

"Daniel, do you speak Italian?"

He nodded.

"Any other languages?"

He nodded again. "Yes, ma'am. French." He must have his father's gift for languages. So far, he hadn't asked questions about why they were here and who these men were, but he was intelligent and would soon notice her anxiety.

Mercy pulled the chair over and looked out the porthole. The ship lay anchored about a half mile from the dock. The buildings and lights were visible along the shore.

No way to tell how long they would remain in port, but if they headed out to sea, she would have no hope of summoning help to get Daniel to safety.

෧෨෧

Tel Aviv, Israel
Wednesday, July 5

The day wasn't a good one for a funeral, if there was such a thing. Gray clouds opened up with a pounding rain, and the throng that gathered around the gravesite opened umbrellas.

The casket was unloaded, moved silently past the solemn crowd, and laid onto the straps that would lower it into the ground.

Somber, tear-stained faces barely visible under the vinyl rain protectors, waited for the service to begin. Mossad agents turned out in force, as well as Paul Redford and a few of his CIA cronies.

Next to Thomas, Moshe shared his umbrella, his face strained. He glanced over at Shaul's family, and up at the sky, and then spoke so softly Thomas almost missed it. "God's tears for a fallen warrior. He has a special affection for soldiers."

The somber service was in Hebrew, which Thomas couldn't understand, but he got the gist. The mother's wails of grief deepened the chasm of guilt he felt. He'd witnessed death many times, but not since his mother died had he experienced anything this close, this personal.

He replayed that night, standing there in the rain. What could he have done to keep Shaul alive? Should he have realized the battle didn't end in the desert?

That someone was still out there who wanted him dead? Taken precautions? He had thought the attack in Riyadh was about the mission. But it had also been personal.

He could never repay the debt to Shaul's family. Finding his killer would be a start, but it would in no way clear his conscience.

The service ended and Shaul's parents passed through the mourners. His mother stopped in front of Moshe. Her gaze searched his face, and then her composure crumpled. She grabbed his lapels and fell onto his chest, sobbing.

His arms went around her. Holding her close, he whispered soft words in Hebrew. They stood there for a long while before her husband pulled her away and back into the procession.

Thomas, Moshe, and Heim fell into step behind the family. Faces taut with emotion, they made their way to the car that would take them to Ben Gurion Airport.

A ribbon of headlights, blurred by the rain on the vehicle's narrow windshield, illuminated the road in the semi-darkness—the street glossy with a film of water and oil from engine exhausts.

An oncoming stream of tourists and natives departed the busy airport, headed into the city. Rain continued as they drove onto the tarmac at Ben Gurion.

The shroud of overcast sky reflected Thomas's mood. He tried to ignore the depression the funeral brought on, forcing himself to concentrate on the task ahead. Settling the score with Clint Monroe.

Heim parked the big vehicle at an angle to the aircraft.

Thomas opened his door and made a dash for the

stairs. Warm rain pelted his face and rolled down the neck of his shirt before he made it to safety inside the Mossad jet, promising to buy an umbrella when they reached London.

Thomas found a seat near the front, and Heim claimed the one next to him.

Glancing at the gloomy exterior through the porthole, Thomas spoke the words he'd held in since the shooting. "I'm sorry about Shaul."

"Nothing you could have done. Nothing any of us could have done," Heim said.

"I keep telling myself that, but it doesn't help."

"Blaming yourself gets you nowhere. It's a road without an end." Heim stretched. "What are our plans once we reach North Carolina?"

"Search the cabin and Monroe's quarters. Hope we find how he's getting information. Find out who his contacts are."

"Will we have to deal with the trainers and trainees at the camp?"

Thomas shook his head. "There's a four-week hiatus between training camps. That gives the instructors a breather before jumping back into the game. There may be a small maintenance staff. A few of the DIs stay at the compound for a while after a session. Paul says only a handful, and they'll be gone when we arrive. He called them to Langley for a meeting. He's retaining Monroe and Reid in DC to give us time to check out the camp."

Heim reclined his seat and closed his eyes. "The ball is in your court, my friend. Moshe and I are in your hands."

Thomas pulled out his laptop. He'd replaced his computer and basic wardrobe in Tel Aviv. Everything he'd taken to Saudi Arabia he'd dropped at King Khalid Airport.

He went over his strategy for getting onto the training compound until he'd embedded it into his memory. If the camp was empty, no problem. But if and when the action started, he didn't want to have to think about what came next. He'd share the plans with Heim and Moshe, later.

Paul Redford's researchers found the information Thomas expected on Monroe's finances, but Paul failed to turn up any connection to Reid and the money. Langley was still trying to make the link. Video from the Tel Aviv street surveillance cameras had put Reid outside the restaurant, but not Monroe. Proof enough for Thomas.

His boss had not been happy about what he discovered on Monroe, but he had allowed Mossad to accompany him. After Shaul's death, Mossad wouldn't back off. Unofficially, they would have pursued the assassin, just as they'd done with Nazi criminals and the Olympic terrorists.

Two hours into the flight, Heim opened his eyes, as alert as if he'd slept eight hours. "Everything all set?"

Thomas nodded. "Yes." He relaxed against the seat.

25

Naples, Italy
Wednesday, July 5

Ricco Rossellini stepped into his cabin and hurled the glass of wine against the wall, watching the liquid slide downward, and then puddle on the floor. Mad at himself. Mad at Traci.

Why did he still feel such infatuation for this woman? She'd betrayed him, planned to turn him over to the *Gruppo di Intervento Speciale*, and had rejected him in the most humiliating way possible. Yet he still longed to have her back where she belonged. With him.

It wasn't in his nature to put someone else before his own selfish needs. He'd acknowledged his narcissistic mindset to himself long ago. Consequently, he'd always considered himself incapable of loving any woman. But after Lorenz assured him Traci was dead, he'd missed her more than he thought possible. No woman ever affected him like Traci Wallace. Now she was back, and he didn't want to let her go. However, he had a dilemma. She could bring everything he'd worked for down on his head.

His mother, a religious fanatic, his father a fool, had unknowingly provided connections he'd used to amass a fortune. He'd started selling arms to various regimes in Africa, and then through his mother's family connections, to terrorist groups in the Middle East.

If he released Traci, she would likely turn him in to the police now that he had involved the boy. That had been a mistake. She would always be afraid he would harm Daniel. Not that she'd ever shown any motherly tendencies. But that seemed to have changed.

Not the best way to re-establish a long-term relationship.

He didn't understand what had changed her. Or why. He might even have considered giving up his business for her, if she had asked.

He didn't want her to die. But he could never fully trust her. The threat of harm to the boy would keep her in line. But he didn't want her to stay under coercion.

Rationalizing the problem was getting him nowhere. First, she must turn over the pictures. Then they could talk about what happened next.

He strode to the door and jerked it open. The man in the hallway snapped to attention. "Bring Traci to me. I'll wait in the salon."

❧◦❧

Mercy paced the cabin, and stopped at the porthole. About eighteen inches in diameter, too small for her to fit through. She slammed her hand into the ship's hull in frustration. How could she give Ricco pictures she didn't have? He would never believe she couldn't produce them on demand.

Paralyzed by her situation, her mind stopped functioning. Every horrible scenario played out in her thoughts, ending with Daniel's death. She could accept her own demise, but never Daniel's. As she paced, she sent fervent prayers upward asking for wisdom and guidance. Somehow, she had to get Daniel off the ship.

After a while, a moment of clarity came to her—an idea that would buy her some time. When Ricco would return from his fool's errand, she would be in deep trouble. He would be raging mad. But by God's grace, she could ensure Daniel made it to safety.

Keeping her face composed, she put Daniel to bed.

"Mummy, why can't we go home? I don't like it here."

"I know. But we need to stay here a little while longer. It won't be long." She kept her voice soft and controlled. "I'd like to take you home, but I have to wait to talk to our host. Try to sleep, Danny. Tomorrow we'll know something."

Reassured, Daniel's eyes closed and within minutes, his breathing was deep and even—the innocent slumber of a child. She sat by his bedside watching the gentle curve of his cheeks, a softer version of his father's rugged features.

Where was Thomas? Had he arrived at the island? Did he know they were missing?

Fergus would notify him immediately, and Thomas would search until he found his son. Would he arrive in time to save Daniel from harm?

Could she take that chance? She returned to the sitting area and stared through the porthole once more, glad to see ships lay anchored within a quarter mile of the *Fleeting Fortune*.

Without a knock, the stateroom door opened. The tall bodyguard with the cold blue eyes motioned her forward. "Ricco wants to see you."

He took her arm and moved her in front of him. He pointed her towards the door. His touch made her shiver. And if that wasn't enough, she still had to face Ricco. Casting a concerned glance back at the bedroom door, she stepped into the passageway.

The man led her down the corridor, up the stairwell, and then across the deck to the salon, with an impressive view of the bay through the misting rain. The ships in the harbor sparkled like Christmas lights bobbing in the restless sea.

Ricco stood behind a stainless steel and glass bar, a silver shaker in his hand. He removed the lid, poured martinis into two glasses, and handed one to her. "Ah, *cara mia*. I made this just the way you like it." His eyes took in her apparel. "You look lovely. You make jeans and a T-shirt look smart. I guess that's one of the tricks of the fashion trade."

She took the drink, not wanting to upset him. Not yet.

He came from behind the bar and placed his hand on her back. He drained his glass, took hers from her hand, and placed it on the mirrored counter. With one hand behind her neck, the other at her waist, he pulled her to him, and placed a lingering kiss on her mouth.

She didn't push away. Didn't respond.

Still holding her close, Ricco grimaced and looked down into her eyes. "A kiss usually involves two people."

She said nothing.

He pushed her away.

"Let Daniel go, and I'll tell you where the photos are."

He wagged his finger at her. "No, *cara mia*. You tell me where the photos are and when I have them in my hand, I will let the boy go. Where are they? We checked your cell phone. They're not there."

"I uploaded the pictures onto the computer in the London apartment. You know where the apartment is."

He nodded. "Do you have the key?"

She shook her head. "Not with me."

"Never mind. What's your password?"

"John 3:16." That was her sign-on for the computer in her Houston apartment.

His gaze turned dark and menacing. "I warn you, Traci. Don't play games with me. If you send me on a wild goose chase, when I return, I'll start breaking your son's bones until you beg to tell me."

⤜✦⤛

Fergus pulled up in front of the carnival entrance and scanned the crowd for Traci, Daniel, and Hamish. "Women," he muttered. "She's forgotten the time." He retrieved his cell phone and called her number. No answer. Then he called Hamish.

No answer there, either. Something was wrong. Hamish wouldn't turn off his phone. Not while he was acting as bodyguard.

The carnival grounds were closing down for the night, but a few booths remained open, mostly souvenir shops and a few games still looking for suckers.

He searched behind the closed rides, and found nothing. He headed towards the fireworks stands. He almost missed Hamish.

Nearly invisible in his dark clothing. Hamish lay unconscious in the shadows, sprawled on his face under the stands.

Fergus lengthened his stride and hurried to the

prone figure. He dropped to his knees and found the carotid artery. A strong thump beat beneath his fingers, but blood flowed, sticky and warm. It was too dark to examine him properly, but he found the source of the bleeding, a deep gash at the top of the man's skull. He shook the unconscious man to revive him. "Hamish, where are Traci and Daniel? Answer me, man."

Hamish only groaned.

Ten minutes later, he'd deposited Hamish in an ambulance and hurried to the ticket booth, praying he could catch the cashier. He caught her just as she locked the booth.

Barely five feet tall, the tiny woman was in her early sixties, gray hair cut short, and wearing a navy dress that could only be described as matronly.

Please, God. Let her speak English.

"Ma'am, did ye see a blonde woman in a yellow dress with a small boy about six years old...after the fireworks show?"

She held both hands out, shrugged, and spoke with a heavy French accent. "Monsieur, there are so many people..." She hesitated. "Mam'selle, she is very pretty, blonde, no?"

"Yes, with a small boy."

"Oui, I think maybe I see them. She and the boy, they get into a car, very fancy automobile. I think is called Royce, *en noir et blanc.*"

"A black and white Rolls Royce?"

"Oui, Oui. That is it."

"What time, do you remember?"

She gave another shrug. "Not sure of time. After fireworks."

"Can you describe the men in the car?"

She smiled and nodded. "Two men, very *elégant*, very handsome. One very tall."

He pressed the woman for more details and came away with a certainty. Traci left with Rossellini and a very tall man, leaving Fergus with a dilemma. Had Traci planned to meet Rossellini here, or was she taken by force? Her past actions led him to believe it was the former, but he couldn't ignore the recent attempts on her life.

"Merci, Madame, merci." He left the carnival and went straight to the hospital.

Hamish was awake.

A nurse led Fergus back to the examination cubicle.

Police had questioned him and accepted the robbery story Hamish told them.

Fergus wasted no time with civilities. "What happened, man?"

Hamish lowered his head. "I guess I'm losing my edge, Fergus. I let the guy get behind me and knock me cold, and I didn't even get a glimpse of him. Let him take the woman and child I was supposed to be guarding."

"That kind of talk will no help ye now. Take a cab back to the hotel and get some rest. I'm going to start searching." On his way out of the hospital, Fergus called Frank. He could search Naples alone until help arrived. "Get back to the island as fast as ye can and pick up the other three men. Traci and Daniel are missing." Protecting the boy was Fergus's primary responsibility. And he had blown it.

Involving the local police was an option, but one he wanted to postpone as long as possible. Police would mean the press, and if she and Daniel were abducted, it might force the kidnappers to harm the lad.

If Traci deliberately ran off with that Italian scoundrel, it would mean more ugly publicity.

Fergus searched the docks and side streets while he waited for reinforcements.

Frank and the men arrived in Naples a little after two o'clock in the morning. They spread out and continued the hunt.

Finding no sign of Mercy and Daniel, nor of the Rolls, they returned to the hotel at five for a couple of hours sleep before sunrise. The car could have already left the city.

If he hadn't heard from the kidnappers by noon, he would have to contact the Italian authorities. He inhaled a deep breath, picked up the SAT-phone, and made the call he dreaded.

There was no answer.

26

London, England
Wednesday, July 5

Thomas placed a call to Chip Nelson while they were still in the air. The kit with all his supplies was with the freight headed back to Edinburgh. He had to pick up a replacement at Chip's shop in the back alley of London's warehouse district. At precisely noon, he arrived at the CIA supply depot.

Chip answered the bell seconds later. "Wasn't expecting to see you so soon. You on another assignment?"

"Nope, same one. I need to replace the kit you brought, but this time I need the gun."

"What?" Chip looked at him, askance. "The reports I'll have to fill out." He groaned.

"Chip, you're such a cry baby."

"Yeah, well walk a mile in my moccasins, Wallace. You know how the government loves paperwork. It's job security for a couple'a thousand bureaucrats in dark rooms in D.C."

Thomas rubbed his hands over the stubble on his face and grimaced. "How can I make it up to you, Chip?"

The supply agent faced him, a bright smile on his face. "How about a week on your private island?"

Thomas shook his head. "Can't do that. It's my

home, not a hotel. But when the mission is over, I'll bring back both kits and buy dinner for two at the restaurant of your choice."

"Anyplace?"

"Anyplace," Thomas said.

"Wallace, I love you." He made as if to hug Thomas.

Thomas backed away.

Chip raised his hands and grinned. "It's gonna cost you, buddy."

"I know, Chip."

∂∽∾

CIA Training Camp, North Carolina
Thursday, July 6

The plane landed in a cavern of darkness relieved only by the runway lights as they flashed down the tarmac. The small jet eased to a stop and the unfasten seatbelt signal flashed red.

Thomas and his companions, dressed in black, descended from the aircraft and stood at the bottom of the stairs, the crickets' crescendo almost deafening.

Heim shrugged into his backpack and stepped onto the runway. "Lead on, goy. This is your bailiwick. Moshe and I will be right behind you."

"Sure you're up to this, Heim? You haven't been a foot soldier for a long time."

"Don't worry about me, Wallace. I can do this in my sleep."

Moshe slapped him on the shoulder and chuckled. "Stay awake, OK? I may need you to cover my back."

Eyes adjusting to the darkness, Thomas searched

the shadows. It took only a few seconds to spot the camouflaged vehicle Paul had left for them.

Thomas started the engine, and it roared to life.

Maximum humidity hung in the air, and Thomas's T-shirt stuck to his back. He didn't complain. It was better than the dry heat in the Saudi desert that made him feel like a wrung-out sponge.

The training camp lay twenty miles north of the airstrip, and they made good time on the deserted gravel road. Lightning streaked across the eastern sky, barely visible through the thick forest. They were headed east.

He didn't mind getting wet, but the NV goggles didn't come with wipers.

Headlights on the vehicle spotlighted a wall of insects in their path, leaving a splatter of bug guts on the windshield. Rain would just smear it.

Heim looked up. "I hate rain."

Thomas laughed. "Afraid you'll melt, tough guy?"

Heim harrumphed. "Ten of us could take out a full platoon of regular army."

Thomas shrugged. "Maybe, but I wouldn't try it with Rangers."

Heim pulled his cap down. "Maybe."

Thomas parked a mile from their destination, and they moved away from the road into the woods. Low hills and shallow valleys lay between them and the compound.

As the group pushed through the forest, heavy raindrops began a slow pounding on Thomas's cap, rapidly increasing to a full-scale deluge. Cloud cover, rain, and the canopy of trees made the darkness absolute. He'd run every foot of the familiar terrain during training, and the night vision goggles lighted the way.

Paul Redford had given Thomas the gate entry code, and they moved easily into the compound. He scanned the darkness for the Dobermans. They would be on high alert the minute the gate swung open.

Chip had included a spray deterrent he assured would stop the dogs in mid-stride without permanent damage. However, the downpour would render it useless unless he got close enough to blow it down the dog's nostrils. He could lose an arm before that happened.

The dogs were his first indication something wasn't right. They didn't show.

He held his hand up, and the two Mossad agents stopped behind him. Motioning them to spread out, he withdrew the P229 gun from his shoulder holster.

Night vision goggles in place, they moved silently into the trees along the drive.

Filling his lungs with a deep breath of moist air, Thomas waved the two agents to move forward.

Four instructors lived on base at the compound, but Paul assured him they were away for a week in D.C.

And Thomas didn't believe the entire training camp was infested with traitors.

They knew he was coming. An unexpected complication.

He and his two friends might be outmanned, but not out-classed.

The first bullet sailed past his right ear. Gunfire exploded around him. No need to worry about Heim and Moshe. They were soldiers and knew to take protective cover.

He returned wild shots to provide cover until he

could put the nearest tree between himself and the firefight. Green shadows took human form in the trees around him, closing in. He took aim at the closest man, sending two quick taps into his chest.

A cry sounded, and then silence.

Thomas crouched and moved to a new position. Bullets plunked into his tree cover, sending wood chips flying.

A muzzle flashed on his left flank, and another target went down. Moshe's handiwork.

The darkness would have been impenetrable without the glasses. Two down and no way to calculate how many were still out there.

Keeping as low as possible, Thomas moved towards the cabin in the center of the compound. Another green figure moved into his field of fire. Two more taps.

With the barrage of gunfire that followed, he couldn't tell if he hit the target. The noise was deafening. Seconds later, the man stumbled and fell.

Two men splashed across the clearing and dashed into the cabin. His clip half-full, Thomas followed, moving from tree to tree until he stood about twenty feet from the cabin's main entrance. Within minutes, gunfire behind him ceased, and he felt, rather than saw, Heim and Moshe move up behind him.

"You guys OK? All the targets down?" he asked.

"Yes and yes," Heim shot back. "What's up?"

Thomas whispered. "Two men ran into the cabin. There may be others inside. They're probably getting set for a standoff. They'll have a ton of ammunition at their disposal. Not to mention great advantage to shoot from the high ground. You guys don't happen to have a couple of flash bang grenades, do you?"

"Nope, didn't think I'd need them," Moshe said.

"Yeah, simple operation, right? OK, we go to Plan B. Cover me, I have an idea."

He'd remembered a roof skylight from when the instructors sent the recruits to the shack to store supplies in the attic. Holding up one finger, he dropped his backpack and removed the climbing equipment.

"Cover the front and back doors. When you hear the first shot, come running. I may need you to save my life again."

Minutes later, nylon rope and crowbar in hand, Thomas secured the cord to the chimney. The wet nylon slipped in his hands, but he scaled the building to the roof's edge without incident. He swung one leg over the lip and pulled his body over.

For a moment, he considered removing his boots for stealth. The tile was slippery under the leather soles. If the goons heard any noise, they might just send a hail of bullets through the ceiling leaving him no place to hide. He decided to keep his boots on.

The skylight came into view. He knelt beside it, and pried the seal around the glass loose. Water ran into the cracks, around the casement, and then dripped onto the cardboard boxes in the room below.

He scanned the rooftop and moved with efficiency, using a small crowbar to finish loosening the window seal without a sound. In short order, the glass lifted out, and he set it on the wet asbestos tiles, along with the tools.

Mercy's face flashed into his mind. Visions of London and Paris swirled in his thoughts like clips from a well-loved movie. He shook his head to clear the vision. No time for distractions.

The room below the skylight was in total darkness. Water dripped so loudly through the portal he feared the men below would hear.

He wiped raindrops from the goggles and pulled them back in place. Flat on his stomach, Thomas listened for sounds that someone had detected his entry. Nothing but silence below. His gaze roamed the attic floor. Wooden crates were stacked within feet of the ceiling, the area almost full, with only narrow aisles for access.

After snapping a full clip in the Sig, he returned it to the shoulder holster under his arm and put an extra clip in his pocket. He brought the nylon cord over to the opening, let out the play, eased onto the closest crate, and then to the floor below. After plumbing his memory for the layout of the first floor, he waited until satisfied that he'd embedded the floor plan into his mind.

The attic stairwell bypassed the living quarters on the second floor, descending straight to the ground level. He pulled the Sig from the holster and moved down the steps. The staircase narrowed, eerily quiet as he moved downward and halted at the closed door at the bottom. The knob released without a click.

The great room he remembered lay on the other side of the door. To the right were two large plate glass windows. To the left, a bar and sofas grouped around the fireplace.

One man, his back to Thomas, guarded the front, the second man probably stationed at the back.

He shoved the door open, sending it bouncing against the wall.

Brad Reid whirled towards the noise and hesitated.

Thomas fired a shot in the air and shouted, "Freeze Reid, or I'll drop you where you stand. I don't want to kill you, but I will. Drop it now."

Taking Reid out wouldn't be hard. Visions of the evening Shaul died crystallized his purpose for being here. Reid not only assassinated Shaul Lobel, he was possibly directly involved in the deaths of Aref's comrades in Iran. Those men would have died a slow painful death. Their only crime, love of country. No sleep would be lost over the death of Brad Reid.

Reid didn't stop.

Instead, he raised the Glock.

Thomas fired, sending the 9mm slug slamming into Reid's shoulder.

Reid stubbornly held onto the weapon.

Thomas held his revolver steady, aimed at the assassin's heart, almost wishing he would make a move. Even the score for Shaul.

From behind him in the stairway, Monroe said, "You drop it, Wallace."

27

CIA Training Camp, North Carolina
Thursday, July 6

Hiding in the living quarters on the second floor, Monroe had come up behind him.

The mantel clock's tick sounded despite the roar of the storm and occasional thunder. No one spoke for a couple of seconds.

Thomas lowered the gun but didn't drop it.

Monroe motioned him away from the doorway. "You think I'm kidding, Wallace? Drop the weapon."

"Take him, Clint," Reid spewed a volley of profanity. "Blow out both knees. He ruined my shoulder."

"Not here. Not now. When the rain stops we'll march him into the woods and you can take your revenge." He turned his attention back to Thomas. "Where are your friends?"

"I'm all that's left. How did you know we were coming?"

"I'm not stupid. Redford was nervous. I knew something was up and came back to clean out my files, just in case."

"And those dead guys on the lawn. Who are they? Not agency trainers."

Monroe shook his head. "Mercenaries I brought in. I expected more efficiency from them." His face twisted into an ugly grin. "Perhaps I should have run them through the training program here."

Lightning brightened the sky and Moshe's silhouette passed the large plate glass window behind Reid.

Both men, focused on Thomas, missed it.

Monroe growled. "I'm not going to tell you again to drop the gun, Wallace."

Monroe didn't want to kill him here or he would already be dead.

Thomas could take one of them, but not both. He had to trust Moshe to get the second one. Reid would be the easiest target. His wounded shoulder would throw his aim off. That was a maybe, not a certainty.

Dropping to the floor, Thomas squeezed the trigger twice rolling back against the wall as he fired.

The force of the bullet spun Reid around, his legs twisted, before he did a face plant into the tiled floor.

Moshe blasted the shotgun through the window, knocking Monroe off his feet. Glass shards erupted inward, covering Thomas and Reid.

Monroe tried to raise his weapon but not before the Israeli emptied the other barrel into his chest.

At the same time, shots echoed from the back, a grunt, followed by the sound of a body hitting the floor.

Heim entered, his firearm lowered to his side. He nodded at the back door. "Another bad guy. You OK, Wallace?"

Thomas rose, brushing glass from his hair. "Yeah."

"Good," Heim said. "I'll clear the building."

Moshe glanced down at Reid's body. "Too bad you had to kill him, Wallace. I was hoping for a little alone time with him."

Thomas shook his head. "It's better this way. It won't keep you awake nights."

Moshe kicked Reid's gun away. "It wouldn't have bothered my sleep." He didn't smile.

"Where'd you get the shotgun?" Thomas asked. He placed his Sig back into the shoulder holster.

"Dead guy out front gave it to me."

Thomas laughed. "Nice of him." The cell phone in Thomas's pocket vibrated. He retrieved it and scanned the screen. Paul Redford.

Abort. Monroe back at base. Confirm.

Great timing, Paul.

Thomas pulled up the agency chief's number and pressed call, quickly explaining what just went down.

Paul yelled through the phone. "I told you to abort."

"You sent the message a minute ago, Paul. The fight's been over for five. Bad timing. You should have kept Monroe in DC and we wouldn't be having this discussion."

"He disobeyed orders, left without telling me. I think he knew something was up."

Thomas kept silent—let Paul work it out.

"What a mess. You know who Reid's father is, right? And Congress doesn't like us, anyway."

"I don't think the Congressman will be interested in pursuing an investigation. Reid had a sniper rifle with him. Same model as the one that killed Shaul. I'll bet the family jewels it's the murder weapon. He won't want that to go public. Might hurt his chances for re-election."

"You don't have proof of that."

"We have the videos from Tel Aviv showing Reid in the area and now we have the gun. That's good enough for me. Have your cleanup team comb this place until they find what you need."

Paul waited in silence on the other end of the line. Finally, he heaved a resigned breath into the phone. "OK, hang round until I get a team in there. Tell Heim and Moshe to go back to the plane. I'll clean up the mess."

Thomas called the two Israeli agents over and filled them in on his conversation with the CIA chief.

"OK. We're on our way," Heim said. "We'll wait for you at the landing strip. We'd get a cold reception from the Mr. Clean Team. Two foreign operatives at the scene of a bloodbath wouldn't go over well. Especially with two dead CIA agents in the mix."

While waiting for Redford's team, Thomas searched the cabin. It didn't take long to prove Paul's position was covered.

Monroe had bugs everywhere in the great room, attached to the latest in recording equipment. That's how he'd learned about Aref's undercover presence in Iran. Monroe had recorded Thomas's conversation with Paul that last day at the training camp.

The clean-up team arrived by chopper within two hours and landed on the helipad behind the cabin. They spread out like ants on a sugar cube. The agency's technical whiz-kid, Chase Stabler, headed for the desktop and switched on the computer. Thomas had worked with him in the old days. "Hey, Thomas. Haven't seen you in a while."

Thomas smiled. "If I'm lucky, you won't see me again, ever. Just came back on special assignment."

"You responsible for all the bodies?"

"I had help."

"You must be slowing down. You use to do this

kind of thing all by yourself."

Stabler was inside the computer in seconds.

Thomas looked over his shoulder. "Find anything?"

"In here?" Stabler asked, and then shook his head. "Not yet. But he's dirty. I hacked his and Reid's financial records when Paul called earlier. This baby should seal his coffin."

"It's already sealed. One of the body bags out there belongs to Monroe."

Monroe's records would have enough damaging evidence to hang him and Reid, had they survived.

If he knew Paul Redford, when he finished with the crime scene he'd classify the two men as heroes who died defending the compound from terrorists.

The Langley team would report whatever Paul Redford told them.

Thomas didn't care. They'd dealt with the two men responsible for Shaul Lobel's death, saving taxpayers the cost of a trial and incarceration. Justice served.

Thomas found the agent in charge. "I'm leaving. You've got the con."

He took Monroe's car, parked in the back of the cabin, and headed to the airfield. With luck, the weather would allow them to takeoff. On the way, he called Fergus. "Meet me in London tomorrow morning. I'm coming home."

"I've been trying to reach ye," Fergus said. "Traci and Daniel are missing."

"When?"

"Fourteen hours ago, in Naples."

"Have you notified the authorities?"

"I was about to when you called. I waited to see if

ransom was involved."

Thomas swallowed the lump that almost choked him. His greatest nightmare had just come true. "Call them. I'm on my way."

28

Naples, Italy
Thursday, July 6

Mercy gazed through the porthole as the launch pulled away from the yacht, the sea like liquid gold reflecting the morning sunlight. A temporary respite from the rain. Nearby ships bobbed gently in the bay's calm waters.

Ricco and his thugs reached the wharf, disembarked, and headed for the airport. She glanced at her watch. 9:30 AM. The countdown had begun.

Twelve hours max to get Daniel to safety.

Thank God, he had healed from the surgery. However, that didn't ease her apprehension. Only six years old—too young for such a dangerous task. But the alternative was too horrible to comprehend. Having him fall into an enraged Ricco's hands would be unthinkable.

In the light of day, her plan seemed more ominous than it had last night. It put Daniel into a different kind of danger, alone in the ocean. Once he was in the water, she couldn't help him. God had provided a calm sea. She could never have sent him out in a storm.

Daniel was an excellent swimmer, better than most grown men, better than she was, but still...she paced and prayed, unable to handle the terror alone.

She glanced again at her watch. The minutes

slipped away too quickly. Time to commit to a course of action or abandon the plan altogether. But there really was no choice. It was the only way to get Daniel off the ship.

Inhaling a shuddering breath, she called Daniel away from the television. Hands around his waist, she lifted him to the bed so he could see through the porthole. "I need you to be very brave, Daniel. Do you see the white ship with the candy-striped deck chairs, the one closest to us? Do you think you could swim that far and climb aboard?"

"Y-Yes, Mummy. But I want to stay with you."

She swallowed, took a deep breath, and let it out slowly. "Danny, this is important. There are some very bad men on this ship, who plan to hurt you. I need you to swim to safety. Contact the police. They'll help you find your father. Can you do that?"

His eyes widened. "Yes. I'm a good swimmer." He was so little, and so brave.

Her throat constricted. "I know you are."

If anything happened to him, how could she live with...? Best not to think about that now.

She decided to wait until after the noon meal. It would waste three precious hours, but she'd notice yesterday that the guards started drinking after lunch. They wouldn't be as alert. She didn't want to run the risk of them spotting him in the water.

When she and Daniel finished eating, she asked the porter for a plastic baggie to keep the half sandwich Daniel didn't finish. The porter gave her a quizzical look but brought one later and picked up the tray.

As soon as he was gone, she found pen and paper in the lamp table drawer and quickly wrote a note.

HELP! URGENT!
My name is Traci Wallace and this is my son, Daniel. We were abducted by a man named Ricco Rossellini and taken aboard a yacht, The Fleeting Fortune. *Send help. Contact Thomas Wallace.*

She listed Fergus's cell phone and the satellite phone numbers at the bottom. Fingers trembling, she sealed the note inside the plastic bag. Using Traci's name made sense. She was a celebrity and that would lend an added sense of urgency to the message. No one would be rushing to rescue Mercy Lawrence.

At the bottom of the closet, she found three life preservers. Two large, one small. She pulled out the smallest and slipped it over Daniel's head, securing the buckles on the chest, making sure they wouldn't come open. She placed the note in the life preserver's waterproof pocket. She zipped it closed.

"Mummy, I don't need this." He fingered the life preserver.

"I know it will slow you down. But I think you need to wear it. Just in case."

He nodded, resigned, but not happy.

With shaky hands, she removed the top bed sheet and carried it to the porthole. She tied one end under his arms, and showed him how to untie it, giving him time to practice twice. "Swim to the boat. If there is no ladder, yell for help until someone pulls you on board. Give the note to an adult. Keep asking for the police until they come, or the people take you to the police station."

He smiled and patted her cheek. "I'll come back for you."

Taking his hands in hers, she shook her head. "No,

Danny. Only if you bring your father, or the police, with you. You are *not* to come back here alone. Do you understand me?"

His gaze searched her face, and he gave a solemn nod.

She pulled him close for a final hug. "I'm very proud of you, Daniel. Always remember that I love you very, very much."

He climbed onto the bed.

She helped him through the porthole and then lowered him into the water.

Tears she'd held back flowed as his tiny fingers untied the sheet, and he swam away.

Vision blurred, she watched the small orange blob make its way across the water.

Time crawled until finally, activity on the target vessel indicated they saw the boy in the water, and they pulled him onboard.

Mercy tasted blood. Without noticing, she'd bitten into the fist she'd held clenched against her mouth. One thought calmed her.

Daniel was safe.

Now all she had to worry about was dealing with Ricco when he arrived from London, empty-handed.

By God's grace, perhaps the police would arrive before Ricco.

છ૦ન્જ

At six-thirty, a knock sounded on the stateroom door, and Mercy jumped. Distracted with getting Daniel out of harm's way, she'd lost track of time.

"Just a minute." She dashed to the bathroom, turned on the shower, returned to the sitting room, and opened the door. She'd left cartoons on the television to avoid suspicion from the steward.

The porter they'd had since she came on board, maneuvered inside, a heavy tray on his shoulder. "Where is the boy?"

She busied herself clearing the table. "In the shower. Leave it. He'll be out in a minute."

"Bring him out. I'm supposed to make sure you are both here." His thick Italian accent made him sound perpetually angry.

Dread kicked down her spine. The longer she concealed Daniel's absence, the better her chances. She turned, feigning anger, and planted her fists on her hips. "I am not dragging my son from his bath so you can take a head count. Really, where else could he be?"

His scowl deepened and he hesitated a fraction of a second, deciding whether to push it or not. He mumbled something that sounded like curses, and left.

She paced the cabin, her nerves taut as a fishing line with a hundred pound marlin on the other end. If the police didn't arrive before Ricco returned, she would be dead. Eyelids feeling like eighty-grit sandpaper, her fertile imagination envisioned a thousand ways her next meeting with Ricco could go, none of them pleasant.

Too restless to sit still, she took a shower and changed clothes. The hot water soothed her frayed nerves, but the relief was only temporary.

At ten-thirty, the launch returned.

What could be keeping the police?

She held her breath, listening as Ricco shouted words too far away for her to understand, but she felt the force of energy in the air as he stomped down the passageway towards her.

Courage she'd never known swept through her, and she realized she wasn't afraid of this man. Not now.

His hold over her had been broken.

Daniel was beyond Ricco's reach now.

He could only threaten her with Heaven.

Not that she wanted to die, but her fate had always been in God's hands. She crossed her arms and stood waiting for him.

Ricco kicked the door open, his eyes bright with fury. He strode across the room, followed by the tall man with the icy blue eyes.

Ricco grabbed both her arms, his fingers digging into her flesh, and shook her like a rag doll. "I warned you, Traci. Where's the boy?"

She lifted her chin. "He's gone. You can't touch him."

Ricco turned to the tall man and screamed. "We'll see about that. Lorenz, search the ship. Find him."

She stood her ground. "It won't do any good. He's been gone since noon. He's safe in the hands of the police."

His arm came back and he delivered a stinging slap that sent her reeling across the room, bouncing onto the sofa. One side of her face numbed. He charged across the room and took both sides of her shirt in his hands, jerking her to her feet. "I want those pictures, Traci."

Her hand went to her jaw, and she wiggled it. Feeling returned with stabbing pain. "There are no pictures. They never were in my procession. I'm not Traci Wallace. This entire fiasco since I left Bermuda has been a horrible case of mistaken identity."

He pulled her closer. "I don't think so."

She shook her head. "My name is Mercy Lawrence. I live in Houston, Texas. I can't deny the uncanny resemblance, but no matter what you do to me, I can't tell you where to find the pictures."

With one quick jerk, he ripped her shirt down, exposing her right shoulder, pinning her arms to her side. He stared at her for a moment. His pupils dilated, and something she didn't understand passed across his face. Shoving her back to the sofa, he eased into a chair across from her, and exchanged a look with Lorenz. "It's...true. What you're saying." Ricco shook his head, his gaze roamed around the room and then landed back on her shoulder. "You're not Traci. You don't have the tattoo."

"Tattoo?"

"A small silver scale, we both shared the same astrological sign, Libra." He opened his shirt and revealed the sign on his own shoulder. "We got them the same day on Capri." He lowered his head, resting it in his hands, and then raised it again to look at Lorenz. "Traci...she is dead."

A shudder of relief washed over Mercy. Ricco believed her. She pushed herself upright and pulled her shirt together. "What makes you think Traci's dead?"

He didn't answer the question. "Lorenz, stay with her." He stood and walked to the door. He turned and glared at her. "I'll decide what to do with you later."

The door bounced against the frame, the lock broken.

Within minutes, the groan of the anchor lifting filled the cabin, and the ship headed out to sea.

&०९

Wallace Island, the Aegean Sea
Friday, July 7

Thomas left the house and headed for the beach, unable to bear the cavernous rooms that no longer echoed with Daniel's laughter or were brightened by Mercy's smile.

Frank stopped him. "The weather is getting worse, boss. We need to wait until this blows over."

"I can't wait, Frank. I'll give you an hour to work out a flight plan to take us over or around the weather. Then we go. Regardless."

His chest was hollow, empty like the house. He wasn't sure he could fill it again if anything happened to Mercy and Daniel. Only one burning need remained. To find his family and bring them home.

A dark sky hung overhead. Gray clouds boiled above, damp and alive with expectancy from the coming squall. Waves pushed in, battering the shore.

Wind whipped his hair and clothing, but he pushed farther down the coast. Emotions caused his brain to stop functioning—his head stuffed with intense feelings that stifled his powers of reason. If he'd been here, instead of traipsing off to save the world, Mercy and Daniel would still be safe at home.

He'd grilled Fergus endlessly for details on their disappearance, but in the final analysis, there were no clues to follow. All they knew was Ricco Rossellini fit the description of one of the men his family left the carnival with. Twenty-four hours ago. They could be anywhere.

Heavy rain pelted his head and face, soaking his

shirt and trousers, plastering them against his skin. He ran, screaming into the wind, pushing himself faster and faster until he ran out of beach. He reversed and returned to the villa, headed to the shower. When he finished, the hour was up. A rap sounded at the door. "What do you want?" he shouted.

It was Frank. "The plane's ready."

"So am I. Have you notified Fergus?"

"Yeah. He's waiting in the foyer."

"Then let's roll."

In the entryway, Fergus moved into step beside him.

"We're flying to Naples. I'll check in with the Italian police on the way. Either way, we'll tear that city apart until we find my family."

"Ye don't think she just left with Rossellini? It's happened before."

"Not this time, Fergus. Not this time."

On the flight to Naples, Thomas rose and walked back to the stateroom, too anxious to sit still.

Maggie had texted a message she was sending an e-mail attachment. He had no time for business but sat down at the computer station in the stateroom. He might need to make a copy. It would be simpler from the desk. The printer paper tray was empty, and he opened the desk drawer.

In the center compartment, he spotted a tiny black thumb drive. He rose and took it to Fergus. "This yours?"

The Scot glanced down. "Not mine, lad. The puppy found it under yer bed. Traci put it away for safe keeping."

Thomas bounced the USB drive in his palm. It didn't belong to him. He returned to his seat and connected it to his laptop.

It took a minute for the file to open. Pictures of Ricco Rossellini and most of the terrorists on the ten-most-wanted list moved across the monitor—al-Qaeda leaders relaxing aboard Ricco's yacht. Traci must have taken the photos. Why hadn't she turned them over to the authorities? Or to him?

The pictures brought up a link to a video. Thomas clicked on the site and Traci's face appeared. "Thomas, if you're watching this you know what I stumbled onto. I wanted to give it to you, but you were in Edinburgh, and you've been so angry you wouldn't take my calls. I hid it on the plane, knowing you would find it.

"I'll meet you back on the island after I finish this photo shoot for *Harper's*. We need to talk, Thomas. About us and where we go from here. You won't believe this, but I do truly love you. I always have."

The screen went dark.

He sat in silence for a long while.

These were the photographs Mercy told him Ricco had been after.

Traci hid them, knowing Ricco couldn't get access to the plane. Smart girl. And probably the reason she went into hiding. She should have come to him. Despite their differences, he would have protected her.

Paul Redford could take this information and use Rossellini to capture the entire network.

Thomas saved the file and sent it to Paul on his secure line. The fasten-seatbelt light came on. He returned to the cabin and buckled up for landing.

Rain beaded on the aircraft's window as they taxied onto the Naples Capodichino Airport runway.

Frank pulled into terminal two as the satellite

phone rang.

He picked up the phone. "Thomas Wallace."

"Mr. Wallace, this is Captain Galluzzo with the Naples Police," he said in surprisingly good English. "We have your son."

Thomas's breath caught. "Is he all right?"

"*Si*, he is fine."

"My wife...?"

There was a pause.

The captain cleared his throat. "The boy had a note. We'll discuss it when you get to police headquarters."

"I'm at the airport now. I'll be there as fast as the weather and your traffic laws allow." He disconnected and signaled to Fergus. "The police have Daniel. Make sure a car is waiting as soon as we're off the plane."

29

Naples, Italy
Thursday, July 6

They made the trip from the airport in twenty minutes despite the foul weather.

Lightning flashes through the tinted windows brightened the police station as they pulled to the curb. The building sat in the middle of the block, almost indistinguishable through sheets of rain, an old structure with nineteenth century Italian architecture, the stones gray in the dimming light. Steps rose four feet from the sidewalk to the entrance. Lighted basement windows faced the street.

Thomas grabbed his umbrella and charged into the police station, Fergus right behind him. "I'm Thomas Wallace. Captain Galluzzo is expecting me."

The man behind the desk nodded. "*Si*, he is waiting in his office." He picked up the phone and within minutes, the captain entered the reception area through security doors to the left.

Thomas met him halfway. "I want to see my son."

The captain offered his hand. "Perhaps we should talk about your wife first, before you see the boy."

He gave the man's hand an absentminded shake and then waved at Fergus. "This is my security chief, Fergus McFadden. What about my wife?"

"Come back to my office. I'll fill you in on everything we know. You can read the note."

The office was small, with well-used wooden furniture. A desk, two chairs, and a file cabinet. A single window provided a view of the bay, the scene gray and hazy through the fogging casement.

"How did my son escape?"

"From what he told us, your wife let him out a porthole, and he swam to the nearest boat. He's a very brave boy. The note was tucked into his life vest. He gave it to the people who rescued him. They contacted us immediately. We had copies of the abduction notice, and we brought him here."

He pushed his glasses up on his prominent Roman nose. "Doctors have examined him. He seems to have suffered no physical damage from his experience."

One sheet of paper lay in the center of the desk.

The captain's hand shook slightly as he handed Thomas the note.

Thomas scanned the paper. He didn't move except for the rise and fall of his chest.

Mercy had put Daniel's life before her own safety.

His actions since he'd taken her from Bermuda had been less than gallant. Now, he prayed he'd get the opportunity to say he was sorry.

"Why didn't you rescue my wife?"

"It was a hostage situation, Mr. Wallace, or so we thought. We couldn't charge in and put her life at risk."

"What do you mean, you thought?"

A shadow passed over Captain Galluzzo face. "We were watching the boat when we received this." He reached into his desk drawer and pulled out a fax sheet. "Is this your wife?"

Thomas took the sheet. It was a morgue photo of a dead woman. Lead settled in his chest and choked off his breath. Skin ashen, hair tangled, it was Mercy. Still lovely, even in death.

A chill spread through his gut. When he could finally speak, he laid the picture back on the desk. "How is that possible? She wrote the note...?"

"We haven't received the coroner's report. They're faxing the autopsy results here." The captain hesitated for what seemed an eternity, and then said, "I assume that after the boy escaped they decided to kill her."

The Italian shifted, making the chair springs squeak. "After we found your son, we sent out pictures of your wife. The police in Capri found this." He tapped the morgue shot. "The body was unidentified until they received our inquiry."

Beside him, Fergus clasped his shoulder, his brown eyes suddenly pooled.

Thomas stared at the picture. It was easy to recall her face in life. Soft, warm, and beautiful. He stood and gave the chair a violent shove. Had she suffered? She'd needed him and he wasn't there. How could he ever tell Daniel? The boy had just found the woman he thought was his mother only to lose her again.

He'd been married to the wrong woman seven years and had only begun to realize the happiness possible with Mercy. Now it was too late. If he'd left her in Bermuda, she'd be alive.

She had died because of the pictures Traci had taken. And where was Traci? Obviously, in hiding somewhere. But where?

Thomas gazed across the desk at the captain. "What will you do about Rossellini?"

The captain held up his hand. "Don't do anything hasty, Mr. Wallace. Rossellini's yacht left port around eight o'clock tonight. Our navy is watching the yacht's movements. We lost visual sight in the storm, but they've tracked the boat on radar. It seems headed for Capri. Now that we know your wife isn't aboard, we can send a tactical force in and arrest him for murder and kidnapping."

Ricco Rossellini killed Mercy and kidnapped Daniel. He wouldn't escape judgment in a justice system gone mad.

Thomas would see to that. He took another long look at the morgue picture, etching it in his memory. He wanted it there when he came face to face with her killer. He rose and turned to the door. "I'd like to see my son now. I'm going to send him home."

The captain walked Thomas to the door. As they stepped into the hallway, a clerk handed the captain an envelope, and he passed it on to Thomas. "Your copy of the death certificate."

Thomas slipped it into his pocket and went to get Daniel. He wasn't going home.

Daniel would get on the plane with Fergus for safekeeping while Thomas took the high-speed ferry to Capri. He could be there in a little more than an hour.

The Wallace jet in Naples would serve as a good alibi if needed.

He had information the police didn't have. Yet. The location of Ricco's villa on Capri.

∢∟

Capri, Italy
Friday, July 7

Inside the cabin, the motion of the sea's turbulence paralleled Mercy's emotions. Wind lashed waves against the porthole. Rain pounded the deck above her head. She sat on the sofa, Lorenz across from her in the chair, his long legs stretched out in front of him, feet crossed at the ankles, never taking his eyes off her.

"Where are you taking me?"

He stared, never blinking. "You'll know when we get there."

"Your English is very good. Did you spend time in the States?"

No reply.

She tried a friendly smile. "Why don't you just let me go? The police are looking for the yacht, even now. They know Ricco abducted me. Think about it, Lorenz. As long as you hold me, they will put forth all their efforts to rescue me. Make your escape plans, leave me on the boat or wherever, call and tell the authorities where I am. All their manpower will come to find me, giving you a better chance of getting away."

He laughed. "Are you worried about me? I'm touched." He was enjoying this. "We'll get away, whether we let you go or not. Besides, Ricco has plans for you." He propped his feet up on the coffee table. "You found out about dear Edda, I understand."

Mercy didn't expect that. "Edda? You knew—Of course, you did. She worked for you."

"Very clever of you to figure that out. She was really quite easy to seduce, a middle-aged woman looking for romance."

"And you'll let her go to prison without a backward glance."

He snorted. "Why should I care? I originally recruited her to find the pictures at the villa. But when Ricco decided he would rather have you dead...Edda stepped in. She didn't like you, anyway."

"You were the shooter on the ridge."

"Is this true confessions time?" Lorenz shrugged. "I wouldn't have missed if it hadn't been for that meddling old man."

The yacht's motors slowed and then stopped. The unmistakable sound of the anchor dropping into the sea filtered into the cabin, followed by the splash of the launch as it hit the water, and then bounced against the yacht's port side.

She stiffened as her nerve endings sparked. She didn't want to die.

Lorenz sat like a cat watching a mouse hole, waiting for her to try something.

In a battle of strength, she would lose. She motioned to her ripped shirt. "I need to change."

He nodded. "Leave the door open. Hurry. We'll be leaving soon."

Leaving for where?

Gait unsteady, she crossed to the bedroom and opened the closet. She quickly slipped into a long sleeved sweater and took down her purse. She needed a weapon, something to give her an edge.

She scrambled through the bag's contents and pulled out a metal fingernail file. Not much, but it might work. She slipped it into the back pocket of her jeans. In the bathroom, she found a small trial-size can of hairspray, and stuck it into her purse.

Movement made her glance into the mirror. The Italian henchman loomed, staring. He leaned against the doorjamb. "Looking for something?"

She ran a nervous hand through her hair. How long had he been watching her? "Yes, my toothbrush."

He chuckled and placed his hand on the back of her neck, pushing her back into the sitting room. "I don't think you'll need to worry about a toothbrush."

Minutes later, she was on deck. Despite an umbrella, the storm soaked through her clothing as the wind whipped rain sideways. The downpour ran into her eyes, blurring her vision.

Lorenz pushed her in front of him and started her down the ladder.

Ricco waited in the launch. Halfway to the bottom, Ricco put both hands around her waist and lifted her into the bobbing vessel.

Lorenz and two men from the crew followed her onboard.

Fighting the waves and swells, the small boat made its way towards the pier. Fifteen minutes later, they reached the dock where a car waited.

Forced into the backseat between Ricco and Lorenz, she couldn't see through the dark, rain soaked windows but sensed they were climbing into the hills. Her wet clothes stuck to the leather seats, and she shivered.

Ricco fingered the wet sleeve of her sweater. "You're cold, *cara mia.* My apologies. I would give you my jacket, but it is equally wet. You'll find warm clothes at the villa."

Her teeth chattered. "Y-your villa. Is that where we're going?"

He pointed at the windshield. "Yes, it's just ahead. Traci loved it here."

30

Isle of Capri, Italy
Friday, July 7

It was after midnight when they approached a white stone wall that seemed to encompass the property. The rain had slowed to a heavy mist, but exterior lighting brightened the night, framing the view in a foggy haze. The second floor was visible above the high fence.

The man next to the driver got out and opened a heavy iron gate. The car moved up the illuminated drive and stopped under the portico at the villa's entrance.

Ricco turned to Lorenz. "Take her to Traci's room. I'll join you there."

The cold-eyed thug clenched his hand around her arm and pulled her from the car. He led her inside and up to the second floor. He stopped at the first door on the right, and shoved her inside. He held up his hand. "Wait here."

He peeled off his wet jacket and tossed it on a chair. His gun was tucked into a shoulder holster. Moving across the room, he checked the door leading to the balcony and then opened one of the window blinds and looked outside. From there, he moved into the bathroom.

Her hands trembled as she stood in the bedroom

doorway. Some instinct warned her this man was infinitely more dangerous than Ricco.

The bedroom, like the 18th Century palazzo, was furnished with a Tuscany motif. Decorative tile floors and massive dark furniture filled the space. A king-size bed with an enormous carved headboard sat centered on the wall. Bed coverings were in earth tones of deep brown and red. A large wrought iron chandelier with simulated candle lighting, hung from the beamed ceiling. Gold, ruby, and brown damask fabric covered pillows on the tan sofa and love seat in front of a stone fireplace. So much splendor. So much evil.

Lorenz came back into the sitting room. "Get changed. The closet is just off the bathroom."

Hoping there might be a window, she was disappointed to find only a large glass-block wall that allowed in light, but no egress.

She found jeans, a thick pullover, and dry tennis shoes in the walk-in-closet, glad for the warmth they provided.

Traci seemed to have left clothes everywhere she stayed for any length of time. The scattered wardrobe had served her well.

Taking a handful of tissues from the box on the vanity, Mercy wrapped them around the file's blunt end, and placed it into her jeans hip pocket, then tucked the hairspray canister into the hand warmers sewn into the front of the sweatshirt.

When she returned to the bedroom, Ricco had already arrived.

He set a pot of tea and three cups on the coffee table. "I brought you some hot tea. I also brought brandy you can add if you like, or drink it straight. It will take away the chill. Sorry I can't provide a snack.

The villa has been closed for the summer." He shrugged. "I have no staff here at present."

She shook her head, refusing the cup he offered.

"It's safe to drink, *cara mia*. I'm not an ogre. I don't use drugs to capture a woman's affection." He offered the tea again.

This time, she took it. The hot, sweet liquid stopped her trembling and gave her a boost of energy.

Ricco walked across the room and placed one hand on the hearth, the other held his tea. He turned to face her. "You must be wondering what's to become of you." He didn't wait for her answer. "I've decided to release you, let you return to wherever you call home."

Before she could absorb his words, Lorenz jumped to his feet. "You can't do that, Ricco. She knows who we are."

Ricco shook his head. "The police know who we are, and will soon know about this place. The moment the boy reached safety, they knew."

"They don't know me. Look, I'll take care of her, just as I did Traci. Consider it a parting gift."

Too much information came at Mercy too fast. Her gaze darted from Lorenz to Ricco. "He killed Traci? Daniel's mother is dead?"

"Yes. I'm sorry to say. You won't believe it, but I truly am sorry."

"How? When?"

Ricco shook his head. "It doesn't matter now."

Lorenz gave a tight smile. "I took care of Traci months ago, although I guess you could say she committed suicide. She ran from me and fell off the cliff. Your demise will be handled more efficiently, I assure you."

"It's over, Lorenz. I'm going into hiding in

Pakistan or Syria." Ricco shrugged. "Not my preference, but it probably had to happen sooner or later. You're welcome to come along, but a man with your impeccable taste would probably find it rather crude."

The assassin looked at her. "No, I'll stay here. I have other plans."

Ricco walked across to where she sat and cupped her face in his hand. "I'm truly sorry to have put you through all this." He gave a short laugh. "It really is too bad you're not Traci. It would make the desert nights much more bearable. *Ciao, cara mia.*"

He shot Lorenz a hard glare. "Let her go." He walked to the door, and his hand reached for the doorknob, just before the back of his head exploded.

Mercy screamed, staring at the gun in Lorenz's hand, momentarily frozen. She was so scared she hyperventilated. From somewhere she found the strength to run, but he stood between her and the doorway.

He stepped forward, his gaze never leaving hers. He re-holstered the gun and never paused as he closed the gap between them. His arm snaked out and grabbed her left wrist.

She twisted free, feeling pain radiate up her arm into her shoulder. Her legs came against the bed behind her. She twisted, leaped onto the bed, and moved back against the headboard. Her legs wobbled as her feet sank into the mattress, but she retained her balance.

If he leaped on the bed, she could go off either side and make a dash for the door.

A macabre dance ensued. He moved to one side, she in the opposite direction. At the side of the headboard, she grabbed at the post and the round ball came off in her hand. If her aim was true, perhaps she could stun him long enough to get the gun.

Lorenz stopped and a smile lifted the corners of his mouth. "What? You think you can harm me with that? You can't escape, you know. Do you want me to shoot you?"

"That wouldn't be my first choice," she said with a boldness she didn't feel, "but I figure it's in your long range plans."

Lorenz eyed her up and down. "Not right away. It would amuse me to tame some of that spirit. Who knows? You might convince me not to kill you."

She lifted the wooded ball and hurled it with all her strength. It found its mark, bounced off his head and rolled away. As soon as the object left her hand, she made a dash for the door. She almost made it.

His hand grabbed her hoodie and slammed her back against him. The assassin shoved her back towards the bed.

She couldn't win this fight.

He had a gun and strength on his side.

God, help me.

When she hit the bed, she rolled to the side and bounced to her feet. Before she could run again, he caught her left arm, causing her to wince in pain.

He turned her to face him. "You want to make this a fight? OK by me." He leaned towards her, pulling her closer.

Mercy grasped the hairspray canister inside the shirt pocket and placed her finger on the nozzle. As he bent forward, she blasted both his eyes with the alcohol and hydrocarbon liquid.

He roared with rage, cursing. Clutching at his

eyes, he released her.

Grasping the nail file from her pocket, she stabbed his right hand, and bolted for the door.

She bounded over Ricco's body in the doorway, and ran down the stairs.

Screaming curses followed her. "You'd better run fast, little girl. Because when I catch you..." The sounds of breaking glass and crashes told her he would soon follow, and the grounds' exterior lights would make it difficult to hide.

Outside, the fine mist offered no concealment. She did a three-sixty turn. Which way to run? With a snap decision, she ran towards the garage. *Please Lord, let there be a car with keys in the ignition.*

Two vehicles sat side-by-side, a sports car with the top down and no key, and the Jaguar sedan they rode in to the villa. *Please, please let there be keys.*

Jerking the driver's door open, she scanned the ignition. Nothing.

Lorenz's voice sounded outside in the quiet night. "Mercy, I'm coming. Playing hide and seek will make it more fun when I catch you. And make no mistake, I will find you."

Heart pounding in her throat, her breath came in short, panicked gasps. She had to slow down, get control, or he would hear her labored breathing across the courtyard. Inhaling five deep breaths, she let the air out slowly. The terror inside lessened. She silently closed the Jaguar door and moved back to the garage's side entrance.

She hoped that he would go to the gate entrance, thinking she would head that way. He could also be outside the garage door, waiting for her.

On tiptoes, she moved back across the garage to

the tool bin, selected a heavy wrench, and then moved back to the door.

She peeked around the doorframe into the courtyard. No visible threat. The wrench gripped so tightly her fingers felt numb, she ran towards the palazzo's shadows. Her feet slipped on the slick stones and she landed on her knees. Pain shot through her legs and warm blood seeped down her right shin. She grabbed the wrench again and hobbled to the building, pressing her back against the cool limestone.

The gate lay about a quarter-mile away. The only cover was the huge, stone flower urns dotting the landscape between the villa and freedom.

With her wounded knees, she would be an easy target, moving from vase to vase. She had to try.

Lorenz still had the gun, and he would use it.

She stepped around the villa's corner towards the gate, poised to dart to the nearest urn.

From behind, a large hand covered her mouth, stifling her scream.

31

Isle of Capri, Italy
Friday, July 7

Thomas arrived early at the Mergellina Dock. The Aliscafo hydrofoil didn't leave until 23:10. That would put him on Capri in forty minutes. While he waited for departure, he rented a car. He would drive it onto the ship and be ready to roll when the boat docked on the island.

He pulled into the queue as the huge white ship glided to the wharf. Vehicles on board disembarked. A white-coated steward stood in the rain at the ramp, directing cars into bays. Travelers were few this time of the evening, and Thomas parked on the lower level.

Following the steward's directions, Thomas pulled into the slot indicated, cut the motor, and decided to remain in the car for the short trip. He leaned against the seat with a feeling of throbbing urgency he couldn't shake.

Mercy was dead.

The reality of that twisted his gut. His eyes filled with tears, and he tasted their salt as they rolled across his mouth. He shook his head, pushing away the ache, folding the hurt deep inside. He had to concentrate on what lay ahead. All he could do was find some kind of justice for her death.

He withdrew the copy of the death certificate that

Captain Galluzzo had given him. Unable to read it then, he needed to wait for the shock to wear off.

The report Paul Redford had sent was still in his jacket pocket, also unopened. He withdrew the documents, and switched on the dome light, death certificate open in the faint glow above him.

He had to translate Italian to English as he read. The Italian equivalent of a Jane Doe, most of the spaces on the form were filled in with approximate and unknown, spaces such as age, address and burial site—until he came to the cause of death.

Trauma, multiple fractures, hemorrhagic shock, and cervical fracture.

The car's interior closed in on him as the clinical description of her death sank in. Clenching and unclenching his hands, he realized he'd read the entire document without taking a breath. Then it hit him. He'd missed something.

He read the death certificate again, his breath coming faster. His gaze bounced back to the date of death. One week after Traci disappeared. Almost eight months ago.

Under cause of death, the authorities noted possible suicide. Fishermen saw her go off the cliff and pulled her from the water. Too late to save her life.

Thomas knew Traci too well to believe it had been suicide. She wasn't the type to take her own life. She'd loved life too much. Someone had pushed or driven her off the precipice.

He lowered the window, letting the damp ocean air wash over him.

The woman in the morgue was Traci.

Mercy was alive and still in the hands of Ricco Rossellini. She had told him the truth from the beginning.

He ripped the Redford report from the envelope and jerked the papers free. A yellow sticky note in Paul's almost illegible script clung to the first page.

Here's the information you wanted. This makes us even.

Paul

Thomas moved closer to the light and read the report twice. Everything came into focus, all the missing parts were there. How and why he had mistaken Mercy for his wife. Anyone could have made the same mistake. In fact, everyone had done so. That didn't absolve his guilt.

Questions filled his mind, questions he might never know the answers to. How Traci's body remained unidentified for so long? Small morgue? Limited funds to investigate? Thinking someone would surely inquire about her?

He hadn't checked hospitals and morgues, only because she left with her lover. He thought she didn't want him to find her.

A heavy mixture of grief and joy battled inside him. He didn't love Traci. Her infidelity had killed that part of him. The burden of grief, and the effect her death would have on Daniel and Nanna, almost overshadowed the elation that Mercy, by God's grace, was alive.

The hydrofoil slowed, and within minutes, the ramp was in place for departure. He was the third car off the boat. The open window helped clear his mind.

If Mercy was still alive, she faced imminent danger.

Ricco had killed once. He wouldn't hesitate to do so again.

Thomas floored the vehicle, taking the slick curves at top speed, headed east into the hills.

Ricco's palazzo sat at the end of a winding road like a bright jewel atop the knoll, a massive estate with a two-story edifice surrounded by high stone walls. The villa lay well back from the unmanned gated entrance. Walls would be wet from the storm, and he'd have to scale it without the equipment in his backpack.

When he first began to look for Traci, he'd climbed the hills overlooking the estate. Hiding with binoculars, he'd watched the activity on the grounds. Driven by jealousy, pride, and hatred, he became little more than a peeping tom.

She'd been dead by then, but he hadn't known that, and he'd spent the long night watching for signs of her. Had he found her there, he was unsure what might have happened. It had not been his most shining hour. He'd told himself he did it for Daniel. His motives had been less than altruistic. Enough. That was the past.

Now he must focus on finding Mercy. Her life depended on it.

If memory served, the exterior lighting stayed on until daylight. If there were hidden cameras, he'd have to disable them before going over the wall. Becoming a spotlighted target wouldn't help Mercy.

Minutes later, he parked next to the gate and located the two cameras that panned the front entrance. He picked up a handful of mud and rolled it into balls, then pulled the car directly under the security cameras. Standing on the automobile's roof, he plastered the lenses with mud.

If guards watched the monitors, they'd know company had arrived. They would rush to secure the gate.

He hid the car and jogged around the wall and up into the hills, back to his old perch. The rain made his recon position a mudslide. He slid down the hill and crashed with a thud on top of the wall. Scrambling to his feet, he jumped to the ground, landing fifty feet from the palazzo.

Rain settled into a fog-like mist that worked in his favor, giving a little unexpected cover. No stars. No moon. But the exterior lights still haloed in the gloom.

No surveillance equipment in the back of the property, at least none he could see from his position. The absence of cameras would give him an edge.

In a crouch, he moved into the dark bulk of the house's shadow.

There had to be a back entrance for the household staff.

He stood still, waiting and listening. No dogs but there hadn't been any during his last visit. A good thing. The trusty dog-be-gone canister Chip had given him was at home in his backpack.

Boots on stone pavement brought him to a halt. He moved closer to the building and flattened against the wall.

A short figure, dark pea coat and knitted cap, rounded the corner, an AK-47 slung over his shoulder.

Thomas waited until the man was within arm's reach, grabbed his neck and held him until he became unconscious and slid to the ground. He stuffed the man's cap into his mouth, removed his belt and tied his hands behind his back. No reason to kill him. He was just a foot soldier.

Finished, Thomas pulled the body into the shadows.

Close. Sentries were a new addition.

A muffled shot sounded inside the villa.

As Thomas bolted towards the front entrance, another sentry came into view, heading the same direction. Thomas launched at the man, hitting him at the knees and heard a bone crack. The sentry grunted as they both crashed onto the wet grass.

Thomas rolled, gripped the man's gun hand, and twisted it until the weapon wrenched free.

The guard struggled for purchase on the wet lawn. He didn't make it.

Thomas hit him with the butt of the rifle, knocking him out cold. No more trouble from this guy. With a broken leg and a headache, he would stay put for a while.

Shouts and curses echoed from inside the villa. The front door flew open and Mercy rushed out, turned in a circle, and then dashed towards the garage.

A man burst out the door, dodged into the shadows and shouted. "Mercy, I'm coming. Playing hide and seek will make it more fun when I catch you. And make no mistake. I will find you."

Thomas's jaw tightened, teeth grinding. When this man fell into *his* hands, the fun would begin. He made a U-turn, skirted back around the villa, and approached the garage from the opposite direction.

Calling out to her wouldn't be wise. Best if the gunman didn't know he existed. He had to find Mercy before the thug did.

He slipped into the garage's side entrance, and hesitated a moment, letting his eyes adjust to the darkness. "Mercy!" he whispered.

No answer.

On the opposite side of the carport, a thin shaft of light from an open doorway revealed her outline. Two vehicles lay between them.

He whispered her name again, but she didn't hear him. Urgency drove him forward.

The gunman was just outside waiting for her.

Before he could catch her, she hesitated a moment and then eased out the door.

Thomas sprinted to the doorway in an instant, just as the man grabbed Mercy from behind.

"You should've known you couldn't hide from me."

Thomas stepped into the open, his weapon aimed at the gunman. "Let her go."

The man turned and faced Thomas, Mercy in front of him, his gun pressed against her neck. "And who might you be? Not polizia. No uniform."

"Thomas, shoot. Don't worry about me. He's a hired killer. He murdered Traci, and he just killed Ricco. Don't trust him."

"So this is the great Thomas Wallace, who wasn't man enough to keep his wife at home. He won't kill me, Mercy. He's weak. Besides, he knows I'll kill you if he tries."

The taunt was meant to unnerve him. Thomas smiled. "You know who I am. Care to introduce yourself?"

"I guess you deserve to know who's going to kill you. The name's Lorenz Lucci." Lucci turned his head and shouted over his shoulder. "Biagio, Enzo, get over here!"

Thomas kept his tone cool, firm. "Are those the names of the two unconscious sentries?"

Lorenz raised an eyebrow. "Perhaps I'll have to revise my estimation of you. Maybe not so weak." His pale eyes glittered in the half-light. "So what do we do now, Mr. Wallace? We have a standoff. If you shoot me, I kill her. Why don't you drop your gun and maybe we can make some financial arrangement for her release?"

"Don't trust hi—" Lorenz jammed the gun in her neck.

"You have until the count of three, Lucci, to let her go before I kill you."

Lorenz laughed. "You don't mind if I kill her? I hadn't really considered that. She isn't your wife, after all, is she?"

"One. Two."

With full force, Mercy brought the wrench in her right hand down on the gunman's knee.

He cursed and lifted the muzzle from her neck. Thomas fired twice, putting both rounds between Lorenz's eyes. The impact sent him tumbling to the stone pavement. His eyes opened and then went blank.

Mercy stood in place. Stunned. Eyes wide and searching. Her gaze shifted to the man on the ground and then back to Thomas. She took three steps forward, and Thomas met her there. His arms wrapped around her, and she buried her face in his chest. Shudders rippled through her body.

After a moment, she looked up at him. "Daniel...he reached safety? He's all right?"

"Yes, he's on board the plane with Fergus. Waiting for us."

"I was so frightened for him, Thomas. Ricco said he would...I had to get him away."

He smoothed strands of hair away from her face

and tilted her chin. "You did exactly the right thing. If you hadn't, you'd both be dead."

Her brows drew together, and she expelled a tired breath. "However are we going to explain about his mother...about me?"

"We'll have to talk to him soon but not tonight."

She leaned into him again and then looked up, a question in her eyes. "What were you going to do on the count of three?"

He grinned down at her. "I knew you would save me. I saw the wrench in your hand, even if your friend didn't."

She slapped his chest. "And if I hadn't used the wrench? You would have let him shoot me?"

"No, I had a plan B. I would have shot his gun hand, and then put one between his eyes."

"You were willing to risk my life on your plan B?"

With both hands framing her face, he looked into her eyes. "I would never let anyone hurt you." He pulled her in closer and whispered a truth from his past. "You were never in danger as long as I had the gun in my hand."

32

Isle of Capri, Italy
Friday, July 7

Sirens wailed at the villa entrance. Within minutes, police crashed the gate.

Thomas and Mercy met them in the driveway.

The two disabled sentries were gathered off the lawn and loaded into ambulances. For the next hour, Thomas explained what had happened, more than once. Either he explained it badly, or they were too dense to comprehend. Meanwhile, he and Mercy stood in the misting rain, getting wetter and more exhausted by the nanosecond.

He gave the officer his most patient smile. "Look, Captain, with all due respect, this woman has been through a terrible ordeal. I'm going to take her inside and make her a hot drink until you decide to release us. Contact Captain Galluzzo in Naples. He will vouch for me."

"The captain is on his way here. You cannot go back into the palazzo. It is a crime scene. Only our people are allowed inside."

Thomas shook his head. "The kitchen is not a crime scene. The villa has been closed for the summer. You can send an officer in with us. All I want is to let her sit down and get something hot to drink."

"I just told you, I cannot permit you to go inside. It

is a crime scene."

He had more important things to do than to contend with this bureaucrat. Thomas whipped the cell phone from his pocket and tapped in a number. "This is Thomas Wallace. May I speak to the Prime Minister?"

After a short wait, a man with a distinctive and well-known voice answered.

"Sorry to wake you, sir. But I have a situation here on Capri." Thomas explained the problem briefly. He held out the phone to the captain. "The Prime Minister wants to speak to you."

Moments later, they were inside the massive kitchen full of Old World charm, and stocked with all the modern conveniences. He found Mercy a seat in a booth. "What'll it be, coffee or tea? There's cheese and wine, but I wouldn't trust the cheese."

Mercy's head rested on the table, using her arms as a pillow. She looked up when he spoke. "I'd love a cup of tea with honey and lemon."

"Coming right up. No fresh lemons, but tea and honey I have." Thomas filled the teakettle and set it on a burner and then turned to the young Italian officer who followed them in. "What about you? Coffee?"

The young man gave a shy nod, and pulled out a stool from under the butcher-block island.

While they waited for the drinks to brew, Thomas placed a call to Fergus. The plane awaited them at the Capri airport. He tried to explain the Traci/Mercy situation, but he could tell his mentor was still confused. It would just have to wait for now.

They had settled down with their drinks when Captain Galluzzo strode in. He took one look at Mercy and stopped as if he'd grown roots through the tile floor. 'The woman in the morgue, she was not your wife?"

All Thomas wanted was to get away from here. He would have to explain Mercy to the captain but not tonight. It was too late, the story too complicated, and Mercy was exhausted.

Thomas set his coffee down and motioned for the captain to follow him outside. He didn't want Mercy to hear the truth this way. When they were out of her earshot, he halted. "Yes, Captain. The woman in the picture was my wife." He nodded towards Mercy. "That's her sister. I will return in a few days to Naples and explain everything. Now, I need to take her home. She's been through enough tonight."

"She was the one on the boat...with your son?"

Thomas nodded.

"The note said she was Traci Wallace."

He nodded once again. "She was afraid no one would come if she used her own name."

The policeman fingered his mustache, his bushy eyebrows drawn together in a straight line across his brow. Finally, he shrugged. "I know where to find you."

Outside, Thomas opened the rental car's passenger door, helped Mercy in, and drove to meet the plane.

She leaned back against the seat and spoke in a soft voice. "Ricco was going to let me go after he realized I wasn't Traci."

"How did he know you weren't Traci?"

"I didn't have her tattoo."

"What tattoo?"

"Apparently, he and Traci got matching astrological tattoos. They shared the same sign—a small silver scale on her left shoulder."

"Not surprising I didn't know. Traci and I hadn't lived as man and wife for almost four years."

The Capri airport looked deserted as Thomas parked the car in front of the rental agency and dropped the keys in the slot. They walked the short distance to the plane. As they started to board, Mercy looked down at her sweater, covered with Lucci's blood. "I can't let Daniel see me like this. It will frighten him."

Thomas removed his jacket and gave it to her. "This is covered with mud, but it will do until you can get a shower in the stateroom. I have a T-shirt you can wear."

Fergus met them at the aircraft door.

"Is Daniel awake?" Thomas asked.

Fergus shook his head. "As soon as I told him his mother...uh...was safe, he fell asleep."

"That's good. We can all use some rest." He turned to Mercy. "Do you want that shower now?"

She sank into the closest seat. "No, I might wake Daniel. I'll wait until we get home."

He sat beside her, leaned back and stretched his legs.

Soon, her head rested on his shoulder, both hands clasped around his arm, as if afraid he would leave her side. Her face was dirty, her hair mussed and damp, but she had never been more beautiful.

He smiled in spite of the trauma they'd just gone through.

She had said home.

Wallace Island, the Aegean Sea
Saturday, July 8

No matter what happened in the lives of mankind, God's world kept turning. The tide came in and went ou., The sun and moon still rose and set at their appointed times.

Thomas stood at his office window, Traci's death certificate and Paul Redford's report in hand, amazed at the island's tranquility. Serene, despite the unprecedented disruptions of the last two months.

He had abducted a woman he thought was his wife, brought her to his home, and then left on a black ops mission.

In his absence, Mercy had been shot at, poisoned, and abducted by an arms dealer.

He'd learned his wife was dead, and he had fallen in love with her double.

All this in the space of eight weeks.

Incredible.

Now he must somehow explain the bizarre events to his family.

Mercy and Daniel slept in, as per his instructions that they not be disturbed. They needed rest after their ordeal.

He read the documents once more before placing them in his jacket pocket. He wanted to speak to Mercy first. Privately. He owed her that.

The clatter of dishes and silverware from the dining room told him breakfast was ready. His stomach felt hollow. He'd eaten only one meal yesterday.

There'd been no time to replace Edda, but the house seemed to be running smoothly without her.

Breakfast was on time and the smell of waffles and bacon spoke to his hunger.

He strode down the hall and found Nanna in the dining room. He kissed her cheek. "Good morning, Nanna." At the buffet table, he filled a plate and grabbed a large mug of coffee.

Creases formed around Nanna's eyes, and she gave him a pained stare. "Thomas, I'm so glad you're back. You can't imagine how frightened we were, and how good it is to have Traci and Daniel home safely. I've been so worried…"

"I know, Nanna." He set his plate down, pulled her into his arms, and held her while she cried. When her tears abated, he released her, giving her back a gentle pat. "Everyone's all right now."

She pulled a lacy handkerchief from her pocket and wiped her eye. Giving him a weak smile, she patted the front of his shirt. "I've gotten you all damp."

"Not a problem. After breakfast, we need to talk. There are things I want to explain." He must tell her about Traci, but he could at least let her eat before he broke her heart. That Traci never lived up to her potential hadn't diminished Nanna's love for her.

She dabbed at her eyes again and straightened her back. Ever the English lady. She took a plate and added toast and marmalade. A maid entered and poured a cup of tea for her. "Find me when you're ready."

A woman he didn't know stepped into the dining room and cast him a smile that quickly faded. She came across the room an offered her hand. "I'm Katy Martin, your…wife's nurse."

Fergus must have told her about Traci, judging from her somber expression.

At ten o'clock, he had the cook put together a breakfast tray, climbed the stairs to Mercy's room, and knocked. "Mercy, it's Thomas. May I come in?"

"Yes, the door's open."

When he stepped into the room, she emerged from the bathroom in a white robe, toweling her hair. "You shouldn't have done that, Thomas. I was coming down to breakfast, albeit a little late."

"I thought you might be as hungry as I was." He crossed the room and placed the tray on the bedside table.

"I am, a little. I was just trying to wash away the last seventy-two hours. But I don't think there's enough soap and water in the world." She placed the towel around her neck and sat on the bed, taking a bite of toast.

Paddy rose from a pillow to investigate the breakfast tray. She gently pushed him away, and he settled back into his nest

"I've discovered the best healer," Thomas said, "is to replace the bad memories with good ones."

The corners of her mouth gave a slight tilt upward. "Sounds like a plan. Where do I start?"

He inhaled a deep breath, let it out slowly, and sat beside her. "I don't know where to begin, so I'm just going to jump in. I told you I was investigating your past, remember?"

She nodded.

"I received the information just before I arrived on Capri." He handed her Redford's report. "My sources did a meticulous job. There are things in there you probably don't want just anyone to know."

He stood and paced to the balcony. "You and Traci were sisters. Two years after Traci was born, your father, Christopher, had an affair with a waitress in Houston named Kristi Carpenter. Kristi was your mother. She put you up for adoption. There's a photo of her inside. She bears a remarkable resemblance to your father's wife, Dorothy."

She glanced down at the report but didn't open it. "Well, that explains the resemblance to some degree. Is my mother still alive?"

"No. She died in a boating accident some years ago. It's all in the report."

"And my father, he was OK—" She smothered a sob with her hands.

Feeling helpless, Thomas returned to sit beside her and pulled her close. "Your father, Nanna's son, died in a car crash six months before you were born. I don't think he knew your mother was pregnant. But there's no way to tell since both are dead." He laid his hand over hers. "Perhaps Nanna can help you there. Although I'm sure she didn't know about the affair."

He stood and punched his hands in his pockets. "The report also covers your time in the orphanage, after your foster parents' deaths. And your molestation by a male teacher." His face muscles tensed, making his jaw ache. "Feel free to burn that report."

She sat silent for a long while and then looked up at him, tears pooling in her eyes. "When do you want me to leave?" she asked, her voice low.

"Let's postpone that discussion until after the funeral. I still have to tell Nanna and Daniel you're not Traci and about her death."

"Do you want me with you when you speak to Daniel? I will if you like, but I'll need a little time..."

"We'll talk to him together, later. He'll have questions I don't have answers for. I'll handle it alone for the present."

He reached down and pulled her into his arms, smoothing her wet hair with his hand. The wretchedness of what she had suffered seared his heart. He cradled her close like a wounded bird, trying to absorb some of the pain.

⇆

Mercy lay on her stomach across the bed, her gaze drawn to the cloudless blue sky outside the open French doors.

Light and dark did not always rest with the weather or current surroundings. Darkness lived inside evil men and rubbed off on their victims, sometimes lasting a lifetime.

She had managed to hide the darkness left by her past. Along the way, she found a source of Light that could overcome any darkness. The darkness was her past. The Light her future.

Paddy jumped on the bed and nuzzled her cheek, purring. She sat up and pulled him into her arms. "Whatever happens, Paddy, we're going to be all right."

⇆

Downstairs, Thomas found Nanna on the terrace. "Shall we walk?"

She rose and took his arm. "I know you have something terrible to tell me, Thomas. I saw it in your eyes at breakfast. Go ahead. Waiting will only postpone the pain."

He cleared his throat and led her over to a chair. "Nanna, your son had an affair with an American woman after Traci was born." He passed her an extra photo of Kristi. "Were you aware of that?"

"No, I knew he and Dorothy were having marital problems. But that's not the sort of thing he would have confided to his mother." She gazed down at the photograph and smiled. "Chris was always attracted to the same type of woman. The only thing that ever changed about the women in his life were their names and personalities."

He turned to face her. "There was a child from that affair, Nanna."

She stopped, her eyes widening. The grip on his arm tightened. "That's not Traci upstairs, is it?"

"She's your granddaughter. Her name is Mercy Lawrence. I brought her here against her will, thinking she was Traci. She told me the truth from the beginning. I just didn't believe her. There were a lot of reasons why I didn't buy her story, but it's immaterial, now."

Nanna gazed down at Kristi's picture. "She's Traci's half-sister, yet they are so alike. How is that possible?"

"I can't explain it. Perhaps just a strong gene pool on your son's side. As you saw, Mercy's mother looked more than a little like Dorothy—just a younger version. But who knows?"

Nanna inhaled a long breath. "I think I knew from the first she wasn't Traci. Their personalities were so different." Awareness gleamed in her eyes. "Then Traci..."

He knelt beside her chair and took her hand. "I wish there was an easy way to say this, Nanna. Traci died seven months ago, murdered by one of Ricco Rossellini's henchmen."

Even though she'd expected bad news, the color drained from her features, leaving her skin pale and gray in the sunlight. She hesitated an agonizing moment before she brought her hands up to cover her face.

He'd asked Katy to stand by.

She must have sensed his need. The nurse walked over and patted his shoulder. "I'll take over here, Mr. Wallace."

❧

Thomas climbed the stairs to Daniel's room. One final ordeal.

Daniel played on the floor with Pal.

Thomas sat beside his son on the carpet. "Good morning. So this is your new friend. Have you both had breakfast?"

"Yes, sir. Isn't Pal cute, Dad? He's the best puppy ever. I missed him while we were gone."

Thomas scratched behind his ear.

Tail wagging, the puppy rolled over onto his back.

"He's pretty special all right, almost as special as you." He reached over and tousled Daniel's hair. "I'm very proud of you, Danny, for what you did. Swimming to the other ship was very brave. You were a real hero."

Daniel gave him a shy smile and looked away.

Thomas gathered Daniel into his lap. Explaining to a six year old wasn't easy. "I have something to tell you, and I need you to be brave once more."

As if sensing the seriousness of what was coming, Daniel hugged Pal close to his chest.

Thomas pushed out a deep breath. This was going to be the longest day of his life. "Danny, do you know what an aunt is?"

33

Edinburgh, Scotland
Tuesday, July 11

Thomas led the funeral party through customs and found a horde of reporters, photographers, and onlookers waiting inside the terminal.

"Wallace, how did your wife die?"

"Did she really have a sister?"

"What's the sister's name?"

He leaned in close to Fergus. "Take the family and find my father. I'll try to delay the bloodhounds until you're in the car."

Fergus shepherded Nanna, Mercy, and Daniel past the crowd and disappeared further inside the airport.

Thomas stopped before a microphone. "Traci's son, grandmother, and sister are here to lay my wife to rest. We would appreciate your respect for our privacy while we undergo this painful process. My office will issue a statement later this week. Thank you."

The journalist continued to yell questions at Thomas as he hurried to catch up with his family.

Edward Wallace waited inside a limo parked at the curb.

As soon as the family got inside and Thomas closed the door, the car sped away. They would spend the night at Wallace Manor before the funeral the next day.

He glanced across at Mercy, her face pale in the dim lighting.

Daniel snuggled in close to her.

All Thomas's protective instincts came to the forefront, but there was no way to shield them from the firestorm tomorrow's funeral would bring.

His father's glance traveled from Mercy to Daniel. This would be Edward Wallace's first meeting with Mercy.

Thomas hoped, for her sake, the elder Wallace would conceal his long-standing ill will against her sister.

Traci had dragged the family name through the tabloids, something his father abhorred.

His greeting was civil, if a little stiff.

For now, Thomas would settle for that.

At Wallace Manor, the party moved into the entryway. Thomas shed his coat while his father made sure the staff settled the women into their quarters and provided tea after their long journey.

Daniel bounced into the billiard room and his father and Thomas joined them there.

At dinner that evening Mercy was seated next to his father. After he blessed the food, Mercy echoed amen with the others. His father looked at her and raised one gray eyebrow. "Are you a Christian, Mercy?"

"Yes, sir. Since I was nine. My faith was all that sustained me after the deaths of my foster parents."

"I understand. That's what saw me through the death of my wife, Catherine, four years ago."

Mercy touched his hand. "Thomas told me. I'm so sorry."

Edward Wallace's voice wavered slightly when he

spoke. "You have a degree in geology. Do I have that right?"

"Yes, sir. I worked for Sabine Oil during the summer while I was in college. My supervisor there became my mentor. When he decided to retire, he suggested me as his replacement. It was almost unheard of, but they gave me a shot at it. However, I wasn't able to accept the job. I wound up on Wallace Island instead."

"I guess you know oil equipment is the family business. If you ever decide to use that degree of yours young lady, we can find a place for you at Wallace. Right, Thomas?"

Thomas nodded.

"I appreciate that, sir."

Thomas eased out a long, silent breath.

Mercy had just received the family seal of approval.

ॐॐ

Edinburgh, Scotland
Wednesday, July 12

After breakfast the next morning, Thomas joined the family in the foyer. They clambered into the black limousine waiting in front of the manor for the thirty-minute drive to the chapel.

He glanced at the somber faces as they neared their destination.

Nanna's elegant face showed no emotion. Her upbringing didn't allow her to reveal the sorrow.

He squeezed her hand. No way to spare her the pandemonium and the distress it would bring. The innocent always seemed to bear the most pain.

The limo stopped at the church entrance and flashbulbs lit the gray morning. The burial of Traci Wallace had turned into a circus, as he feared it would. The passing of an icon couldn't go without a media frenzy.

An overflow crowd stood in the rain outside the church. Whether curious, or out of respect for his dead wife, he had no way of knowing. He hoped it was the latter.

At the gravesite, police kept the media outside the cemetery.

Thomas stood with Daniel on one side, Nanna on the other. His father supported Nanna's right arm.

The unrelenting rain continued, and Thomas pulled the umbrella close to shield Nanna from the elements. She squeezed his arm and leaned against him.

The black clouds made the mood even more somber.

Mercy held her umbrella in one hand and clasped Daniel's in the other. In black hat and sunglasses, her resemblance to Traci was startling.

And journalists hadn't missed that fact. For obvious reasons, it had been a closed casket service, which added fuel to the speculations that she really was Traci Wallace.

The pastor's last words were lost to him. His thoughts went back to his wedding and the day Daniel was born. He and Traci had shared a few happy times.

She'd lost her way somewhere but had finally realized there were things in life one couldn't overlook. Things like killing innocent people to further a radical religious cause. The significance of terrorists on board

Ricco's yacht must have given her pause. She tried to stop him and died because of it.

Thomas couldn't visualize a patriotic Traci—a side of her he'd never glimpsed–a side he never allowed her to show him.

His failed marriage hadn't been all Traci's fault. Once he learned of her infidelity, he'd shut her out, never considering forgiveness or trying to work out their problems. His injured pride had pushed her away, refusing to pardon her sins. She deserved better from him. He should have protected her from Ricco and his minions.

As the pastor closed with a prayer, Thomas lowered his head and asked God's forgiveness for his failure with Traci.

The service ended and the mourners dispersed. He led the family through the crowd of condolences and sympathizers to the waiting car. His phone vibrated, and he checked the screen. It was from Maggie, his secretary. He took the call.

"Just so you know, conspiracy blogs have sprung up overnight, suggesting someone other than Traci is buried in her grave. The phone's been ringing constantly. They're speculating the subterfuge is to protect Traci from jihadists bent on revenge because she exposed Ricco Rossellini. Want me to keep saying no comment?" she asked.

"That's all we can do, Mag. We can't honor such nonsense with a reply."

"Got it," she said. "You and your family are in my prayers."

He thanked her and disconnected.

Ironically, in death, Traci would be remembered not as a party-girl extraordinaire, but immortalized as a hero. Perhaps she had been. Her cell phone photos were the catalyst that set everything into motion. She brought down Rossellini and her actions would destroy his extremist network.

The most positive result was that Daniel's memory of his mother would be something he could be proud of. Thomas made a mental note to destroy Traci's scrapbook when he returned to the island—to preserve this final image of her.

The limo dropped them at the airport entrance. Thomas guided them through Edinburgh Airport to the private plane terminal. He stopped and picked up one of the tabloids, fresh off the press.

A picture of Mercy arriving at the airport yesterday morning was on the front page with the caption:

TRACI WALLACE: IS SHE REALLY DEAD?

He handed it to Mercy. "Want to read your notices?"

She glanced down and shook her head.

He dropped it in the first trashcan he passed.

ஒ~ல

On the flight home, Mercy removed the hat and sunglasses and took a seat by the window. How had her life become so complicated in such a short period of time? Would she ever be able to unravel all the emotions that tied her to this family?

How confusing it must be for Daniel. He had buried a mother he hardly knew while standing beside a mother he had come to love.

During the service, she'd thought about what Traci's last moments must have been like, facing the cold eyes of Lorenz Lucci. Mercy knew the terror her sister must have felt. She shivered, remembering the evil in Lorenz's gaze, and it left an ache in her chest for her sister.

Mercy exhaled a deep breath and gazed at the window that reflected her own profile. Where did she go from here? She still had no idea if Thomas wanted her in his life. He'd been so busy the last few days with funeral arrangements she'd hardly seen him. She leaned her head back against the seat and closed her eyes. Even if he didn't want her, she couldn't bear to lose contact with Nanna and Daniel.

"Are you OK?" Thomas took the seat next to her.

"Yes. I think so. It's been a really horrible day. I don't know how you stand all the photographers and reporters screaming questions at you."

"It's never easy. You just accept it as a part of life that must be dealt with."

"Thomas, I want you to do something for me," she said. "Have Edda released from prison. I don't want to press charges. She was the victim of an evil man. I don't think the punishment meets the crime."

"You're sure that's wise?"

"She can't harm me now. And perhaps she's learned her lesson."

His gaze searched her face. "I'll take care of it tomorrow."

Daniel came across the aisle and climbed into Thomas's lap. "May...I still call you Mummy?"

She'd known that question would come, but she'd hoped to avoid it until she and his father had talked. She cast a frantic glance at Thomas.

"How about we wait until later to answer that question, Danny. In the meantime, continue to call her Mummy if you wish. Will that be all right?"

"Yep." He climbed down, walked across the aisle, and talked Fergus into a game of checkers.

Mercy turned her face back to the window. It seemed she had her answer.

&

Thomas strolled to the galley for a cup of coffee. As he poured the dark liquid, his phone vibrated. He glanced at the screen. *Unknown.* He reached to shut the cell off and then hesitated. Only a handful of people had his private number. He pressed the green phone icon.

"Thomas?"

He recognized the voice, but it couldn't be.

"Thomas, it's Shaul."

For a moment, Thomas couldn't speak, a mixture of relief and anger swept over him. "I thought you were dead."

"I will be, if Heim finds out I made this call. But I couldn't let you blame yourself for my death. I know how I would feel in your shoes."

"Heim knew, and he didn't tell me? Why, Shaul?"

"It was his idea. He decided to use the incident for an undercover assignment he's sending me on. He thought it would be best if everyone thought I had died. Even Moshe doesn't know." Shaul paused for a moment. "The bullet pierced the kevlar vest, barely missed my spine and cracked a couple of ribs, but the damage was minimal." He chuckled. "It only hurts when I breathe...literally."

"This ruse is a little cruel on your family and friends, don't you think?"

"Yes, I especially hated the effect it would have on my mother. But in the long run, it will make her and others safer. At least that's what I tell myself."

Still reeling from the shock, Thomas slipped into a seat next to the galley. "I appreciate your letting me know, Shaul...and wish you Godspeed on your mission."

"Thanks, Thomas. Sorry we kept you in the dark."

The line went dead.

Thomas had a few choice words he would never get to say to Heim Rosen.

࿅࿅

Wallace Island, the Aegean Sea
Wednesday, July 12

Dusk was falling when they reached home, and weariness washed over Thomas, mental as well as physical. He still owed Mercy the talk he'd promised her. "Let's change into something comfortable. Meet me on the terrace in twenty minutes."

She turned for the stairs. "Yes, I'd like to get out of these heels."

Right on time, she emerged looking more relaxed in slacks, a long-sleeved cotton sweater, and tennis shoes.

He gave her an approving glance. "Care for a walk on the beach?"

She nodded.

He clasped her hand.

They took the path that led close to the incoming waves, stepping around the driftwood gently pushed ashore by the tide. Fingers of clouds drifted across the rising moon, casting shadows in their wake.

"You asked when I wanted you to leave."

She glanced over at him and nodded.

He led her over to a rocky plateau and lifted her to sit on a smooth boulder. "Tomorrow. I want you to leave tomorrow—"

" —I'll be ready in the morning." She tried to jump down from her perch, her eyes bright with unshed tears.

He held her in place. "You didn't let me finish. I want you to leave tomorrow—with me. To get a marriage license. That is, if you're willing to marry an overbearing Scot who frequently jumps to the wrong conclusions. I would like to marry you tomorrow, but I can wait until the furor over Traci's death slips off the tabloids. Even though Traci and I were separated for four years, it would seem insensitive to rush this too soon."

"You needn't explain, Thomas. I understand. I need to return to Houston to take care of some things, close out my bank account, dispose of my furniture, and my car." Her eyes glittered in the moonlight. "You're not just asking because of Daniel—because he wants me to be his mother, are you?"

He lifted her to the ground and held her close. "We haven't known each other long, but I'm very sure this is right. You belong here. With me." He drew her closer. "If I let you get away, my son would never forgive me. And no, it's not for Daniel. I fell in love with you that first day in Bermuda. When you decided to fight against the odds."

❧❧

He traced her cheek with the back of his right hand. Relief washed over Mercy. For a moment, he had her guessing. The stubborn man had finally said what she'd been waiting to hear. That he cared for her—that he loved her.

She smiled. "It took me a little longer than that. Until Paris. Maybe a little sooner. When you brought Paddy to me as a Mother's Day gift."

Laughter rumbled deep in his chest. "Perhaps I should ask if you're agreeing just to become Daniel's mother."

She looked up and slipped her arms around his neck.

His lips met hers halfway.

When the kiss ended, she looked up into his eyes. "Guess you'll just have to trust me."

34

Wallace Island, the Aegean Sea
Saturday, September 14

Mercy sat up in bed, her eyes open wide. This was her wedding day.

Paddy had been asleep, curled next to her. Her sudden movements sent him scampering for cover.

What had she done to deserve so much happiness? Of course, she'd done nothing. That was the amazing part of God's grace.

She dashed into the bathroom, humming.

She and Thomas decided not to go formal for the occasion, inviting only people on the island. Thomas flew in a hairdresser from Rome. Wise decision. She was so nervous she couldn't hold a brush.

To keep the press in the dark about the wedding, Katy had gone to Paris to order a simple white ballerina length dress for her "niece." No veil. They didn't want to deal with helicopters buzzing the island for photos. That would have spoiled their plans for simplicity.

Thomas's connections in Scotland allowed him to get the marriage license in secret.

Were all brides this nervous on their wedding day? Her anxiety came from the fact they hadn't known each other very long. But it felt right. They had crammed a lot of living into that short time period.

Thomas's father, Edward, although a little cold in the beginning, had soon warmed to her. He appeared to be a kind man. Knowing her father was dead, he'd ask if he could give her away. That pleased her.

Katy stuck her head in the door, followed by the beautician. "You need any help, Missy?"

"I'm good, Katy. Thanks."

"Then I'll go get the rest of the wedding party organized."

An hour later, Katy and Nanna walked in. "The men have already—" The two women stopped and stared.

"Until Webster invents another word for stunning, it will have to do. That's what you are, Mercy Lawrence. Stunning," Katy said. "The tiny flowers in your hair are the perfect touch. I hope Thomas Wallace knows how lucky he is."

Heat rose in her cheeks. "Stop, you're making me even more nervous than I already am. It's a good thing I have a nurse in the bridal party. In case I faint."

Nanna, elegant and regal in gray silk, walked over, tears in her eyes. "You are a radiant bride, Mercy." Her grandmother held out a strand of pearls. "This is your something old. They belonged to your great-grandmother. I was saving them for Daniel's bride, but I think now is the time to pass them on to my granddaughter."

Mercy turned to face the mirror and her grandmother fastened the perfectly matched pearls around her neck. They cast a warm glowed against her skin. "Thank you Nanna...I'm honored to wear them." She pulled a tissue from the box and wiped her nose. "We'd better leave before I ruin this hard fought illusion."

The three of them went downstairs for the short trip to the chapel. Nanna took her arm and smiled. "Too bad Father Paul couldn't be here to see Thomas in church."

"Some sow, some water, and others reap the harvest," Mercy said. "Sad that he couldn't come back for the wedding."

Nanna gave a sad nod of her head. "He had to remain in Rome for his renal therapy. But he sent his blessings."

❦

Thomas stood near the chapel altar, waiting for the bridal march to begin that would signal the beginning of a new era in his life.

Fergus was at his side.

Both stood in full kilt regalia.

Piped in music filled the small church, provided by the sound system. No organ or piano.

Much different from his first wedding.

Nerves assailed Thomas. Mercy was a gift he didn't deserve. He couldn't mess this one up.

Frank escorted Nanna to the front pew. He'd seated the villa staff and islanders earlier.

Strains of Felix Mendelssohn's "Wedding March" filled the air and Thomas turned towards the aisle.

As maid-of-honor, Katy came first, followed by Daniel as ring bearer.

And then Mercy stepped into view. His father, resplendent in his kilt and war medals, held her arm.

Thomas's mouth went dry and he swallowed hard.

Mercy floated towards him, a vision of

indescribable loveliness. Even more important, the beauty wasn't just skin-deep. She was as beautiful inside as out.

His father smiled, handed Mercy over to him, and then took his seat beside Nanna.

Mercy leaned close. The smell of lavender soap and orange blossoms followed her. "Nice knees," she whispered.

He struggled to keep from laughing out loud. Life with this woman was going to be fun.

కాళ్ళ

After the ceremony, they returned to the villa for the reception. The house was filled with flowers and well-wishers. The staff had provided vast quantities of food and drink, most of which were consumed.

The guests began to leave, and Mercy found herself alone with Thomas for the first time that day. She turned in a complete circle and gazed at him. "Where did everyone disappear to?"

He took the glass of punch out of her hand and led her into the foyer. "Dad went back to Edinburgh. Nanna and Daniel have gone to visit an old friend of hers in London. Fergus and Katy went along as chaperones." He grinned. "Maybe it's the other way around.

"Since you didn't want to leave Daniel for a long honeymoon, I've arranged to have this place to ourselves for an entire week." He picked up the SAT-phone from a nearby table and punched in a number. "Maggie, this is Thomas. If you call me in the next seven days, you're fired."

Her peal of laughter through the phone line

reached Mercy before he disconnected.

After returning the phone to the table at the bottom of the staircase, Thomas lifted her into his arms. "You must promise not to gain weight if you expect this service often."

"I promise to *try* to not gain weight. Are you trying to impress me by carrying me up this long flight of stairs?"

"Yes."

She laughed. "If I do gain weight, you could always install a chair-lift, and I could sit in your lap as we glide up."

"I'll keep that in mind for when I'm eighty."

When they reached the landing, he nodded down the hallway. "I had your things moved to the master suite at the end of the corridor."

"You did?"

He grinned. "I did."

Mercy smiled and placed a light kiss on the corner of his mouth. "That was very thoughtful of you."

"I know."

Paddy sauntered to the open doorway of her old bedroom and yawned. His gaze followed Thomas as he turned away towards the other end of the hall.

Pal scampered up beside Paddy and licked his face. The old warrior crossed his eyes and turned back into the bedroom. Paddy would be fine.

Mercy added another kiss. "You're very sure of yourself, aren't you?"

He laughed and she felt the rumble in his chest. "Always. It's a character flaw. Shouldn't I be?"

"Confidence is good. But I wouldn't want you to become conceited."

When they reached the door, Mercy removed one

arm from around his neck and turned the knob.

He shouldered the door open and stepped over the threshold.

His gaze said everything she was feeling.

Thomas leaned forward, his lips only inches from hers. "Welcome home, Mercy Lawrence Wallace."